BLACK SHACK ALLEY

BLACK SHACK ALLEY

JOSEPH ZOBEL

TRANSLATED BY
KEITH Q. WARNER

A THREE CONTINENTS BOOK
LYNNE RIENNER PUBLISHERS
BOULDER & LONDON

Published in 1997 by
Lynne Rienner Publishers, Inc.
1800 30th Street, Boulder, Colorado 80301

Originally published as *La rue cases-nègres* © 1974 by Présence Africaine, Paris
First published in English in 1980 by Three Continents Press, Inc.

ISBN 0-91447-868-0
Library of Congress number 78-13852

Printed and bound in the United States of America

 The paper used in this publication meets the requirements
of the American National Standard for Permanence of
Paper for Printed Library Materials Z39.48-1984.

6 5

Contents

Foreword:
We All Had a M'man Tine

I don't precisely know how we came to read Joseph Zobel's *La Rue Cases-Nègres*—we never read local authors. Césaire was only known then as the showpiece of Martinique for he was an exemplar: the Black man who, at election time, left his audience in open-mouthed dazzlement with words that another of our (to us unknown) authors had earlier described as "the French of France/the Frenchman's French/French French." Fanon, who had just written on the question of why we did not read Black authors, remained unknown for a long time also.

It was in Fort-de-France, a sun-drenched colonial town whose citizenry's level of literacy is demonstrated by bookstores supplied with the latest in French books and magazines, that *La Rue Cases-Nègres* appeared; first in an off-street bookstall and later on main street.

The works of Martiniquans were not banned; it was simply not profitable to stock a product that no one bought or read. To see the work of someone one knew was from the colony aroused feelings of anguish and collective apprehensions since, *a priori,* a colonial writer could only imitate one of France. The belief that the colonial writer had been laughed at in the metropole, and with him Martinique, was unbearable. Cultural sterilization from within had given the colony a rigidity as to what was proper to the point where the place seemed to be aptly characterized by a tireless "I heard that you didn't go to your violin lesson/a banjo/You said a banjo/You really said a banjo/No sir/You must know that we do not allow here/neither ban/nor jo."

It had been the wish of the Black people of the colony to link themselves to the metropole as early as the French Revolution. It was felt, and this was particularly true of the people of colour who had battled with the white Creoles since the eighteenth century, that amalgamation with France was the only hope for cultural viability, as well as security. Based on the acceptance of this latter premise the people of colour and the descendants of the freed slaves both wagered their existence upon France's assimilationist tendencies; betting at the window of their identity with self-alienation. Concomitantly, and as a result of the apotheosis of France by the colonials, the biological and phenotypical proximity of one to the rulers became a panacea. In this regard, Césaire has denounced the "saved ones" as:

> those who are not at all consoled at not being made in the likeness of God but in the likeness of the devil, those who believe that one is black as one is a second-class clerk anticipating better and with the possibility of rising above his state; those who beat the drum of surrender before themselves, those who live in their own pit; those who cloak themselves in proud pseudo-morphoses; those who say to Europe: "Look, I can bow and scrape like you, I can pay compliments, in short, I am not different from you; pay no attention to my black skin, it's the sun that has burned me.

At the time *La Rue Cases-Nègres* first reached Martinique, the acceptance of a system of colour-coded determinism (either voluntarily or passively) underlay the basic structure that undergirded and perpetuated the *modus vivendi* of the colony. Everyone was drawn into the vortex of this all encompassing colour syndrome. It had become the *raison d'être* to escape from the mark that once tied one to the oblivion of slavery which was itself tied to the land of José Hassam, the central character of Zobel's novel.

Not surprisingly, therefore, bookshops were empty of the works of Martiniquans despite the increasing publication in Paris of local authors who participated in the great international literary movements of the period between the two world wars.

The classroom too was devoid of topics relating to the colony except in regard to its relationship with the metropole. Along with José, we really did memorize and recite in unison a phrase to the effect that "our ancestors were the Gauls." This was truly, as Sartre has said, the golden age of assimilation.

Education was part of the 'burden' France had assumed on our behalf. Bordeaux (which had been the major town in the triangular trade) was the center of education for all of the French colonies. All curricula and major exams were prepared for us in that city. The curricula were steeped in the French tradition of classical education in which Latin, French, and French history were the major subjects. The courses of study fit perfectly with and reflected the French notion that Africans had been devoid of culture and France had a duty to impregnate their descendants with her own culture. European history, more specifically, French history, was a particular subject which the metropole utilized to show itself in the best light. And Africa, when not projected as a barbaric continent, was depicted as "an extension of Western conquest."

It is with this "bovaristic" background in mind (protected as we were against our self-awareness) that the advent of *La Rue Cases-Nègres* can be seen as son important to the people of Martinique. The fact that the novel was obviously autobiographical and that the author had gone, or, like us was still going, to the Lycée Schoelcher was immensely appealing. Suddenly Zobel became the biographer of every kid who could read or who had thrown a rock at the *béké's* mango trees and had run from his overseer. However, an even more significant aspect of the work was in its opening of our consciousness to the sort of revival that had not reached the colony following Césaire's pronouncement of the "New Negro," under French rule (which to his later chagrin was to be popularized as "the movement" of Negritude).   *La Rue Cases-Nègres* thus became our personal *Return to My Native Land.*

We all had our own M'man Tine (José's grandmother in this story) and since she was in the book written by someone from here, we were immediately prepared to identify with her and her grandson. We had, in fact, grown up with the toils of the Antillean woman—as much a fixture in our lives as the surrounding seas. The strength of a M'man Tine or Délia (José's mother) amply compensated for the lack of a male parent. For, in her function as both mother and father, the seriousness of the Antillean matriarch is unsurpassed. The reader might recoil at the harshness of punishments which M'man Tine meted out to José. But that too is traditional. It is supported by M'man Tine's monomaniacal desire to see José escape from the vicious circle of *La Rue Cases-Nègres* plus the belief that a mother only wants what is best for her child. Indeed, it is true and we say "a mother's thrashing never hurt anyone."

In her almost desperate efforts to inculcate her children with the abhorrence of ever becoming a sugar cane field hand like herself and to physically raise them out of the environment she has always known, a M'man Tine will do almost anything. She will work incomprehensibly hard in the *béké's* field, bending low to cut the cane at the roots, in the sun or rain; rising to chop off the leafy cane head, from dawn to dust, every day except Sunday, half-a-day Saturday and certain religious holidays. She then goes home to prepare supper, her back tormenting her, in no mood for any nonsense perpetrated while she was at "work." By the time she reaches forty, she is known as "la vieille" (the old woman). Meanwhile most of her subsistence salary has returned to the all too conveniently placed plantation's store. She usually dies , her wish unfulfilled. For soon, the children must help out in the only plentiful and nearby employment available: the cane fields.

To see M'man Tine, then, in the pages of Zobel's novel confronted us with the realization that a part of ourselves had remained with the "petites-bandes" against which M'man Tine had thrown the power of the town's school, to raise her charge above her own lot. Anguish followed recognition and if one of us threw a rock in the Fort-de-France mêlée of 1959, it was surely in response to this.

The sugar mill of Petit-Bourg, where M'man Tine laboured, and those at Lareinty, St. Marie, Lamentin and Rivière-Salee comprised the economic centers of the colony. Concentrated in the hands of "ten" *béké* (creole) families, the dependence of Martinique upon them was total until the introduction of metropolitan aid to dependent children. The impotence of the worker in the face of Martinique's slave-ocracy— if not always characterized by Julien's "What am I waiting for to croak, damn it!"—is in any event a sure base for self-recrimination and false perceptions of the masses as its own oppressor. Thus, outbursts such Mlle Andre's "this is why I am not afraid to say that I detest this race whose colour I have" are not uncommon. This is the theme upon which Mayotte Capecia fabricated her life and wrote the autobiography, *La Négresse Blanche.*

From obtuse premises and strayed interests, Martinique has existed anomalously still a colony of *rues cases nègres* where the people "toiled and moiled like slaves for the *bèkès;* they put up with them painfully, but did not bear any malice toward them." The latter statement is a befitting epitaph to the Black masses of the colony who have not listened to Jojo's harangue: "What the hell are you waiting for to set fire to the damn cane fields? Can't you see it's that that makes it miserable to be black!" You will notice José's surprise at Jojo's outburst: "You, Jojo, you said that?" The ultimate confrontation is, therefore, never envisaged. The church whose powers M'man Tine believes in as much as she does in the school, has enveloped the community of Petit-Morne with an infectious fatalism which has gnawed at the source of all revolts and which "has removed all blame from the oppressor." To us, "the cause of misfortunes and poverty is attributed to God: He is fate." Sighs are as common here as the nagging cries of the black birds.

Submission is the characteristic which marks a pious community and in a colonial context piety becomes obedience to the colonial situation itself. The people of *La Rue Cases-Nègres* must, therefore, participate in their own exploitation or, as Sartre has said, "share in the responsibility of a crime of which they are the victims" since their salvation for being Poor-Black was in the very enslavement which provided them with Christianity.

The schematic result is that the French Catholic Church, which was given the monopoly of religion by the Code Noir as early as 1685, has cemented France's colonial policies at the grass roots level with its requirements of submission to the *béké*. Consequently, cutting other than the sugar cane from which the Metropole and the *békés* derive their profits with the cheap labour of M'man Tine, is contemplated only in fits of frustrating rage directed in the end against members of one's own community. There has not yet been any substantial attempt to recover one's humanity here since 1870 when the southern part (mostly the drier region) of Martinique revolted against colonial rule and was defeated.

A notable exception occurred from 1941 to 1949. Again in the southern part of the island, a field hand by the name of René Beauregard—or Mister René as he came to be known—took it upon himself to breach the *béké's* hold on the lives of the people of Rue Cases-Nègres." For eight years, sheltered and fed by the people of the region in spite of a price put on his head, Beauregard's exploits dominated the consciousness of the whole colony. He challenged, as no one has done since, the established structure of the colonial order with uncanny coups of survival and surprise attacks against his enemies. The colonial regime vainly made attempts to discredit him in the eyes of the population: he was twice condemned in absentia to hard labour for life and three times—also in absentia—to death. Finally, trapped and wounded, in the early hours of October 1, 1949, Beauregard cheated the colonial guillotine with a well-placed discharge of his gun to his rebel's heart.

Diametrically opposed to la rue cases-nègres is la Route Didier which, José reminded us, was built through the toil and labour of M'man Tine. This area just behind the lycée stretches up to the coolness of the Balata Hills in a "Petit Paradis" on earth—a splendor so breathtaking when compared to the rest of the island. There it is cooler; the sky seems bluer and the sun less hazy; it is peaceful and the villas and houses are fenced with hedges of hibiscus and other multi-colored flowering plants. Everything is more plentiful in "Petit-Paradis" except, perhaps, as in South Africa, the vacuum cleaners which the army of maids and gardeners have rendered superfluous. Fanon surely must have thought of Didier in his depiction of the settlers' town. It is exactly as he describes it; "a brightly lit and asphalted town, where the garbage cans overflow with unknown [to the masses] scraps, never seen, not even dreamed of. The colonists' feet are never visible, except perhaps in the sea; but no [Black person] is ever close enough to see them. These feet are protected by strong shoes although the streets of their town are neat and even, with no holes or stones. The settlers' town is a well-fed town, a lazy town; its belly always full of good things. The colonists' town is a town of white people, of foreigners."

The "white people" of Didier are the wealthy *békés*, descendant-inheritors of the large plantation owners, whose names often carry the ennobled 'de.' Having been enriched by slavery and sugar cane, this group of Creoles still dwell at the apex of the colonial pyramid where they have walled themselves with their privileges against all.

Zobel's novel, however, is more than the tale of centuries of colonialism. Read his work. You will also discover, in the hills of the Antilles, devoid of any exotic appendage, a viable sustaining African culture.
— *"Abouhou!"*
— *"Biah!"*
It is the world of Médouze, the story teller, where the night stories like those of the griot are told to entertain and teach. It is also where, upon death, one goes to Guinea to enter the realm of the ancestors.

We had listened to Médouze with some curiosity and had met José, and since then heard the strangled shouts of others. But in Martinique we mostly remain "blind" and our "hands are over our ears."

Christian Filostrat
Howard University
June 1979

Introduction

La Rue Cases-Nègres was first published in 1950, at a time when it was not yet fashionable to delve too deeply into the past of black people and their relationship with their white masters or even with their fellow blacks. True enough, by 1950 the landmark publications—in particular those of the négritude movement—had already made their appearance and their mark. Among them were René Maran's *Batouala* in 1921, Aimé Césaire's *Cahier d'un retour au pays natal* in 1939 and Jacques Roumain's *Gouverneurs de la rosée* in 1944. Joseph Zobel, therefore, was not a true pioneer, but most certainly mastered the "tradition" of which he became so readily a part.

Like so many of the novels written by prominent black writers, *La Rue Cases-Nègres*, translated here as *Black Shack Alley*, is an autobiographical-type narrative. The initial tendency toward autobiography no doubt stemmed from the fact that the writers were without much literary tradition, hence the relative safety of the narrative centering on the personal adventures of the author. Zobel himself claims that his novel was inspired by Richard Wright's *Black Boy* and that "everything in it is autobiographical, but the story was patterned after my own aesthetics of composition.

Autobiography also means a genuine look at the milieu in which the author grew, at least if the author is faithful in his portrayals. Herein lies, however, the crux of an ever-recurring issue: where does fact end and fiction begin? After all, the novelist is not a historian in the true sense of the word, nor is he a sociologist. How then can one accept what he says about his society and milieu without the nagging feeling that it is severely, and quite understandably, biased? One is here reminded of Alex Haley's *Roots*, which caused great controversy simply because some critics refused to see fiction as having a basis in fact, prompting Haley to refer to his work as one of "faction"—the very critics, one might add, who see nothing wrong in accepting Shakespeare's doctored versions of historical fact.

By and large, black novelists, anglophone as well as francophone, have sought to use whatever they wrote to make certain statements, implicit or explicit, on the social milieu of their time or that of their work.

Consequently, one finds large doses of social commentary alongside the straight narrative and the better novelists are those who marry these two elements with greatest effect. Zobel's *Black Shack Alley* must rank him among these.

*

Black Shack Alley portrays the reality of life in the French West Indies in the years between the World Wars. It deals specifically with life on a Martiniquan plantation as well as with the struggles of the poor, black lower class in the ensuing shift to an urban setting in Fort de France. It is important to understand the rôle of the plantation in the colony, as Martinique then was. In his essay, "The French West Indies: Dualism from 1848 to the Present," Professor Brian Weinstein has noted this rôle:

> The plantations or *habitations* of these former colonies created racial classes and were the key to a permanently dependent economy. In spite of their humble origins, often as indentured laborers and soldiers of fortune, many whites became rich while the blacks were kept down as slaves. The poor whites allied themselves with the rich. All groups lived in and around the cane *habitations,* the products of which—sugar and, later, rum—had to be sent to France. In the eighteenth and early nineteenth centuries the *habitation* was an autonomous unit within the colony: the white owner lived surrounded by his black slaves who cultivated and cut the cane and transformed it on the spot into sugar and rum. A little land set aside for food crops supplied some of the needs of the population. Social life revolved around this unit. 'The principal social groups were created within it, others on its periphery in symbiosis with it. Finally, there were those created in reaction to it, but no element in the complex tableau of this society appeared independent of it.' [1]

Not much of this had changed up to Zobel's time and thus we find that the novel exposes, simply but forcibly, the problems confronting the poor blacks, the social milieu with which the author was most familiar and about which he felt he could write most effectively.

The novel is divided into three almost equal sections. Part I deals with the early life of the narrator, José, as he grows up on the plantation and sees him through to the start of his Primary School years. It is to the author's credit that he has avoided the pitfall of allowing the adult that is writing to filter through to the narrative of the young child. As a result, José's descriptions sound genuine and authentic, truly in keeping with the type a child would give and not at all inconsistent with the fact that beyond these it is the adult that is analysing in retrospect.

It would, for example, be somewhat artificial to have the young José make certain telling comments on the state of the society—these are introduced gradually as José matures over the length of the novel—so these are put into the mouths of other characters. In this respect, Médouze's account of his father's troubles in the post-slavery period is typical. In fact, it is this account that brings out one of the rare impulses to violence that we see in José: "I had this maddening desire to hit the first *béké* I set my eyes on," he concludes.

Part II shows José in Primary School and takes us up to his preparation for and success in the examination that sends him to Secondary School, the *lycée*. In order to take better care of him during this period, his grandmother, M'man Tine eventually leaves Petit Morne and Zobel uses this occasion to introduce us to a wide variety of pen portraits of the typical plantation society in Martinique prior to World War II. José once more looks on at the adult world with eyes of innocence, allowing events to make, in a way, their own commentary. However, we witness the gradual awakening of the young narrator to the complexities of class distinctions and other social inequalities, an awakening that comes full circle in Part III.

In this section, José is shown in the urban environment of Fort de France where he is re-united with his mother Délia as he works his way up to the *baccalauréat*. It is a new type of life that José and his companions see in this setting. Contemporary Fort de France is shown in its vivid realism, one that comes from an eye for significant detail which Zobel obviously possesses.

The reality as portrayed by Zobel comprises several facets. Among the more outstanding are the following: *The black/white relationship.* The whites remain virtually unseen throughout the novel, though their invisible presence manifests itself from very early. The local white, the *béké,* owns all the plantations, of course, along with everything on them and is kept in his position of superiority by the labor and merchandise therefrom. The workers are aware of the exploitation of the white masters but cannot do any better—witness the scene on payday when some of them grumble and remonstrate over the abysmally low wages.

José has very little first-hand contact with whites and is naturally conditioned by his grandmother's opinion of them. In her way of thinking, the whites had come from France "where people had white skins and spoke something called 'French'; a country . . . where all sorts of beautiful things were made." Consequently, José is puzzled to see a white Christ on the cross; in his innocence he thought that treatment of such cruelty was only meted out to black people.

In Fort de France, José realizes that the blacks and whites are worlds apart. He sees them only occasionally:

> . . . one hardly ever saw the house-owners in Route Didier.
> On mornings, at middays and on evenings I saw, in the back of
> luxury automobiles, a man with a pink complexion, comfortably
> installed. At times, it would be white women, dressed like
> hummingbirds. Or else it would be children looking like angels at
> Corpus Christi. Occasionally I would hear them (the women in
> particular) give orders to their servants in a stuck-up, pretentious voice
> and in an accent that—I knew not how—associated platitude to
> pedantry.

For all this, he cannot get over the difference in attitude towards
them as shown by the blacks he has known—those from the country
and those from Fort de France. The rural blacks "did not prostrate
themselves" before the whites, "whereas those in Route Didier formed
a devoted category, dutifully cultivating the manner of serving the
békés." The urban blacks, however, have other more practical reasons
for their apparent submissiveness—antagonizing the whites could
mean instant loss of job and home.

Of course the black-white dichotomy was not the only one. In a way,
there are two others: white-mulatto and mulatto-black. With their fairer
skins and less kinky hair, the mulattoes formed part of a buffer group, a
sort of middle management. As José himself sees later on, the
mulattoes are in a quandary, being neither one nor the other, resented
by both blacks and whites:

> When you think that those little bastard mulattoes, born of those
> unions, who don't even have the right to call 'papa' in public or to walk
> up to their béké fathers, grow up with the arrogance of not having a
> black skin, and never miss an opportunity to hark back to the white
> side of their origins.

In the final analysis, though, it is the mulattoes who have won out, as
can be seen so plainly in many of the other West Indian islands, and this
precisely because of the "middle" position they occupy.

Upward mobility. Whereas the whites control the economic
structure of the society, the blacks' only possible means of upward
mobility is through education. Meaningful business enterprises were
out of the question.

We see José striving to acquire for himself the basis of a sound
education and what is more trying to pass this on to his buddies
Carmen and Jojo as well. One is therefore not surprised to see him
spend his vacation poring over all sorts of books. And even though he
does at times wonder about the purpose and significance of what he is
studying and the examination for which he is preparing, it is clear that a
sound education marks the beginning of a new life, away from the slow

death he saw consuming his grandmother, a life such as the returning Sorbonne graduate is about to pursue.

The sequel to this novel shows José on his way to France where he furthers his education, the natural result of his success at Secondary School. Non-whites usually chose the "safe" professions—law, medicine, teaching, etc.—prior to returning to form part of a budding professional middle class. It is unfortunate that the note of optimism on which this aspect of the novel ends is cruelly belied by the realities of the contemporary situation in the French West Indies as well as many of the other islands as a whole. The very education to which the youth aspires still serves to no avail in the face of rampant unemployment and unemployability. In many instances, both educated and uneducated are either under- or unemployed.

The portrayal of the lower class. The group that receives the brunt of Zobel's attention is the lowest on the social hierarchy. This is the group that works hardest but for the smallest gains. It is also the group that looks around for something to relate to in the society. Even Africa is a distant dream and not a reality except for the dances and other cultural vestiges that have survived. It is noticeable that the only time that the blacks are openly happy and carefree—for a while—is when they dance the *laghia* on weekends.

Apart from these times of festivity, there is little else to rejoice over. Life is a constant struggle for the adults and the only other respite is religion. Christianity provides the hope that things will eventually work themselves out, although if that fails there are always their African-oriented beliefs. These appear in the form of powerful superstitions but are nonetheless part and parcel of the everyday existence of the blacks.

One reality of life among the lower class blacks that is highlighted in the novel is the power of the women in the absence of the father-figure. In both crucial periods of José's schooling he is without the guidance and protection of a father and consequently the women in his life assume very important rôles. This fact makes the novel interestingly comparable to those that portray similar situations outside of the confines of the French West Indies.

*

The heavily matriarchal setting puts into sharp focus the two women that occupy the greater part of José's existence.

M'man Tine, in her own simple way, does what she deems best for her ward. From her he receives his first appreciation of life on the plantation as well as the rudiments of good upbringing. It is she, too, who inculcates in him the urge for self-improvement and independence.

She is shown as poor but proud, hardly socializing, except when absolutely necessary, and extremely particular about her humble shack.

Deep in her heart, she wishes she could do more for José whom she loves dearly and thinks of constantly. "M'man Tine would say," the narrator tells us, "that she could not put anything whatsoever to her mouth without keeping some of it for me." The floggings, therefore, stem not from the cruelty of a wicked grandmother, but rather from the loving guardian who in this way assures herself of success in the task of raising a well-behaved child. José's drive to succeed must be seen as his desire to make M'man Tine happy. She is thus made into an omnipresent central character.

The important rôle played by her in José's life is evidenced by the profound effect her death has on him, even though by then he has lived away from her for some time. It is most telling that he cannot picture her face—only her hands:

> It was her hands that appeared to me on the whiteness of the sheet. Her black hands, swollen, hardened, cracked at every joint, and every crack incrusted with a sort of indelible mud. Cramped fingers, bent in all directions, their ends all worn and reinforced with nails thicker, harder and more shapeless than the hooves of God knows what animal that had galloped on rocks, in scrap iron, in a dung heap, in mud.

Délia is at first pictured as being at work in the béké's houses in Fort de France, having precious little to care about, but she certainly rises to the occasion when it presents itself. It is through her stubbornness and self-sacrifice that José is able to continue at the lycée, despite his partial scholarship.

She takes over from M'man Tine and in many ways acts as an extension of her, only in an urban environment as opposed to the rural plantation one M'man Tine knew. She is determined that nothing will stop her son from receiving a secondary education, not even *their* bureaucratic machinery:

> *They* are too wicked! It's because we're black, poor and alone in the world that *they* didn't give you a full scholarship. *They* fully realise that I'm an unfortunate woman and that I couldn't pay for you to go to the lycée. *They* know only too well that giving you a quarter scholarship is the same as not giving you anything at all. But *they* don't know what a fighting woman I am. Well! I'm not giving up this quarter scholarship. You will go to *their* lycée!

That José makes it, then, is due in no small way to the efforts of his mother.

*

Zobel was once asked whether he considered himself "the novelist of négritude." His reply was quite simply: "No, I'm a creative artist. I don't feel that my négritude is a uniform or a function to which I must sacrifice my individuality." The question was posed no doubt because of the controversial nature of the debate over négritude, some seeing in it a literary movement, some an ideology and others a philosophy. The interviewer wanted to find out whether Zobel considered himself among those francophone writers staking a claim for racial equality and identity, for cultural acceptance, for the rejection of Euro-centric bias, in short for all that was championed by Senghor, by Césaire and by Damas in the 30's. Ever since the négritude debate, black francophone writers have been plagued with questions such as the one posed Zobel and his reply was well put.

This does not mean, however, that his novel is devoid of commitment, relevance and black consciousness. Yet, at no time does the reader get the impression that these elements are taking hold of the novel, that Zobel is using it as a cover for his set ideology. His comments fall naturally into place and it is only occasionally that we see outbursts such as:

> . . . who was it who created for the cinema and the theatre that type of black man, houseboy, driver, footman, truant, a pretext for words from simple minds, always rolling their white eyes in amazement, always with a silly irrepressible smile plastered on their faces, provoker of mockery? That black man with his grotesque behavior under the kick in the backside proudly administered by the white man, or when the latter had him hoodwinked with an ease that is explained by the theory of the 'black man being a big child'?

There are further comments on the type of education being dished out in the former colony—an education obviously meant for metropolitan French students but unthinkingly dispensed to the colonials without any adjustments. Nevertheless, it seems that the very fact of writing the novel was sufficient commitment for the author. Indeed, what more eloquent statement on the working conditions on the plantations than the previously quoted passage describing M'man Tine's hands? As is the case with so many of the better novels, what is not said speaks just as effectively as what is.

Inevitably, comparisons will be made with other novels of the same type. One of the more striking resemblances has to be with George Lamming's *In the Castle of My Skin,* set in Barbados and published in 1953. Lamming's novel is also about life in a village in colonial times, about poverty, about class and color and about growth and change in a

West Indian society. It too has an appeal that is both contemporary and universal.

Another comparison can be made with Camara Laye's *L'Enfant noir,* also published in 1953. The genesis of both novels is remarkably similar: the author alone in France, having problems of re-adaptation and thinking of his homeland, of his childhood and his loved ones. Since Zobel also wrote his novel while working in France (the French edition carries the signature "Fontainebleau, 17 June 1950"), one can be tempted to ask the same question that some critics have asked with respect to Laye's novel. Does Zobel tailor what he says to suit the tastes of the French among whom and possibly for whom he was writing? In all fairness to Zobel, it does not appear so. And, of course, the *béké* was a different breed altogether, with a different socio-political background, so that the metropolitan white could easily divorce himself from Zobel's portrayals.

Zobel's impact in this novel can best be summed up by referring to the old saying that we can best know where we are going once we know where we have been. Zobel helps us see more clearly where we have been. In this respect, the novel takes its place alongside many of the fine autobiographical works that have made their mark on the West Indian literary landscape.

*

When in 1974 Présence Africaine re-issued *La Rue Cases-Nègres,* scholars were relieved at finally being able to have this classic readily available. Prior to that, there were only a few preciously-guarded original editions and a rather expensive reprint. Now that the situation with the original French text was improved, it was not long before it was painfully clear that those who did not read French were, from all reports, missing an important piece of West Indian writing. In particular, the need was felt for an acceptable translation into English.

Zobel himself, in a personal letter to the translator, echoed this feeling: "Must I tell you how happy I am over the publication of *La Rue Cases-Nègres* in English? It is not my ambition to see myself translated into dozens of languages, but I did find that the absence of an edition in English was a void that I'm grateful that you have filled at last."

The problems involved in translating a work of this sort are, I presume, fairly well known. To quote a colleague: "Translation demands . . . over and above linguistic skill and literary talent, the actor's ability to impersonate an author and interpret him to the new public."[2] First of all, the title. The choice was either a straight translation of the orginal, as in Sembène Ousmane's *Les Bouts de Bois de Dieu* becoming *God's Bits of Wood,* or another title altogether, as in Jean

Giraudoux's *La Guerre de Troie n'aura pas lieu* becoming *Tiger at the gates*. We opted for the former. Then, to translate "Nègres" as "Negro" did not seem in keeping with current semantic trends, and "Shack" for "Cases" gave it a catchy ring with "Black." "Alley" was chosen over "Trace."

Secondly, Zobel's narrative moved constantly from the historic present to the other usual past tenses. The historic present was excluded in an attempt to unify the style in English. Another liberty taken was the occasional toning down of the rather heavy use of the adverbs "puis" and "alors." True enough, they indicated the narrator's concern with keeping his story-telling in sequence, but all those "thens" grated somewhat in English. The problem, therefore, was to find an English style that reflected the West Indian context, the "French" atmosphere and the author's concern for authentic dialogue.

Most French West Indians have another language beside standard French—*créole*. In fact, for many this is the only language. *Créole* is widespread precisely among the class of people with which Zobel deals. We see, for example, that one of the complaints made against José's association with one of his companions is that the former was speaking *créole* with him. Ironically, this came from someone who spoke nothing else but *créole*, a good example of the duality within the society with respect to language.

It is to be understood, then, that much of the dialogue that Zobel put into standard French was in all probability uttered in *créole*, the most natural language for many of the types portrayed. The solution for the novelist writing for a wider reading public is to find a standard French, since not every reader will understand *créole*, that approximates *créole* in tone and rhythm. Hopefully, the resulting renditions in English will give some feel for the use of the non-standard language.

Thirdly, a few words have been left in the original for effect and atmosphere. These are mainly names of trees, fruits, games and elements of French West Indian folklore, where even the "official" English term would have very little meaning for readers outside the restricted geographic confine of the novel. At any rate, many of the terms have a built-in explanation and a short glossary is provided.

Biographical Note on Joseph Zobel

Joseph Zobel was born in 1915 in the village of Petit-Bourg, Martinique. He attended secondary school at the Lycée Schoelcher in Fort-de-France and had intended becoming an interior decorator but was unable to do so as he could not get a scholarship to pursue his studies in France.

In 1937 he worked for a while as Secretary/Accountant in the Department of Bridges and Highways (*Ponts et Chaussées*) and the following year returned to his alma mater as Supervisor. At about this time, he began to write and published some of his short stories in a local newspaper *Le Sportif*. He wrote his first novel *Diab'là* in 1942. It is set in the fishing town of Le Diamant where Zobel had worked in 1937. However, the Vichy government, then in power in Martinique, forbade the release of the book. It was finally published in 1946.

When Martinique joined Free France during World War II, Zobel was appointed Press Attaché to the Governor. Soon after the war in 1946 he published another novel *Les jours immobiles,* as well as a collection of short stories *Laghia de la Mort ou Qui fait pleurer le tam-tam?* Also in 1946, Zobel made the inevitable voyage—he went to France. He studied at the Institute of Ethnology and the Sorbonne and followed courses on Dramatic Art.

He taught at the Lycée François 1er in Fontainebleau and it was while there that he published *La Rue Cases-Nègres* in 1950. This work was to win that very year the *Prix des Lecteurs,* awarded by a jury of some one thousand readers. The sequel, *La Fête à Paris,* followed in 1953 and thereafter Zobel began a series of conferences and poetry readings. He took part in many radio plays and was instrumental in acquiring for poetry a greater share of radio time in France. He also travelled to Switzerland and Italy.

In 1957 Zobel followed in the footsteps of at least two other illustrious francophone West Indians—Félix Eboué and René Maran. He went to Africa, choosing to work in Senegal. At first, he assisted in setting up the Lycée de Ziguinchor, then in 1958 went to the Lycée Van Vollenhoven in Dakar where he developed Literature and Elocution courses. He was then chosen to re-organize the *Ecole des Arts de Dakar* in 1961, moving the following year to Radio Sénégal as Cultural Advisor. In this capacity he founded and headed the station's Cultural Services and was in charge of the training of announcers.

Another collection of short stories, *Le soleil partagé,* was published in 1964, followed in 1965 by a collection of poems *Incantation pour un retour au pays natal.*

After many years in Africa, Zobel retired and returned to France in 1976 but sees his stay there as only a preparation for his permanent return to Senegal. He claims that he had even made all preparations to return to Martinique at the end of his administrative stint in Senegal, but "twenty years among the Senegalese do not allow me to withstand any other transplantation."

In 1978, a re-written *Laghia de là Mort* was re-issued by Présence Africaine and *Les Mains pleines d'oiseaux,* actually a reworking of his previous *Les jours immobiles,* was published by Nouvelles Editions Latines. Two other novels and a collection of short stories are in press.

Zobel has also released a record: *Joseph Zobel dit trois poèmes de Joseph Zobel.*

Keith Q. Warner

June 1979
University of the West Indies
St. Augustine, Trinidad & Tobago

[1] In Martin Kilson & Robert Rotbert. *The African Diaspora.* Cambridge: Harvard University Press, 1976. The quotation at the end is from Jean Benoist, "Types de plantation et groupes sociaux à la Martinique," *Cahiers des Amériques Latines,* 2 (1968), p. 139.

[2] Brenda Packman, "Some Problems of Translation in African Literature," in C. Heywood. *Perspectives on African Literature.* London: Heinemann, 1971, p. 65.

[3] I am indebted to Raymond Relouzat's short study of *La Rue Cases-Nègres* (Martinique, no date) for much of this information. Some was also supplied by Zobel in personal correspondence. For further reading, see Randolph Hezekiah, "Joseph Zobel: The Mechanics of Liberation," *Black Images,* Vol. 4, Nos. 3 and 4 (1975), pp. 44-55.

Glossary

Ajoupa: little hut or tent.

Akra: cake of flour and codfish, etc. fried in oil.

Baccalaureat: examination sanctioning end of secondary studies, equivalent of "A" level. Familiarly called the *bachot.* (In U. S. terms it would be a "certificate" showing completion of two years of Junior College.)

Bakoua: large, wide-brimmed straw hat.

Bananes macang'ya and **bananes naines:** types of bananas; the latter are green (unripe) which are cooked as regular vegetables.

Béké: local white.

Bel-air: type of dance.

Brevet Elémentaire: Elementary School Teacher's Certificate.

Caisse des Ecoles: School central office.

Canalier: trench digger.

Canari: earthenware cooking pot.

Certificat d'Etudes Primaires: sanctions end of primary schooling.

Choux caraibe: legume, called "tania" in anglophone West Indies; literally: Caribbean cabbage.

Corrosol: soursop.

Coui: calabash.

Cric . . . crac: introductory calls prior to starting tales; widely used throughout the Caribbean; of African origin.

Créole: the popular form of French or Spanish spoken in the Caribbean; increasingly accepted as the standard language of, for example, Haiti.

Entonnoir: local game.

Faire nika: to try a good-luck charm.

Graisses: type of seasoning.

Habitation: plantation.

Laghia: type of dance, of African origin.

Lelé: swizzle stick.

Mabi: drink made from bark of a certain tree.

Macata: species of tropical tree.

Madras: gaily-colored head-tie.

Manger-coulies: wild parasitic plant.

Mansfenil: tropical bird.

Messieurs-dames: Ladies 'n gentlemen.

Migan: old plantation dish, usually made with breadfruit.

Morne: hill (not used with this meaning in standard French).

Nègre, Négrèsse: used by the blacks as terms of endearment.

Palma Christi: type of plant.

Pataclac: local game.

Petite bande: team of young workers.

Pois-doux: type of wild fruit.

Pomme-liane: passion fruit.

Quimboiseur: doer of evil, *obeah*-man.

Rouge et noir: local game.

Séanciere: person capable of predicting future and divining cause of troubles.

Shasha: maracas or "shack shack."

Titim (Timtim): riddle, usually accompanying stories.

Tonnerre!: literally "thunder" but used in swearing.

Toloman: pap.

Transat: popular name for *Compagnie Transatlantique*, operator of ocean-liners taking passengers to and from France from Martinique, Guadeloupe.

Violon d'Ingres: used to refer to something that is dearly loved; literally "Ingres' violin."

Zombi: spirit, jumbie.

BLACK SHACK ALLEY

Part One

Whenever the day had been without incident or misfortune, the evening arrived with a smile of tenderness.

From as far off as I could see the approach of M'man Tine, my grandmother, at the end of the wide road that took the blacks into the cane fields of the plantation and brought them home again, I would rush off to meet her, imitating the flight of the *mansfenil,* the gallop of the donkeys, and with shouts of joy, carrying along the entire group of my little friends who, like me, were awaiting their parents' return.

M'man Tine knew that once I'd come to meet her, I must have behaved myself properly while she was away. So, from the bodice of her dress, she would take some tidbit which she would give me: a mango, a guava, some coco-plums, a bit of yam left over from her lunch, wrapped in a green leaf; or, even better than all that, a piece of bread. M'man Tine always brought me something to eat. Her work companions often made this observation, and M'man Tine would say that she could not put anything whatsoever to her mouth without keeping some of it for me.

Behind us there appeared other groups of workers, and those of my friends who, recognizing their parents, rushed off to meet them, doubling their shouts of joy.

While devouring what I had to eat, I let M'man Tine continue her conversation, and I followed her quietly.

"My God, thank you; I've made it back!" she sighed, placing the long handle of her hoe against the shack.

She then removed the small round basket of bamboo slats perched on her head and sat on a stony outcropping in front of the shack which served as a bench.

Finally, having found in the bosom of her dress a rusty tin box, which contained a limestone pipe, some coarse tobacco and a box of matches, she began to smoke slowly, silently.

My day was also at an end. The other mamans and papas had also arrived; my little friends returned to their shacks. Games were over.

To smoke, M'man Tine occupied almost all the space this huge stone offered. She would turn to the side where there were beautiful colors in the sky, stretch out and cross her earth-stained legs, and seem completely engrossed in the pleasure of drawing on her pipe.

I remained squatting beside her, gazing steadfastly, in the same direction as she, at a tree in bloom—a completely yellow *macata* or a blood-streaked flamboyant—the colors of the sky behind the hills, on the other side of the plantation, whose glow was reflected even beneath us. Or else, I looked at her—on the sly—for she told me time and again, often vehemently, that children must not stare at adults.

I really enjoyed following the curves of her old straw hat, its form crushed by her basket, its rim water-soaked and made wavy by the rain. It would be pulled down over her face the complexion of which was scarcely any lighter in color than the land of the plantation.

But what amused me the most was her dress. Every morning, M'man Tine would have to sew something on it, all the while grumbling that there was nothing like cane leaves to eat away at poor black women's clothes. This dress was nothing more than a squalid tunic where all colors were juxtaposed, multiplied, superimposed, blended into each other. This dress which, originally, as far as I could remember, was one of simple flowered cretonne, intended to be used for communion, the first Sunday of every month, then for mass every Sunday, had become a thick padded tissue, a heavy ill-fitting fleece which nevertheless seemed to be the outfit most suited to the root-like hands, to the swollen, hardened, cracked feet of this old black woman, to the hut we lived in, and to the very *habitation* in which I had been born five years ago and which I had never gone far from.

From time to time, neighbors passed by.

"Amantine, you're having a nice smoke," they said by way of a greeting.

Without even moving her head, without so much as glancing at them, M'man Tine replied with a grumble of satisfaction, and remained imperturbably lost in the pleasure of smoking her pipe and deep in her reverie.

Can I say whether she was dreaming, whether she let herself go, at that precise moment, whether the smoke from her pipe carried her off somewhere else or altered in her eyes the entire panorama of the plantation?

When she was finished smoking, M'man Tine would say:
"Good!"

But it was rather a cry of great effort, a personal exhortation.

Then she would put her pipe next to her tobacco and her matches in the small tin box, get up, take her basket under her arm and enter the shack.

It was already dark inside. Yet, in a wink, M'man Tine had examined the entire scene, deciding whether I had moved some utensil or done any damage.

But, after days like that one, I wasn't afraid. For lunch, I had had just the amount of cassava flour and the small bit of salt codfish she had left me. I had not used too much oil, and couldn't find the sugar tin which she must have stashed in a hiding place only the devil himself could unearth. I had not broken any plates, and had even swept the smoothened earth floor of the hut, so as to clean up the specks of flour that had fallen while I was having my lunch.

The truth was, innocence and reason had possessed me all the time that M'man Tine had been gone.

Satisfied at finding everything impeccable, M'man Tine asked herself under her breath (she often spoke to herself in this fashion):

"What am I going to do tonight?"

Standing undecided in the semi-darkness, she yawned at length.

"Left to me," she said in a tone of complaint, "I wouldn't even light a fire, I'd put a pinch of salt on my tongue so the worms can't attack my heart, then go straight to bed."

For she was tired, tired, she said.

But thereupon, breaking her torpor, she busied herself, taking from her basket a breadfruit which she cut in four, peeling each quarter which she then cut into two "squares." This operation was still amusing to my eyes—the filling of the *canari,* an earthenware cooking-pot, in the bottom of which M'man Tine placed first of all a layer of peelings, followed by the 'squares' of vegetable, a pinch of salt, a piece of salt codfish, and finally filled with water.

In addition, she often brought back from the field where she worked a bundle of greens and this methodical filling was rounded off with a layer of this grass covered with peelings in a criss-cross fashion.

Outside, a leaping flame, pushing its way up between three black stones, already provoked in the inside of the *canari* a most healthy-sounding rumbling and shed in front of the shack a tawny, vibrant glow in which M'man Tine and I sat, she on the huge stone and I quite near to the fire in order to put bits of wood in it and kindle the flame upwards into a roar.

"Don't play in the fire," M'man Tine shouted, "you'll pee your bed."

And all around us on the plantation, there were in the darkness of the night similar fires, cooking *canaris,* making the façades of the shacks and the faces of the children come alive with all those reflections that give fires at night so much seductive appeal.

M'man Tine hummed one of those monotonous songs that continually rose from the *habitation* and which I sometimes sang as well, along with my friends, when our parents were away.

I thought that the sun was an excellent thing because it took our parents off to work and left us to play quite freely . But night was also a marvellous thing when flames were lit and songs were sung.

Some evenings I didn't want to remain a long time waiting for my dinner. I was hungry and found that M'man Tine was singing too much instead of checking to see if the food in the *canari* was ready.

On such evenings, it was so painful to wait while M'man Tine prepared the sauce to go with the breadfruit. How slow she seemed to me as she took a small earthen saucepan, rinsed it (oh! how M'man Tine loved to wash and rinse everything!), cut up some small onions, grated some garlic, went for some thyme behind the shack, took some black pepper from one of the many little bits of paper tied up in balls in a corner, some pimento and four or five other seasonings! How long I found the time all this remained browning before the vegetable soup, the piece of cod, and the greens were poured in. And it was never good right away. Always a bit of clove to be added; and it had to simmer a bit more!

M'man Tine lit her kerosene lamp, and the table was lit up amidst all the shadows, including ours which, enlarged out of proportion, weighed on the wretched walls of the shack.

She was sitting on a narrow chair near the table; the large ware bowl with blue and yellow stripes from which she ate with her fingers, was between her knees, but she insisted that I put my aluminum plate on the table and that I use a fork, 'like a well-bred child.'

"Is your belly full?" she asked me when I was finished eating.

Three breadfruit 'squares' had filled me till I felt about to burst; and I scarcely had enough breath left to say in a clear voice: "Yes, M'man."

Then M'man Tine gave me a small calabash full of water, and I went to the threshold of the door to rinse out my mouth, taking care to shake the water vigourously between my cheeks and to spit it out as violently as possible.

While doing the dishes, M'man Tine kept talking to herself under her breath, and I remained sitting on my chair listening to her as if she were speaking to me. In this way she went over her entire day: the incidents, quarrels, jokes on the plantation; she became so seriously indignant that I was afraid I'd see her break the *canari* or the bowl she was in the process of rinsing. Or, she sniggered so gustily that I too burst out laughing. And she would stop suddenly to ask me: "What are you laughing at, you li'l devil?"

At other times she was not angry, but talked on and on in a deep, vibrant voice; and not fully understanding what she was saying to herself, I leaned over to see if there weren't tears running down her face. For I felt myself in such anguish! . . .

I remained staring steadfastly at the lamp for a long time, and allowed myself to be entertained by the little moths that darted against the flame to tumble backwards on the table, dead or singed beyond ever flying again.

And my eyelids grew heavy and my head at times seemed to slip off my neck down to the table, when I would catch myself just in time.

Now, M'man Tine was constantly drying and putting away her utensils. On more than one occasion, she moved the lamp in order to clean the table. When, oh when, would she get up from that corner where she had stooped to fix some bottles?

Then, I deliberately rested my head on the edge of the table.

Finally, M'man Tine shook me by the shoulder, calling me in a loud voice so as to chase my sleep away. Holding the light in her hand, she took me into the bedroom.

I was drunk with sleep and nothing made any more impression on my senses. M'man Tine undid a large bundle of rags which she spread for me to sleep on over a sheep skin lying on the ground. She undressed me; I barely mumbled the words she had me repeat to the glory of God. I perceived everything as from the depths of troubled waters. When finally I said "Goodnight, M'man" and collapsed onto my bedding, I was like a drowned man coming back up to the surface.

*

But, on most occasions, the day ended badly.

On mornings, as soon as I was up, I picked up my mattress of rags and went to spread it out in the sun, on the huge stone in front of the hut, for it was nearly always wet in certain spots. M'man Tine, at that time crouching in the corner of the shack where there was a small earthenware stove, of the type that used wood coal, was preparing her coffee. Through the window of the room, the daylight poured onto her back, which showed a withered skin through the holes in an old dress that had become as perforated as a net, and that she slipped on to sleep in. On the fire, water was singing away in a small jelly tin, and with it M'man Tine sparingly wet the little filter on the ground.

After changing my night shirt for a long drill smock which was what I wore every day, I moved beside M'man Tine so I could watch her draw the coffee.

She collected the first drops in a little porcelain mug, added a pinch of sugar and then stood leaning against the door-frame, one hand on her hips. From this spot, running her eyes over the horizon, she described what the weather was like, or would announce:

"The folks in Petit-Bourg can count on eating fish to-day, for the fishermen from Diamant will come back with their boats full . . . You see those little clouds: looks like the seines will be bursting . . . "

And she punctuated her words with small mouthfulls of coffee which made her click her tongue.

At such times I knew how careful I had to be not to disturb her, not to ask her anything whatsoever. She would fly into a rage. She would shout: "The sun is scarcely up, I've not even had a drop of coffee in my stomach, and this child is already tormenting me!"

In a large, thick porcelain bowl with blue and pink flowers decorating it, M'man Tine had given me some cassava flour soaked in light, very sweet coffee, and with my little metal spoon I put it all away, sitting on the threshold of the shack.

All during this time M'man Tine kept turning over and over on her knees her working dress, examined the complicated patchwork and hastily did a few urgent minor repairs. She then became very zealous in her movements to and fro, thus appeasing my sneaking impatience to see her set off. For outside, the trees, the fields, the entire savannah were already bathed in sunlight.

Finally, M'man Tine said to me:

"At noon—you know? When the plantation clock is about to strike—you'll take a glass of water and pour it on this plate of flour. It already has oil and cod on it, all you have to do is to stir it up properly and eat."

She showed me the plate which she placed at the edge of the table, where I could reach it; then, once more stepping up her preparations, she made herself a similar lunch in a calabash bowl which she very carefully placed in her bamboo basket with a few other things—among them the old black stockings she used as mittens and covering for her legs to protect her from being scratched by the cane leaves and, at times, a calabash full of fresh water.

She then filled her pipe and lit it, put on her wild straw hat over her kerchief, pulled tightly around her waist a raggedy string, and said to me:

"I'm off to see if the Good Lord still gives me strength to struggle in the béké's canes! See how clean the shack is, and your clothes as well . . . no tears . . . and no mess in front of the shack? . . . And don't go knocking about. Try and behave yourself so I won't have to get vex tonight!"

Thereupon, she took two puffs on her pipe, filling the shack with smoke, bent down at the same time, raised the small bamboo basket which she placed on her head and, taking hold of the hoe as she started on her way, went through the door, saying:

"I'm off!"

Free at last! Free for the entire day.

But I did not dash outside to enjoy my freedom as yet.

Sitting on the doorstep, I allowed a few moments to pass. In her haste to leave, M'man Tine had very often forgotten something which she returned to fetch. In such a case, she must find me as well-behaved as when she left me. Then, assured that all was fine, I went outside, taking care to close the door properly.

Those of my friends whose parents had already left were in a group in front of the shack. They greeted me with great enthusiasm, and we waited for the others.

Black Shack Alley comprised some three dozen ramshackle wooden huts, covered with galvanize, standing at regular intervals at the side of a hill. To the top there stood, majestically, the house of the manager whose wife ran a little store. Between "the house" and Shack Alley, one found the overseer's little house, the mule compound, the manure pile. Below Shack Alley and all around, stretched vast fields of cane, at the end of which one could see the factory.

This whole area was called Petit-Morne.

There were large trees, groups of coconut trees, palm trees lining paths, a river lazily flowing through the grass of a savannah. And it was all so beautiful.

At any rate, we children enjoyed it immensely.

While waiting for the group to be complete, we had fun right there, and our shouts and our laughter called to arms those who were missing.

How many were we? I don't think we ever counted. We did notice when someone was missing: we each had our favorites and indicated their absence if they were not there; and we also sensed when everybody was present.

First of all the leaders: Paul and his two sisters, Tortilla and Orélie. Gesner, my good pal, and Soumane, his younger brother. Romane and Victorine, as fearless as boys; Casimir and Hector. And myself. For I was also one of the gang.

Then came a trail of urchins who could be rather cumbersome under certain circumstances. You know, just a bunch of noisy brats, who could't even run about without scraping their elbows and knees in the dirt, who couldn't even climb trees or jump over a stream.

But we "bigger ones" knew the paths and the spots where you could catch crayfish with your bare hand, under the babbling rocks in the streams. We knew how to pick guavas and husk dry coconuts. And cane ready for sucking, that was our specialty.

Now it was just the moment when we could extract the greatest pleasure from the sun-filled freedom afforded us by the absence of our parents.

Furthermore we were the only ones with clothes on. Old men's jackets floated on the backs of the other boys and were ripped asunder during their frolicking; or vests with so many holes in them that they in no way covered the frail bodies that pretended to wear them.

As for the girls' dresses: a cord slung over the shoulder from which fringes loosely hung that hid nothing at all.

And everybody bare-headed with woolly hair made red by the sun, noses running with a greenish substance like teams of slugs, knees skinned like fowls' feet, feet the color of stone displaying toes that were swollen with chiggers.

At 12 o'clock, Hector announced, "I'm having *bananes naines* for lunch, with codfish and oil. Maman cooked them before she left; it was still warm a li'l while ago."

The food question was always uppermost in our thoughts.

"As for us," said Paul, speaking for himself and his two sisters, "we have a large *canari* full of rice mixed with 'red butter.' And our maman told us we could have some flour if we're not filled."

"But you don't have any meat," Soumane pointed out.

"No, they don't even have a bit of codfish!"

"Last night, my maman made a good meal," Romane declared, gesticulating like a big woman: "bread-fruit *migan* and a pig snout. It smelled real good! And that's what I'm having at midday."

When the menus failed to excite greediness, it was because we were not yet hungry. Besides, we were busy roaming from shack to shack. Not an adult left in Shack Alley!

Certain huts were even uninhabited, closed or wide open, for all the workers on Petit-Morne did not live in Shack Alley.

We were alone and the world was ours.

We examined everything, destroying this or that at our fancy, uprooting plants—the awful worm-grass especially, from which were prepared such bitter brews—and throwing pebbles in the barrels of drinking water. We could have pissed in them if we had wanted!

But often those who had plenty to eat, not being able to resist—and yielding to the desire of the other comrades, took the rest of us home and sharing their meals with the most carefree generosity.

Then, finished, the entire gang would set off.

At random. From guava tree to plum tree, from coco-plum field to cane field. We crossed savannahs, joyously stoning the cows. We sometimes came across patches of greenery where the *pomme-lianes* grew in abundance.

"Ay, Trénelle far again?" Gesner enquired.

We came to a halt; those who were lagging behind caught up.

"Sure, it far. Why?"

"Because last night my father brought me some mangoes big so. Said he found them on the Trénelle road."

"Then it can't be very far."

"Suppose we go down there!"

"Why not?"

It was perhaps far in actual fact, but didn't we have the whole day to get there and back? And then, in a gang, just like that you covered a good bit of road without even realising!

At the foot of the Hill, we met a cart full of manure and pulled by four oxen squeaking its way through the ruts. Gesner, Romane and I immediately jumped up to the rear. The others, clinging as best they could, had themselves towed while the weakest among us followed in a trot.

Silence, so the driver wouldn't realise what was happening!

The driver, for his part, standing to the front of the cart, goaded on his oxen, swearing to high heaven. His invectives were too stinging for us to repeat.

Intoxicated by these forbidden words, Gesner added others of his own invention.

It was a maddening round of chattering.

But while the cart continued on its way with its harsh din of clashing wood, its clanging of chains, the squeaking of its axles mingling with the crunch of clumps of dry earth under the wheels, there suddenly appeared before us the driver, brandishing his goad.

"Bunch of li'l run-away niggers, you! . . ."

The gang scattered, to regroup a little farther on.

And to help us regain our nerve, we showered insults at the disappearing team, all oblivious and bumping along the road.

"This is not the right road," Gesner suddenly observed. "We should have gone down to the cross-road over there, behind, and taken the path going in the other direction, like that."

Indeed, we were no longer headed in the right direction for Trénelle. That damned driver had led us astray.

We then retraced all our steps. So bitter was our annoyance that we did not even glance at the guava trees along the way. We knew from experience though that trees lining "traces" never kept their fruits.

We bigger ones walked so briskly that the smaller ones were soon out of breath behind us, just as they had trailed along behind the cart earlier on.

"The overseer!" Orélie shouted.

Everyone ground to a halt. Barely time to catch the white parasol just visible at the crook in the road before we dove into the ditches. And with a loud crackling of grass and scratching straw raking my head, I tried crawling on all fours to reach the deepest part of the canefield.

And such a noise rumbling all around as if the overseer's mule were galloping towards me scared me so much that my heart was about to burst.

And I rolled into a furrow, completely exhausted, lost.

Unable to move, I remained with my head buried in the undergrowth.

Gradually, my heart beat less quickly and I listened.

No further rustling of straw.

Faintly, the trot of the disappearing mule on the parched, porous earth of the road reached me. The last noise subsided. Nothing further. Nothing, but my heart still beating so loudly that it could give me away.

"Ay! Gesner, Romane, Ay!" I called quietly.

A slight rumble reached me.

"Can you still see him?"

"You can barely see his parasol."

It was Paul talking.

Then with eyes filled with wonder, I discovered the countryside. I had just lost all notion of where I was. My impression was that I had covered on all fours an infinite distance and I expected as I emerged from the brushwood to find myself in a far away and unknown place.

Gesner and Romane were already on their feet and announced that the danger was over.

"Where is Tortilla, and Casimir?"

In vain we shouted in all directions, there were some who did not reply.

This was always the case when our outings underwent alarms of this nature! In the ensuing panic, some spurted off in the wrong direction.

In that case, too bad for them.

We returned to the cross-road to set off from there.

"But this time," Gesner proposed, "we're not following the road."

Instead we crossed a canefield lying fallow.

"I'm sure there are *manger-coulies.*"

And, of course, in such an abandoned field we always would find bits of shrivelled up sugar cane, good enough to be appreciated so late in the season.

But this hike, no *manger-coulies,* no canes. Nothing but weeds and wild flowers.

What of our missing friends? We now caught sight of four or five of them straggling towards Shack Alley.

As for us, all the obstacles cluttering up our plans could not keep us from pursuing our adventure to its end.

We were already far away when the lunch bell sounded at 'the house.' It was so far off that it was only faintly that we heard its announcement.

"They're going to devour their lunch," said Paul, alluding to those who had returned. "Perhaps they'll even go and steal ours."

"Makes no difference," said Romane, "they'll not have tasted all those lovely mangoes we're going to feast ourselves on. And we're not going to bring any back for them. Not one; not even the skin."

In the blazing sun, our rags flapping in the breeze, we crossed the field. We followed another 'trace,' chattering away, stopping now at every shrub to raid its fruits—ripe as well as green—to quell a hunger that was awakening in us and which we were scarcely aware of, spellbound as we were by the perils we had so valiantly faced since our departure, and stimulated by the daring of our initiative.

We roamed idly about a great deal, then remembering what our aim was, we hurried on, resolutely taking one path to the right or another to the left as we came upon it.

It was a place where the road is nestled deeply between two red humid plots of land, with tall ferns rising very high above our heads, leaving just a crack to allow one a glimpse of the sky. It was so strange that we spoke in hushed voices, trying to walk side by side.

We had never seen a road like that!

Always, when one least expected it, small balls of earth would detach themselves from above and come tumbling down at our feet, taking our breath away.

We advanced slowly, not speaking, and couldn't help glancing back over our shoulders every two or three steps.

Wasn't it as if this half-tunnel threatened to come thundering down on us, or seemed to close up as we passed? Our march was more and more halting and unassured. As for me, I was choking from not daring to speak.

We were afraid.

Suddenly, a shout of terror, then every man for himself! Turning back we shot off using all the strength in our legs and multiplied the shouts of panic from our rest of the group with our own.

Long after coming out of the tunnel, we kept on running without once looking back, charging on straight ahead of us until we ran out of breath. But it was impossible to stop. We trotted, exhausted but urged on by tear. Our fright was so violent that we could not pull ourselves together. Fear had so shaken us that we were drained of all adventure, of any pride.

And running desperately we circled back towards Shack Alley. Once there, what heroism dominated the account of our exploits in the eyes of all those who had not gone along with us! Even our state of panic was proof of our bravery, for:

"We ran! Oh, how we ran! Look, feel my heart."

Wide-eyed, they admired us. It was we who had gone so far, who had come to know the terrible road they couldn't even imagine, who had avoided danger thanks to our bravery and endurance!

To our prestige were added the little fruits we had sampled, the water-course we had discovered, the *pois-doux* we had come across, to which we would pay a return visit when they were ripe.

And to crown our happiness our parents would be none the wiser. That night we would not be beaten.

The fear was gone, we were hungry now.

No, our friends had not eaten everything. So, we began with the rice from Paul, Tortilla and Orélie.

We had invaded the shack. Tortille began the distribution, surrounded by our out-stretched hands.

How pleasant it was to be all back in the shack, in the absence of our parents! Orélie, beside herself with joy, showed us the bedroom whose appearance was enhanced since Symphor and Mam'zell Francette, her parents, had bought one by one four boxes and some lengths of wood with which they had built a frame onto which were piled rags covered with cretonne.

Children always slept on the 'front room' floor, on old clothes used for bedding. There was nothing else in the bedroom, but we were content to remain there as it was quite a privilege for us to crowd into this room reserved for adults. It was so dark and gave off a strange, intimate odor, an odor of perspiration—the smell of plantation workers!

*

It was my turn now to share my lunch.

But I had no intention of eating the way M'man Tine had prescribed: soak cassava flour with water, stirring in oil, etc.

I did not like flour with water. In M'man Tine's presence, I made an effort to overcome my repugnance, and that was all. Cassava flour was something I liked as a dessert. Either kneaded in a bowl with brown syrup until it formed a thick, delicious mass, or mixed up with granulated sugar in a paper cone from which you poured the stuff into your mouth. M'man Tine was not unaware of my predilection, even. And then, today, I felt some inexplicable urge to be part of some fantasy.

So, I invited the gang in to eat flour and sugar.

The sugar was in a tin; but where to find that box, that was the problem! M'man Tine was a genius at finding hiding places and at stashing away her sugar tin without my seeing.

It was true that I too had the cleverness to ferret out a hiding place. But it wasn't easy since she constantly changed it.

For instance, just day before yesterday the sugar tin was there on that shelf. I had only to take a chair, climb onto the table and reach out my arm.

Today it was no longer there.

At my feet the entire gang, puzzled, looked at me and waited.

"My m'man doesn't have a sugar tin," said Gesner. "It's only on Sundays that she buys two cents worth of sugar to make coffee. But if she had one, I don't think she'd succeed in hiding it from me."

And, resolved to take an active part in the search, he shouted to me:

"Look on all the girders, and around. Mothers love to hide things on girders. They imagine we can't climb."

But I didn't find anything and, discouraged, came down from atop the table.

Thereupon, everybody launched into a frenzied search for that sugar tin in every nook and cranny of the hut. The entire bedroom underwent such upheaval, M'man Tine's humble bed so disrespectfully handled, the utensils banged against each other and resounded so violently that I was seized with fright, incapable of any initiative, powerless to control the violent search by my friends.

"Stop, get out!" I felt like shouting.

But I was afraid.

Heavens above! I had felt it in my bones: a sound of broken dishes.

The blue and yellow bowl!

The bowl in which M'man eats her food!

"Is you who pushed my arm."

"Is you who made me do it. You did so, like that, with your hand."

Romane was after Paul. Paul accused Gesner.

The others were dumb with stupefaction.

I burst out sobbing.

"Your maman going to beat you?" Romane asked me.

"I'll say that it was you who came here to steal," I said angrily.

"You mustn't," said Tortilla. "You'll say it was a hen; a frizzle hen that came in, jumped up on the table and broke the bowl when you chased it outside."

Everybody claimed that this explanation was valid. But for all that I could not be consoled.

I was so angry that I wanted to give them a good pummelling, to chase them from M'man Tine's shack which they had dared rummage through so wildly.

Nevertheless, I did nothing of the sort. I controlled myself.

"Friends," I said to them. "I think that M'man Tine took her sugar tin to the field with her; she mentioned that the other day."

"Well, we'll eat the flour as it is, with codfish," cried Tortilla.

On afternoons, from a certain hour, we hardly left Shack Alley. Everyone knew that when our parents were doing task-work they could arrive at the moment they were least expected.

Thus we devoted our time to the innocent game of chasing dragonflies, for example. For on afternoons there were many of them about and in all colors. They alighted on the dry bushes, on the dead branches of the old cotton trees, on the stalks of bamboo planted behind the shacks for the yam and bean shoots.

As for me, I knew all the dragonflies that haunted the sun-filled afternoons of the *habitation:* the big ones as red as berries, or light maroon, with lovely transparent, straight wings, just right for one to squeeze delicately between two fingers. The smaller ones, brown with wings that were short and yellowish or with a black stripe across; very agile, these were, sensitive to the approach of our hands, wild! Finally, more aristocratic and of rarer stock, the 'needles,' so slender and light that one could scarcely make out the little ball of fine gold that formed the head and the periwinkle gauze that sustained their flight.

We knew that the large ones were easy to catch and that all we had to do was to allow them to settle and wait for them to fold the wings ever so slightly. Easy for me who knew how to walk on the tips of my toes without making any false moves and who possessed the art of muffling the crunch of dried leaves under my feet. Me who could judge without error the distance and time to stop, to reach out my hand and stretch my body flexibly, to close my thumb and index finger on the wings of the little creature at rest. Easy for me who could, on a well-endowed branch, catch a dragonfly in each hand, almost at the same time.

Be that as it may, those were the first ones the novices managed to catch. Whereas one needed expert fingers and great experience to catch the short-wings which, agile, mistrustful, remained in a nearly raised position, ready to fly off at the slightest rustle, at the most cautious of approaches. All the same, one succeeded every now and then.

But nobody, not Gesner, not Romane, not even I myself, nobody had ever caught a 'needle'!

Thus we considered them a species not meant to be touched.

In the afternoon we amused ourselves by surprising these dragonflies by taking them for a run, their wings imprisoned between our fingers. Then we released them when they could no longer fly, for the mere pleasure of recapturing them, mutilating them and giving their bodies to the ants.

At last came the moment when, tired of everything, we did not dare undertake any new games; as if the disproportionately lengthening shadows that blended into the ground also penetrated our hearts with all their melancholy.

Tortilla left us to go and wash the *canari* from which we had eaten the rice with her, and Romane, whose tattered rags were once more in shreds, made little knots here and there so they could hold up around her.

It was only then that I became aware of the state of disorder M'man Tine's shack was in.

On the table, I had placed the pieces of the broken bowl.

Everything had been turned upside down and I couldn't even put the objects back in their proper place.

On the ground, cassava flour and dust were mixed into one and I swept in vain. It remained encrusted in the cracks in the smooth earth floor.

I wouldn't have the courage to say that it was a hen that broke the bowl. M'man Tine wouldn't believe a word. Everything betrayed me.

Ah, yes, that evening, misfortune would be my lot.

And there were Gesner and Soumane coming back, visibly tortured by anxiety.

"They're going to beat us, friends; our clothes got torn," said Gesner.

"That's how it was this morning," Tortilla told him after looking at Gesner's rags.

"You must be mad! This big hole wasn't there this morning, nor this piece hanging here. And the shoulders didn't fall like that."

"And look at me," Soumane added, "look how my clothes are torn in the back. Was Mamzé Romane who did that while running on the road to Trénelle. She wanted to get in front of me, and she held me like that, she pulled and rip!"

And myself!

All worked up over the broken bowl, I hadn't looked at myself as yet. I hadn't yet noticed that rip behind my overall, from the hem, all along my legs. And those two spots of mud in front, no doubt left from the impression of my knees on the damp ground under the straw when I had fallen in the field.

"That's nothing," Tortilla cried. "What if you were like me . . . Look, in the cane field, all that burst open. Well, I've already tied it up."

Indeed, the dingy jacket clothing Tortilla's body had shrunk, and if I couldn't see that the number of knots that made up the texture of it had increased, I was nonetheless aware that my good friend was all the more naked for it.

I would have wished to do something for my part. Wash out the two spots of mud for example.

"But it won't have time to dry," Tortilla explained to me. "Your maman will find you all wet."

And that would be even more serious.

Make a knot to patch the tear in the overall. I mustn't think about it either; that'll only make it show more.

What to do?

"Well, all you have to do is use the old *nika* charm. You take all the fingers on one hand and put them one over the other . . . "

"I know, I know."

But I had done it once so M'man Tine wouldn't see a wound I had on my knee; well, she had seen it all the same, and had washed my sore in salt water to boot.

"Well, you have no luck with *nika*," Tortilla concluded. "You should try to tie your maman. You take a handful of hay from over there, in the savannah, and you make as many knots as the length of the blades of grass allows, and you hold that tightly in your hand. Then, when your maman arrives, you walk towards her to say good evening, and before saying a word, you drop the hay behind you. I assure you that you'll never be beaten. You maman may quarrel with you, she may swear, but she'll never lay hands on you. She'll quite simply be tied."

We were together once more, united in fear at present.

"Your dress is not torn like my jacket," Paul said to me. "And then, tomorrow, your maman will give you another so she can sew this one. Whereas with me, my papa said that when I finish this one, I'll go about naked."

Indeed, what Paul called his jacket was nothing more than a coarse, grimy lacework whose usefulness escaped me completely. I'd have found him better off and much cleaner entirely naked. Furthermore, I too would have loved to run about in the nude. For I was fed up being flogged for getting my clothes torn. They would burst in the sleeves and elbows while we played and rip in the back as we passed under the barbed wire fences, and the hem would come apart as we ran in the bushes.

Oh, for all of us to be naked!

"Me too, I prefer to be naked . . . "

"Me too!"

Who wouldn't have been thrilled to run about completely naked in the sun!

"Well," Romane ventured, "this very evening, we're going to ask our parents to allow us to run about naked."

Not feeling I was brave enough to make such a request as far as M'man Tine was concerned, I proposed:

"All we have to do is take off our clothes as soon as our parents set off on mornings and put them on again when they're about to return."

"That's not possible," Tortilla interjected. "We mustn't remain naked. We're too big. Our Good Angel will fall off."

"What's this about our Good Angel?"

"Oh, you don't know your Good Angel?"

Tortilla's tone of mockery confounded me even more in my ignorance.

"Well," she cried, throwing back her shoulders suddenly and placing her hand under her belly, "your Good Angel is down there. That's why we do not run about naked!"

By this time there was not a speck of sunlight in the trees nor on the ground.

Night had fallen. Our parents would soon be arriving. We would be beaten. We could sense that from the very manner in which our anxiety increased, in which we were incapable of being talkative and happy. And, in actual fact, I had no confidence in that patch of hay held snug in the palm of my hand, to which I added another knot every now and then.

Oh! If only it were possible not to feel those lashes on my legs! Those switches on the skin of my behind!

We had already given deep thought to the matter. But we only ended up with a few manoeuvres to avoid the onslaught being too long.

"At the first blow," said Orélie, "I begin to bawl. Bawling as if I'm dying. Then, maman herself gets bewildered. She only gives me one other blow: wap! and she shouts: 'Quiet, quiet, now.' I tone down the bawling a bit, keep whimpering for some time while maman is there grumbling, and when her anger subsides, I shut up."

"With me," Romane added, beating his chest, "I'm a black girl with a stout heart. My papa uses a switch on me—not a sound. Maman says I get that from my grandmother who was stone and iron."

Mr. Gabriel, the overseer, passed by on his mule. The daily workers had finished their task. M'man Tine wouldn't be long now.

I wouldn't go to meet her. None of us, I thought, would be going to meet his parents. We were afraid.

We separated, each one returning near to his dwelling place. And we waited.

Already there passed mules upon which sat brutal mule-drivers who whipped them on their rumps and swore to high heavens.

Stooping on the step of the shack, I curled up more and more, consumed as I was by anguish.

How mournful the night seemed, with paths absorbed by the darkness, the galvanized roofs of the shacks assuming a bluish hue, the coconut trees whose branches grew heavy rustling in the gusts of breeze, and that huge flock of men and women drained of all strength wending their way out of the cane fields like ghosts coming out of the darkness for some unknown gruesome ritual!

And soon there would appear before me one of those ghosts, particularly familiar, whose return I feared and which I awaited, and whose voice jolted me out of my sad reverie:

"What's wrong? You're tired from playing on the *béké's* plantation?" M'man Tine asked.

I knew that whenever she began by this sort of questioning, everything ended up badly for me.

Already I was losing countenance and, without realizing it, forgetting Tortilla's recommendations, I limply dropped my knots of hay at my feet.

"Eh! what were you doing at 12 o'clock on the road to Trénelle?" M'man Tine pursued.

I couldn't answer. I hadn't prepared a reply to that.

Furthermore, I had in no way anticipated she would have known.

With my head bowed, I played awkwardly with my fingers.

With her usual gesture, M'man Tine placed the handle of her hoe against the shack and put down her bamboo basket.

"Stand up a bit, let's have a look at you!" she said to me.

Slowly, a crestfallen look in my eyes, I stood up and remained motionless before her, my toes riveted to the ground, not knowing what to do with my hands.

"Wow!" M'man Tine cried. "So this is the state of the clothes I put on you this morning! And your knees have fresh bruises like the backs of pack mules, and there's more straw on your head than any shack in Morne-Mango-Zo!"

Already I couldn't feel the ground under my feet. I was so stiff in my position that my joints hurt.

"So you were part of that convoy that followed the cart in the Grand Etang trace? And you were happy cursing the oxen, spitting out foul words to your heart's content?"

I did not say a word. Besides, the truth of the matter was, those were not questions. They were accusations.

"Well, tomorrow," she declared, "you'll remain as you are, for I'll not have time to sew your clothes."

But far from being relieved, my heart felt a sudden twinge.

I wanted to be the first to broach the subject of the broken bowl, but my attempt to summon up enough courage to lie the way Tortilla had advised me was futile.

Now, instead of sitting outside to smoke her pipe, M'man Tine went inside the shack.

"And you broke the bowl!" she cried.

My head was spinning with fear. In order not to lose my balance, I stiffened my body to the point where my bones almost snapped.

"Eh?" M'man Tine exclaimed, coming towards me. "Come here and tell me what you were doing for the bowl to break," she then said, grabbing me by the arm.

I remained dumb, looking at the two fragments of the bowl in a haze.

"What were you doing?"

It seemed that the moment was ripe to let out with what Tortilla had advised me to say, but I was stiff, right up to my jaw. It seemed to me that even if I were to be beaten with a stick I wouldn't utter a sound.

"Lord," M'man Tine exclaimed once more, "what on earth happened here?"

And turning to me once more:

"What happened to you? What were you looking for?"

My reaction was such that she dragged me from outside to deposit me in the middle of the room, transfixed in my dumb state, head bowed, my eyes glued to the ground.

"Well! well!" M'man Tine proclaimed, shaking her head as her eyes ran over the interior of the hut.

"Well! well!" she exclaimed once more in the bedroom. My bed has been turned over like a yam patch. An earthquake couldn't do all that!"

Then leaving the bedroom suddenly, she shouted to me:

"Go into punishment!"

Automatically, I fell on my knees.

M'man Tine entered her bedroom once more, fuming and grumbling in anger.

"What the devil was this little ragamuffin looking for in my things, eh?"

The roughness of the ground began to bite cruelly into the open bruises on my knees. But I followed closely the evolution of M'man Tine's fury. I fearfully awaited the moment when she was going to fall upon me with blows from the first thing she could lay her hands on and I felt almost nothing, save a confusion which overpowered me despite the state of stoic stiffness I kept myself in, there in the center of the shack on my two knees.

All of a sudden M'man Tine fell silent and, as I could not see what she was doing, as I could no longer follow her, I suddenly felt myself losing my balance. I didn't know what was happening.

That awful silence isolated me in my confusion, clearing everything around me, like at times when M'man Tine looked for a broomstick, a *lélé* or a piece of rope to beat me.

I felt like bawling from in front.

From the back of the bedroom the angered voice asked me:

"Ah, you were looking for the sugar? It's the sugar you were looking for!"

I barely had the time to see M'man Tine come from the bedroom before her hand, hard as a clod of earth in the dry season, came into contact with my face.

"O.K., that's the sugar you were looking for!"

And I remained sprawled on the ground, dumbfounded, hearing the thundering of her voice and resigned to receiving a shower of blows.

"Back on your knees!"

Painfully I got back on my knees, glancing sideways at M'man Tine who, with the sugar tin in her hand, uncovered it and examined it.

"The li'l scamp!" she said, "He turned the whole place upside down and couldn't find the sugar; and in all this moving about, he broke the bowl. That's it . . . I mean, my God, I can't even leave the béké's canes without having my blood boil when I return to this old shack. Oh, no! I can't take any more!"

Thereupon she decided once again to send me to Délia, my mother.

For, she said, the Good Lord couldn't thus tolerate my mother enjoying herself in town, behind the chairs of the békés she served, while she was drying up in the sun like tobacco, unable to go to bed in peace for the weighty tiredness in her body.

Then began the endless unfolding of what I had already heard over and over again, every time I made her angry, every time she had just experienced some suffering.

"As for me, when I was small I wasn't a bother to anybody. Far from it. When my mother died nobody wanted me, except Uncle Gilbert. Well, what did Uncle Gilbert do with me? He enlisted me in the *petites bandes,* to uproot weeds from the young canes so I could bring him a few cents on Saturday nights. During this time the plots of land my mother had received from the old béké who was my grandfather were tended by him and he planted whatever he wanted, harvested it, rented a plot here, a half-plot there. From morning to night I remained bent over in the furrow, my head lower than my behind, until the commander, Mr. Valbrum, seeing how I was built, held, rolled me over on the ground and drove a child into my belly. Well, I didn't want to have your mother join the *petites bandes.* I couldn't send her to school because there weren't any schools in the village as yet, but I looked after her till she was twelve, as if I'd been a rich woman. Then I put her *au pair* with Mme Léonce in the village. She didn't turn out bad; she learned to wash, iron and cook.

"Well, Mr. Léonce, the foreman at the factory, when asked by his boss to find him a young person to do the housework, well, he sent your mother, because he was aware that she was a girl capable of working as a servant for a béké, and that his boss was going to reward him himself.

"If she hadn't met your papa who was the Administrator's

coachman, she would probably still be there up to now. But instead of coming and telling me that a man was interested in her, she came to me when she was good and pregnant. I never set eyes on that man called Eugène who is your father and he never set eyes on you either. You weren't born yet when he was caught to go and fight in France. Since the war is reported to be over, no Eugène. All I know, wasn't three months your mother had you there in my bedroom. Up! She left for Fort-de-France in search of a job.

"And I was left to start over with you. Your bouts of sickness, 'twas me. Your worm fits, 'twas me. To wash you, dry you, dress you! While all the live-long day, you invented all sorts of complications for me, as if I didn't have enough with my sun strokes, showers, thunderclaps, and the hoe with which I had to scratch the hard earth of the béké. And, instead of behaving yourself in order to conserve my energy so I can last a bit longer, so as to shelter you, as I did with your maman, you drive me to the stage where I feel like posting you into the petites bandes the way all the blacks do. Indeed, I can't take any more."

Thus, the following week she would go down to the village to ask a "learned" person to write a letter to my mother, telling the latter how impossible it was for her to keep me. If not, she would send me off to the petites bandes.

"Heavens! Take me away! Away from the plantation, from M'man Tine, from my friends, from the savannah!"

As she spoke, M'man Tine had warmed up and despite her utter tiredness, with witch-like zeal, she increased her movements to and fro, busying herself with the many small operations involved in the preparation of dinner.

I was still on my knees in the center of the dark shack.

Outside, the fire flickered madly up and down and from it, through the half-open door, an occasional glow reached me. My knees had grown numb and had no more feeling. I didn't even think of myself any more. My head was spinning as if from some beverage forbidden to children, from all the sad, bitter words murmured by my grandmother and I would have liked her not to stop talking, to relate indefinitely those things I didn't fully understand, but which I felt so cruelly.

My somber reverie was suddenly broken by the angry voice of M'man Tine who shouted to me:

"Beg pardon, so you can come out and allow me to pass."

"P'don, M'man," I muttered.

"Get up, you li'l scamp."

My wounded knees had bled and the clotted blood had welded them so steadfastly to the ground that it was with a muffled shout of pain that I unstuck them.

Hardly was I on my feet before M'man Tine gripped me by the arm and led me outside beside the fire where she had put an earthenware container full of water.

And still grumbling she took off my overall, put me in the container and set about cleaning me up, which proved to be a veritable torture for, because of the grass where I had rolled earlier in the day and the scratches from the cane leaves, my entire body on contact with the water was aflame with burning, stinging, itching, which I translated into grimaces, contortions and groans.

"That'll teach you!" said M'man Tine.

And her rough hands, passing over my bruises like a plane, drew from me cries that evoked no pity since, continuing to rub me down as vigorously as she could, she pressed on my knees, saying:

"Say, look at this young man's knees! . . . Oh no! I can't take any more, I can't take it. Mamzé Délia must come and fetch her child."

After my nocturnal bath, after my late dinner, another torture awaited me: prayers.

"In the name of the Father . . . "

"In the name of the Father," I repeated, making the sign.

"And of the Son . . . "

I knew that 'and of the Son' was in the middle of the chest, on the hard bone concealed there, that M'man Tine had already made me touch in the beginning to cement it in my memory.

"And of the Holy Spirit."

From that point on, I was all confused. My hand flew from one shoulder to the other, not daring to stop on any one.

I looked at M'man Tine, watching for her approval or a reflex of repulsion.

My hand once more started to shake with fear, faltered, touched one shoulder.

"And of the Son," I said, not fully aware of what I was doing.

"Li'l devil!" cried M'man Tine. "You don't find we're wretched enough as it is without your making the sign of the cross wrongside! I told you already that 'And of the Holy Spirit' is on the left shoulder, this one, this one here!" she said tapping my shoulder with my hand held in hers.

That night M'man Tine did not shorten my prayer as she did on some occasions when she was tired or I was sleepy. On the contrary. She started from the 'Let us be in the presence of God!', continued with the 'Our Father,' the 'I salute thee,' the 'I believe in God.' She refused to prompt me, crying "come on, come on!" every time I stopped.

I felt as though I was reeling, scraping my toes and knees in endless tortuous, stony and thorny paths. The 'I Believe in God' in particular seemed to me like a narrow path, curving its way like a snake up a hill whose summit touched the sky.

When at last I reached 'ascended into heaven, and sitteth on the right . . . ' it seemed as if I was then at the very top, standing in the breeze. I then took a deep breath and with the 'from whence he shall come to judge . . . ' I descended the other side of the hill. But alas! only to become hopelessly lost in the maze of all the 'acts' of faith, contrition and hope from which I could see no way out; for every time, according to her inspiration, M'man Tine made me go back to the 'Oh Virgin of Virgins' and ended the prayer on an improvised note—either an 'invocation,' a long litany, or a prayer for 'the dead, friends and enemies' . . .

After that, I had, on my own improvisation, to ask God for "the strength, the courage and the grace not to pee the bed, not to pinch any sugar, to remain in the shack the whole day and not to tear my clothes."

Some nights I made it to the end, somehow or other. But that evening I failed. My knees hurt too much. I was too tired, overwhelmed by my emotions. I was too sleepy. I mumbled for as long as I could, then I collapsed.

Sprawled in my rags which still retained the warmth of the daylong sun, I could make out vague wailings: Gesner or Tortilla, not yet finished atoning for their crimes.

*

Adults formed a world that impressed us above all by its mystery. A mysterious world indeed, where one procured one's own food, where one was not beaten (it was true that Mr. Donatien used to beat Mam'zelle Horacia, his wife, every night; but the latter wasn't backward either when it came to biting), a world where one did not fall as one walked nor as one ran, where one did not shed tears. A strange world! Hence our profound admiration for the men and women from Black Shack Alley. I was particularly fond of those who had no children. I feared my friends' parents even more than M'man Tine. People who beat their children. People who were always blaming us children. Whereas the workers who did not have children would send us on little errands to "the house" (a distraction that was very much sought after by us), and consequently were very kind to us, even spoiling us somewhat.

"The best man in the *habitation*," Gesner affirmed, "is Mr. Saint-Louis."

"Mr. Saint-Louis!" cried Soumane, "I don't like him. The other day, I was passing near his garden. Well, because I pulled a li'l straw from his hedge, that's all, he shouted at me (I hadn't seen him there), shouted at me like a devil. And he sent and told my maman that I was the one who demolished his hedge in order to hunt birds."

"I don't like him very much either," Victorine concurred. "One day, his plum tree was laden and I asked him   for a small one and he said that it wasn't ripe enough, that it was going to give me worm fits . . . Every time you ask him for something, it's not ripe enough."

"And he puts broken bottles all around his garden to make us lame."

"Well!" As for me," Gesner interrupted, "Mr. Saint-Louis gives me everything. On Sundays, he asks me over to his place, tells me to have a seat on the ground in a little corner and when his food is cooked he gives me pieces of yam big like that, with codfish. He even promised to get me a bird's nest with young birds from his garden."

Mr. Saint-Louis was a tall black man whose shoulders moved gently up and down at each step like the back of a horse moving at a leisurely pace. At the bottom of his dark face, almost completely hidden by the rims of an old straw hat, he wore a greyish beard which, for nothing in the world, I would have dared to touch. To go with this straw hat went a pair of trousers rolled up to his calves and on which fell a loin-cloth made from an empty guano bag.

Mr. Saint-Louis' shack was situated behind M'man Tine's. As on one side he didn't have any neighbors, he had enclosed with coconut branches a large plot of land where he would work on Sundays and Mondays.

But nobody among us knew for sure what Mr. Saint-Louis grew in his garden. So compact was the hedge that no one could see through it. One could see above it the tip of a plum tree and an avocado tree, but as for the rest, one didn't know what it was, when it was ripe, when it was harvested.

On several occasions I had heard that it must be a garden where Mr. Saint-Louis grew plants to cure illnesses.

One can well imagine how this garden haunted our imagination and tortured our curiosity. We were afraid of it all the same. Since, in a certain season, the hedge was packed with birds' nests, this garden, despite its aura of mystery and the scientific manner in which it was protected, remained for us an inviolable, but attractive objective.

*

Romane preferred Mam'zelle Appoline. An old woman who couldn't see clearly and who would call us to take chiggers from her feet, something I detested doing. Her feet smelled like a rotten toad.

Tortilla's favorite was Mr. Asselin, Asselin-bread. Someone who never lit a fire in his place. He did not have a wife and existed only on bread, salted codfish and rum. He was the strongest black man in Shack Alley. When he ran, the earth shook. He was also the most naked. Even his loincloth was full of holes. He had huge, white, well-formed teeth. His laughter gave rise to the happiest moment one could ever enjoy. And when he danced the *laghia* on Saturday nights, one didn't want the night to end nor the torches to go out.

My great friend didn't give me anything. He was the oldest, most wretched and most abandoned on the entire plantation. And I preferred being with him to running, frolicking, amusing myself or pinching sugar.

For someone like myself who couldn't sit still one moment, I would remain for hours sitting quietly beside him. His hut was the emptiest and the dirtiest, but I preferred it to M'man Tine's which was one of the finest and best kept in Shack Alley.

"Children must not always be in other people's places," my grandmother used to remind me. "It's bad manners."

But at nights, as I looked at M'man Tine smoking, I longed for only one thing, waited for only one thing: to have the voice of Mr. Médouze call me.

Outside the door that stood wide open to the darkness already accumulated in the shack, a shadow scarcely visible in the distance awaited me—to send me to beg for a pinch of salt from M'man Tine, or to buy two cents worth of kerosine in the shop.

Then in front of the shack we lit a fire between three stones. I was the one who went nearby in search of the twigs that the flame devoured so readily.

While in the *canari* a noisy bubbling converted the wild roots brought back from the cane field where he had worked, the ghost-like form sat on the front step on the shack, at the edge of that terrible rectangular mouth that drank in the night, and I went beside him. He filled his pipe when he was finished, and I went near the fireside to fetch him a flaming twig: as he bent his head over it to light his pipe, the glow cast on his face a hallucinating mask—the true face of Mr. Médouze—with his head streaked with reddish hair, his beard looking like brambles, his eyes, of which one could never see but a small slit, because his eyelids were almost always closed.

The glow from the fireside lit up the entire side of the shack; and Mr. Médouze's body, covered with only a loin-cloth similar to Mr. Saint-Louis', with, around his neck, a tiny sack black with dirt and hanging from a string, looked like a handsome, masculine body that the fire had roasted for a long time and that it now delighted in enriching with all the shades of brown.

He finished smoking his pipe in silence, almost motionless. After a while, as if awaking from his inertia, he cleared his throat, spat and, in a voice that kept failing, he cried point-blank:

"*Titim!*"

Thereupon my attention was immediately revived and my joy exploded in my prompt reply:

"Dry wood!"

That was how our game of riddles began.

"I'm here, I'm in France!" Mr. Médouze proposed.

Pretending to be wracking my brains, I merely looked at him. His steady, calm face once more assumed fantastic expressions in the glow of the flames flickering under the *canari*. He knew, moreover, that I would not find the answer to his riddle and that I was waiting.

"A letter," he told me at last.

A letter? I didn't know what that was; but that only made it seem all the more marvellous. In general, Mr. Médouze, as if to have a sort of revision, started with the most elementary *'titims'*, those to which I already had the key.

"When water climbed up a hill?"

"A coconut," I replied in a flash.

"When water ran down a hill?"

"Sugar cane!"

"When Madame put on her apron back to front?"

"A fingernail."

Then he moved on to the more difficult ones.

"Madame is in her bedroom and her hair is floating outside."

Silence. Prolonged silence. A few puffs slowly taken from the old pipe, and he himself supplied the answer:

"A yam."

That seemed odd to me.

"Of course," he explained, "the yam is in the ground which serves as a bedroom, and its tendrils, like curls of hair, climb on the sticks.

The main attraction of these riddle sessions was to discover how a world of inanimate objects managed to resemble and be identified with a world of people and animals. How an earthenware water-bottle held by the neck became a servant who only served water to his master when the latter choked him. How the manager's parasol looked like 'a shack with only one post.'

Thus, at the mere intervention of Mr. Médouze, the world expanded, increased, teemed in a swirl around me.

When Mr. Médouze finished his pipe, he would spit violently, wipe his lips with the back of his hand, which he also passed over the prickly shagginess of his beard. Then came the most disturbing part of the evening.

"Eh *cric!*"

"Eh *crac!*"

My heart started beating wildly, my eyes were aflame.
"Thrice fines stories!"
"All stories are nice to hear!"
"Who is Dog's mother?"
"Bitch."
"Dog's father?"
"Bull dog."
"Abouhou!"
"Biah!"
I had answered the preamble properly.
Silence. I held my breath.

"Well, once upon a time," Mr. Médouze started slowly, "when Rabbit used to walk around dressed in white calico suit and Panama hat; when all the traces on Petit-Morne were paved with diamonds, rubies, topaz (all the streams ran gold and Grand Etang was a pool of honey); when I, Médouze, was Médouze; there was at that time, an old man who lived all alone in a castle, far, far, far away."

"A liar would say far like from here to Grand-Rivière. My brother, who used to lie a bit, would have said like from here to St. Lucia. But I not being a liar, say that it was far like from here to Guinea . . . eh *cric!*"

"Eh *crac!*"

"That man used to live by himself and was middle-aged," Médouze continued, "but he did not lack anything. One morning, he put on his boots, took his hat and, taking care not to eat or drink anything, mounted his white horse and set out.

"At first, the journey began in perfect silence. As if the horse were galloping on clouds. Then, as the sun came up, the man was himself surprised to hear music behind him. He slowed down; the music became slow and indistinct. He stopped. Silence. He spurred his mount, the music started up again.

"He then realised that it was the four horse shoes that were playing so harmoniously:

'Tis the queen's ball,
Plakata, plakata
'Tis the queen's ball,
Plakata, plakata.

"But what music!

'Tis the queen's ball.' "

Médouze sang. With his deep, grating voice, he imitated one hundred violins, twenty 'mama-violins' (cellos), ten clarinets and fifteen contrabasses.

Overcome by his fervor, I took up the magical song along with him:

Plakata, Plakata.

But, alas! the voice of M'man Tine rang out and came to break our duet. My heart heavy with regret, annoyed to tears, I had to give up the rest of the fairy tale, and to hastily abandon my old friend with a quick 'good night.'

That was what transpired almost every night. I could never hear a story right through to the end. I didn't know if it was M'man Tine who called me away too soon, although she always scolded me for staying too long, or if it was Médouze who did not tell the story quickly enough. At any rate, there was not a night when I didn't leave with my heart and my curiosity unappeased.

In addition to Petit-Morne, to its workers and to ourselves, we knew that the world extended even further, beyond the factory whose chimneys we could see, and that on the other side of the hills surrounding the plantation, lay other similar plantations.

We also knew that there was the town, Fort-de-France, with many vehicles in the streets.

M'man Tine had already told me about a far-off country called France where people had white skins and spoke something called "French;" a country from which came the flour used to make bread and cakes, and where all sorts of beautiful things were made.

On some nights, either in his tales or in his talks, Mr. Médouze evoked another country even further away, even deeper than France, which was that of his father: Guinea. There, people were like him and me; but they did not die of tiredness nor of hunger.

There was no misery as there was here.

Nothing stranger than to see Mr. Médouze evoke Guinea, to hear the voice rising from his entrails when he spoke of slavery and related the horrible story his father had told him, of the rape of his family, of the disappearance of his nine uncles and aunts, of his grandfather and his grandfather.

"Everytime my father tried to relate his life story," he continued, "once he got to: 'I had a big brother called Ousmane, a younger sister called Sonia, the last one', he would shut his eyes very tight and fall silent all of a sudden. And I, too, would bite my lips as if I had received a stab in my heart. 'I was young,' my father said, 'when all the blacks fled from the plantations because it had been said that slavery was over.' I, too, danced with joy and went running all over Martinique because, for a long time, I had so wanted to flee, to run away. But when the intoxication of my freedom was spent, I was forced to remark that nothing had changed for me nor for my comrades in chains. I hadn't found my brothers and sisters, nor my father, nor my mother. I remained like all the blacks in this damned country: the *békés* kept the land, all the land in the country, and we continued working for them. The law forbade them from whipping us, but did not force them to pay us our due."

"Yes," he added, "at any rate, we remained under the *béké,* attached to his land. And he remained our master."

Naturally, Mr. Médouze was then angry and in vain I looked at him with a frown on my brow, in vain I had this maddening urge to hit the *béké* I set my eyes on. I could not make out all he was grumbling and, to console him, I said to him:

"If you were to go to Guinea, Monsieur Médouze, you know, I'd go with you. I think M'man Tine wouldn't mind."

"Alas!" he replied, with a sad smile, "Médouze won't be seeing Guinea. Besides, I have no maman, no papa, no brothers or sisters in Guinea . . . Yes, when I'm dead, I'll go to Guinea; but then, I won't be able to take you. You'll not be old enough; and then, I mustn't."

*

We were at that time familiar with a host of important things our parents had inculcated in us.

"Never say good evening to a person you meet on the road when it is beginning to get dark. Because if it's a *zombi,* he'll carry your voice to the devil who could then take you away at any time."

"Always close the door when you're inside the shack at night. Because evil spirits could pelt stones after you, leaving you in pain the rest of your life."

"And when, at nights, you smell anything, don't say a word, for your nose will rot like an old banana."

"If you find a cent in the road, pee on it before picking it up, so your hand won't swell like a frog."

"Don't let a dog stare at you while you eat. Give it a morsel and chase it away, so your eyelids won't remain stuck down."

I, who knew so many tales and *titims,* was careful not to tell them in broad daylight, for I knew that I'd then run the risk of being turned into a basket.

And we all were careful not to approach Mam'zelle Abizotye, the *quimboiseuse* so as to avoid her evil touch.

Time was simply an alternating of days and nights punctuated by three special days whose names I knew:

Saturday, Sunday, Monday.

Saturday, that was the day M'man Tine left the shack very early so as to complete, at all cost, the week's work; and it was the night the *canaliers* returned very early to Black Shack Alley.

The afternoon was still bright and these men lingered awhile in Shack Alley and gathered to talk in a loud voice. Then, increasing the noise from their palavers and their laughter, they set off once more towards 'the house.'

There followed other strong men who would have been impressive but for the sorry rags that defiled their bodies. Women with supple, rhythmical carriage. Frolicking, laughing young girls, their breasts standing out through the slits in their bodices. And young, bare-backed mule-drivers, astride their mounts trotting nervously between their legs, advancing like dauntless conquerors.

In a flash, the areas surrounding Shack Alley had taken on a new look.

Marketwomen from Petit-Bourg, in long white flowing tunics, had placed their trays and baskets of sweets just about everywhere. Slowly there gathered that earth-stained bunch, tools on shoulders, going to stop in front of the manager's office to await their pay.

Some had bright eyes, open eyes and festive laughter; stocky fellows teasing the girls with smacks on their fleshy buttocks and their round legs and small girls from the *petites bandes* with budding breasts, whispering and giggling among themselves.

There were others who stood around, serious, speaking only to show their impatience to receive their money: it was getting late.

And there were also those who did not say a word and remained sitting on the ground, on the roots of trees lolling, hiding under dull bell-shaped hats full of holes, with eyes that seemed tired of looking at what they saw, but not betraying any sentiment; these limited their movements to an occasional gesture of chasing flies maddened by the running sores on a huge leg, or a swollen broken ankle oozing through a mud-stained bandage.

But what interested me were the trays of the women, which became more numerous and invaded the area surrounding the office and Shack Alley. Then followed the young women selling peanuts. And the women selling hot spicy black pudding. And a huge woman, the most familiar of all, Mam'zelle Zouzoune, who sold her wares from two trays—one with bread, one with fried fish—and from a coal-pot on which she fried codfish *akras*.

Then, suddenly, as if triggered by some unknown force, the crowd in one movement drew close to the window that served as the pay-window, behind which the manager—with the help of his overseer and a commander—was about to hand out the pay.

"*Canaliers!*" the commander announced.

Paying of wages had begun.

"Amédée!"

"Here!" the worker replied.

"Twenty-nine francs fifty."

"Julien-twelve-toe!" the commander continued.

The workers were registered for work under their first names. So the *Habitation,* in order to distinguish several bearers of the same first name, added to each person a picturesque or trivial epithet characteristic of the bodily peculiarities of the individual concerned; or the first name of his mother; of her husband, if it was a woman; or the district the worker came from.

And so—one ended up with: Maximilien-dog-teeth, and Maximilien-big-calves; Rose-full-cucumber and Rosa-Asson; Adrien-Lamberton and Adrien-Courbaril.

"Julien-Achoune!"

" 'sent!"

"Twenty-one francs four centimes."

Julien, having collected his pay, withdrew from the compact crowd, gesticulating like a man engaged in a fight, then angrily threw the money on the ground, stamped on it, swearing by the behind of the manager's mother, insulting God and, mad with rage, picked up the money and moved away grumbling: "What's keeping me from dying, God-damn-it!"

Then it was the turn of the male and female weeders, of the diggers, placed under the heading 'task people,' of the grass cutters, called *'gens z'Héb,'* of the cart and mule drivers; and finally, the entire *petites bandes,* elder brothers and sisters of my friends who on Saturday nights seemed to us so worthy of envy when the overseer handed them rolls of nickel coins and once in a while paper notes like the adults received.

When the paying of wages was finished, the entire group, like water from a drain, moved toward Shack Alley. There were those who were not worried, even happy. But I noticed some who did not hide their disappointment and who paused to take a long look, in the palm of their hands, at what was to be left of their pay once one took out what had to be spent at the manager's store. They shook their heads with a sigh: "Well! Good Lord! . . . " and set off once more at a faltering pace.

Then there were a few, like Asselin, who hardly received anything: a loaf of bread, a quarter pound of codfish, a nip of rum per day, and the rest of the week's wages remained in the plantation store, for in the eyes of everyone Asselin was considered the most extravagant and licentious man in Petit-Mourne.

But once pay-time was over, the festivity began for children. The market-women lit torches under the coconut trees so here and there the night was decked with bouquets of light.

The men bought huge *demi-pains* stuffed with golden *akras,* and the shop had an unending stream of rum drinkers.

The women preferred cakes, and the kids from the *petites bandes* mostly went around munching peanuts.

This carnival went on far into the night, way beyond the time when M'man Tine, having managed to find me in the crowd, dragged me home to the shack.

But even in bed, I would remain awake for some time, for, in the midst of all that bustle, that noise, those bouquets of fire blooming in the night, of all that food, of the stench of feet swollen with elephantiasis, of those rags exuding the smell of old sweat, of that alchohol-drenched sadness, there arose, diabolical and irresistible, the deep, pulsating beat of the tom-tom.

Everything—the purulent feet, the quivering breasts, those male shoulders and frenzied hips, all those glassy eyes and rainbow smiles, all these people, satiated, drunk and forgetting all cares, blended into one burning, invading babel, like a fire, flaring into dancing, dancing, dancing.

*

Sundays were easily recognized as being the day after the night wages were paid, and the day when all the inhabitants of Shack Alley remained at home, of course cutting down our chances to do what we liked.

Then, over the entire *habitation* there reigned a silence that almost made us sick, condemned as we were to playing the part of "well behaved" children, condemned to avoid any noise or foul language.

Our parents busied themselves inside and outside their shacks, cleaning, sweeping, uprooting weeds from the front steps, taking down their beds, putting the boards and rags out to sun so as to kill the bugs, and, inevitably, making us help.

Nevertheless, there was one advantage that, in a way, made up for all the other inconveniences. After lunch, M'man Tine opened the outer door and window to her bedroom to take a little siesta, and no sooner was she asleep than I would dash off to Médouze's place.

I might find my old friend sitting below a mango tree near his shack, or at other times, sleeping inside with the door half-open in the dark, despite the daylight that streamed in through the little hole in the one partition opposite the door.

For furniture the shack had a boulder, the height of a stool, sticking out of the ground, which nobody had bothered to dig out, for luckily, on this stone Médouze had only to place the end of a plank and with the other end resting on the ground, he had made himself a bed.

Lying on this dingy, bare plank, polished by the contact with his skin, the old man would snore away. Too low to receive what little light that there was in the shack, his body formed, along with his loin-cloth, the plank, the stone and the ground, one unified mass, without any protruding detail save the soap-like patch of his beard from which uttered intermittent snores. I would sneak up in silence. But, immediately, he would stir and begin to mutter in a voice that seemed to me impossibly old and rusty:

"It's you . . . I'm not asleep, you know . . . Just trying to rest my old body awhile."

Then, reaching to light his pipe he had placed in a hollow part of his bed-stone, he would rise slowly and painfully, his bones cracking over and over, and we would go outside under the mango tree.

Our conversations consisted of a long series of questions on my part, to which he replied scrupulously.

I asked him, for instance, if the sky and the earth met somewhere.

I was also very interested in finding out where the békés found all the money they were alleged to possess. Médouze then explained that it was the devil who brought it for them.

As it turned out, I already knew by intuition that the devil, misery, and death were more or less the same evil individual, who persecuted the blacks above all. And I wondered in vain what blacks could have done to the devil and to the béké to be so oppressed by both.

Sometimes also, with strings and bits of wood he picked up here and there Médouze would make me a toy, a man or an animal with which I would have fun playing until the time came for him to tell me a story.

*

Sunday . . . Monday.

On Mondays, M'man Tine went to the river and took me with her.

The river was far from the plantation, and we had to walk a long way to reach it.

We left home early, for M'man Tine tried to be the first to arrive so she could choose her favorite spot and settle down at the place where a huge stone hollowed out in the shape of an earthenware bowl could hold the dirty clothes she soaked in it.

On arriving, the washerwomen would string themselves along the shallow parts of the stream and there, singing and chatting, they would scrub away at their patched and tattered clothes.

M'man Tine preferred to be alone because she did not trust those women whose tongues were, it seemed, as clacking as bell clappers.

I spent my time looking for guavas in the woods; or as the months passed, learning how to catch small shrimp by hand in the river.

At midday, a great expanse of linen flittered over with small yellow butterflies shone in the sunlight. After eating my lunch on the grass, I went to a spot where the river was full and slow, forming a curve like a turn in a road, and I amused myself throwing in pebbles which fell into the water with a gentle plop, like big rain drops falling out of a musical sky.

When the sun went out, exhausted, so to speak, after drying so much linen, M'man Tine gathered everything into a small bundle and called me to have a bath. The banks of the river were then too shady and I did not at all enjoy my bath, especially since M'man Tine did not allow me to splash about to my heart's content; instead, she hoisted me onto a stone, scrubbing me vigorously with guava tree sprouts and rinsing me down with a few stinging bowlfuls of water.

In compensation, she would plunge her hands into the water, turning over some stones and surprising a few crayfish which I could roast myself that very night over our charcoal fire.

*

But, despite all that, Sunday and Mondays were, for us children, tough days to get through. To a man, we all preferred Saturdays and the others days when, from morning to night (never mind the showers of blows to which we exposed ourselves!) we were free, responsible only for ourselves, and masters of Shack Alley.

*

"Eggs! Hens' eggs!" Gesner shouted.

I couldn't believe my eyes. Imagine finding so easily in the bushes a nest of grass and straw, and filled with hens' eggs!

I had often heard people complain about hens that made their nests outside. I had even seen one that, after a long disappearance which Mam'zelle attributed to theft, had come back one fine day trailing behind her a brood of chickens. But what a far cry from that to be lucky enough actually to discover the hiding place where a hen had laid her eggs! . . .

The trick was to avoid thinking about whose hen's treasure had fallen into our hands. We counted the eggs: there was one for each of us—except for those who were considered as altogether negligible. The small fries were not too be left out really; we were going to cook our eggs and everybody would get some.

Never had fate so generously spoiled us. Oh, what a marvellous afternoon! And the entire band returned to Shack Alley.

Eggs that we hadn't stolen, that we had found, which had fallen out of the blue, so to speak!

Tortilla put them in a *canari* full of water with a pinch of salt. I was the one who had suggested that she proceed in that way.

I had never eaten eggs. Furthermore, none of us had ever eaten any. Our parents' eggs were for hatching. And the hens were to be exchanged at the store of 'the house' for rice, kerosine and codfish; or sold to the *békés* at the factory.

But I felt that they had to be cooked in a *canari* of water over fire.

At present, the fire was to be lit. Impossible to find matches. Our parents were all smokers and carried away their boxes of matches with them.

But at last everything was ready. A pile of wood was gathered in a flash. Paul had cleaned the fireplace of its ashes and heaped up the small bits of wood in it. Oh for a match to strike, just one match for our joy to be complete.

Soumane, impatient, suddenly took it into his head to do without any fire and, in spite of Tortilla, snatched back his egg. In his grip it cracked and oozed out—the sight of all that egg white lying on the ground filled him with pain and did not entice anyone else to imitate his haste.

What to do? On that entire plantation, whose every nook and cranny we knew, it was impossible to find a single match!

"I know where you can find some!" Tortilla cried. "But 'must be someone who's not afraid to go and get it."

Everyone then felt himself capable of reaching beyond the stars to steal the sun's fire.

"Well!" said Tortilla, "One of you has only to go up to the 'house' and say that his maman has sent for a box of matches on credit."

"But they're not going to believe us. They're going to say that our maman hasn't come back as yet. They're not going to give us a thing."

Who would be bold enough to try such a stunt? I'll admit, shamefully, that I was scared. Even Gesner was scared.

So Tortilla, beside herself, threatened the smaller ones with not a crumb to eat if one of them didn't volunteer to go.

In the end, Maximilienne did.

"You will say: 'Morning *messieurs-dames*,' Tortilla coached, 'my maman asks if you'd be so kind as to send her a box of matches, please.' And if they ask you: 'Wait a minute, your maman is back already?" you will say: "Was since this morning, before she left, she asked me to buy some matches, so she could have them tonight when she gets home, to cook her *canari.'* Don't be afraid, o.k.!" "And don't forget to say thank you.!"

After the fashion of the big people, Tortilla had Maximilienne repeat the correct replies.

Maximilienne was already on her way when Tortilla, changing strategy a bit, called her back.

"Wait, listen! To really make them believe it's your mother who sent you. Ask them for a nip of rum as well."

In the twinkling of an eye, she had found a bottle and Maximilienne set off to Tortilla's repeated recommendations.

Dumfounded, breathless, almost motionless, we watched her climb the slope. Then, suddenly overcome by panic, at the instant when she came into view of 'the house', we darted off into the shack. There we waited, no one daring utter a word.

When Maximilienne returned, out of breath from having run, with the box of matches and the bottle of rum, I felt as if I were transported into a world where children's desires finally came true without the intervention or the censureship of parents. It was as if something unnoticed had just taken place; as if, by the appearance of our messenger, we were going to lead a free, exalted life.

Rum! matches! In our hands, the very hands of those who were said to be too small to use them! To be able to light a fire and partake of that drink we knew only by its smell. Matches! Above all . . . rum! Thus, putting off the preparation of the eggs, Tortilla snatched the bottle and began to share the rum.

"Makes you drunk," she warned, "I'm not going to give you a lot."

With scrupulous stinginess, she poured a few drops in the palm of our hands.

It burned the throat like an ember, but it made you feel like drinking more.

Tortilla, Gesner, Soumane took long draughts from the bottle held above their open mouths. Besides, those three, when it came to sharing, always got twice what the others did.

On that occasion, it didn't enter anyone's mind to protest; our joy was so well shared that everyone had a good laugh. We couldn't stop giggling.

Tortilla struck the sticks of matches one after the other and threw them among us, and we each ran helter skelter, shouting and laughing.

"You're wasting all the matches," Gesner cried. "Let me have some too."

Having pushed Tortilla to the ground, he grabbed the box of matches from her hand. Tortilla, in her desire to recapture it, darted after him and Gesner fled, making us all run in his pursuit.

And everybody sprawled and rolled in the grass, getting up and falling over again, clinging to one another.

Crushed in the melée, the smaller ones cried out, but their cries only evoked laughter and incited battles.

As for Tortilla, now, she only raised herself up half-way and slumped back down, gripping anybody nearby and making him roll over with her. Then the others would run from her and, stark naked on the ground, she would shout and shout, stretching out her arms, trying to stand up, and would roll over bellowing as if calling for help: "Maman, Maman!"

And we laughed at this so much. We really did.

Gesner was another one who couldn't remain on his feet and, furious because we laughed at him, he swore like a cowherd, and peppered everyone he could lay his hands on. He would look for stones to throw at us, and we ran off; but he would slump down in the dust and the entire band would gather to dance in triumph around him. Then his threats scattered us once more.

In this way, we roamed from shack to shack, abandoning one by one and without any remorse, without giving it the slightest thought, those who could no longer walk or maintain their balance and who were reduced to crawling, a cry of despair on their lips, or who grew weary from incoercible laughter.

And the box of matches, hotly disputed, passed from hand to hand, so much so that there was a veritable game of hide-and-seek among us as we tried to discover who had it, as we ran here and there about the huts. A few even had had to give up and, stupified, amused themselves with any little thing.

Consumed by our delirium, evening was approaching and we were not even concerned with our parents' return. The fact that our clothes were now reduced to shreds was the furthest thing from our minds.

Suddenly, I found myself alone after darting away, but I heard such shouting in various places around me that I didn't know where to go to rejoin my mates.

A loud, overpowering din indicated a larger group so I dashed off towards it.

"Fire! fire!" Paul shouted to me as he saw me come up. "We have set fire to Mr. Saint-Louis' garden! No more fence, we're going to see what's inside!"

Already, a huge cloud of smoke rose above the hedge of branches. Everybody was jumping about and frolicking, and that new-found joy also got me to dancing and shouting.

When, through the smoke, the first flame shot skywards, we were overcome with real madness and, had it not been for the heat which kept us away, we would have thrown ourselves body and soul into the glowing fire.

*

The emotion, the confusion, the tears, the anger and the consternation that rocked Shack Alley that night and the following day all over again, had shaken me twenty times more than the whippings, the beatings, the clouts M'man Tine had rained on me.

However, I was so severely beaten, ill-treated, bruised; I saw so many frightened people talking about us, reprimanding us, this bunch of ragamuffins, and repeating in tones that still showed their alarm; 'If Good Lord hadn't put a helping hand!' that I was to reach a stage where I couldn't understand a thing that was going on.

For just when the flames were at their highest and reddest, the adults had rushed up to put out the blaze with pails of water. Then everyone had swooped down on us, carrying us off, threatening us with our separate punishments.

That night, M'man Tine had done nothing but beat me, bawl me out, and weep. She hadn't prepared anything to eat and, I believe, she wept and grumbled the entire night long.

" 'Twas God," she said, "who was good enough to show Horace the smoke rising in the sky."

Horace it was who had sounded the alarm to all the workers.

"As if it wasn't enough to toil and moil from morning to night in the *béké's* canes, these little wretches now bringing more misery on our heads. What am I going to say if the *béké* calls me?

Then M'man Tine turned to talking about my mother Délia, who had never had so much trouble with me, who was living her life in Fort-de-France, protected from the sun and the rain, 'behind the chairs of the *béké*' she served, and who was the furthest thing in the world from imagining the catastrophe I had just caused along with the other little blacks on the plantation.

"Oh! only misfortune dogs poor people!"

I was no longer crying.

My bruises gradually produced a stiffness that slowly took over the rest of my body, erasing from my brain all memory, stealing me blissfully from reality.

I remained several days without leaving bed, without seeing my friends. I couldn't get up nor could I even move an arm or a leg. M'man Tine had put me to lie on her bed; on mornings, before setting off for the fields, she would make me a huge cup of tisane with just a tip of sugar and a large bowl of *toloman* and I remained lying there for the whole day. I slept out ot sheer boredom or tried to chase it with the tisane and the *toloman.* During this time, I thought about Gesner, Tortilla and Soumane whom I had left in a ditch with his hands and feet all running blood, and wondered whether he wasn't still there. I tried to catch the faintest sound in the hope of hearing one of them and guessing what he was up to.

At times, I felt as though I were no longer in Black Shack Alley, as though I could just as well be in one of those countries which were the scene of the tales Médouze would tell. Or, all of a sudden, there would come over me a sort of apprehension that, because of what had happened, the extent and consequences of which I couldn't even measure, Shack Alley had undergone horrible changes.

*

On evenings M'man Tine made me eat vegetables crushed into a pap and gave me warm, brackish tisane in case I had been 'injured.' She then placed in a saucer some rum, salt and a piece of candle, struck a match, and after allowing a beautiful little blue flame to catch, blew it out and rubbed me with the sort of warm ointment she had made.

The first time I went outside to have a fresh look at Shack Alley was both a relief and a great disappointment.

Happy at the fact that my familiar haunt was just as I had left it, I expected all the same, as a result of all I had suffered, to find the landscape in complete disarray and unrecognisable.

Yes, there was a strange impression of emptiness around me. Where were my friends? Gesner, Soumane? Perhaps they too were sick and still confined to the bedroom.

This thought only made me more worried and puzzled.

That very night, M'man Tine said to me:

"I had a letter sent to your maman telling her to come for you; meanwhile, you'll go to work with me . . . , for Mr. Gabriel is no longer allowing us to leave the children alone in Shack Alley during the day."

Then it was that I understood why I hadn't seen my friends; they must have gone to the fields with their parents.

This perspective did not displease me at all. Quite the contrary. It corresponded perhaps to the desire for change that this crisis had sparked in me.

Thus, the following morning, I accompanied M'man Tine to her work. I figured that all the people worked at the same place and that we children would be able to meet and play together. But M'man Tine and I were immersed in sugar cane leaves which the wind made rustle all the day long; for the entire day, we were alone at that spot, not seeing anything outside the field, and I had no idea where I was.

M'man Tine would scratch the ground with her hoe and gather the weeds and fine dirt at the foot of each clump of canes. But the grass seemed hard to cut with the hoe. My grandmother struck hard with the edge of the tool, letting out "umh! umh!" and from time to time straightened up, placing her hand behind her as if to help the pain in her back. And she had a horrible grimace on her face.

I remained sitting beside her bamboo basket, between two clumps of cane she had joined by a knot in the ends of the leaves so we could have more shade. When, having progressed in her work, she could no longer see me behind her she would come back to fetch me and would make me another shelter.

I tried to amuse myself—with the earthworms dug up by the hoe, with snails I chanced upon, or collecting wild grass and spinach for the evening meal.

But, on the whole, I was restricted to a muteness, to a silence, even to a state of immobility that coiled about my body and made me sleep for hours, curled up between my two clumps of sugar cane.

*

I saw my friends only fleetingly on evenings when Mr. Médouze had called me; and every time I met Soumane, Tortilla or Orélie, I had the undefinable impression that neither they nor I were the same as before. There was no friendship in our conversations, only gloom, as we kept constantly looking towards our parents' shacks, for fear of being surprised.

Naturally, the memory of the outrage we had been party to instilled in us a spontaneous mistrust of one another. The floggings we had received, I believed, had broken the ties between us, and we needed a few days to be ourselves once more, to re-establish the friendship and trust that held us together.

But something remained irreparable—we could hardly play; we no longer had time to play.

*

The first week went by in the following manner:

Each child would leave in the morning with his mother, would return at night with his mother, would run errands at the store for his mother, would return to his mother's place, eat, go to bed, till the following morning.

We never had the joy of meeting in the fields. Our parents worked in areas that were very far from one another. M'man Tine was at Grand Etang. "My maman too," Victorine told me. Yet, at no time in the day did I have the impression that M'man Tine was not alone in that vast expanse of sugar cane.

On evenings, on returning from the field, we would come across workers moving through the 'traces' and we would go up to Shack Alley together. But I hardly ever saw among them Gesner, or Victorine, or any one of the others.

Indeed, this new mode of living which I accepted, alas! in all submission, was an awful burden to bear at certain times.

It was with relief that I saw the arrival of the first Saturday following this new state, and like each Saturday, I went to witness the payment of wages.

I was to experience a surprise that left me with an inferiority complex that would long affect me.

When the overseer reached the category 'petites bandes,' what a shock it was for me to hear:

"Tortilla . . . eight francs. Victorine . . . six francs, Gesner . . ."

I wasn't aware that we were to be given money because we went with our parents to work. I was so puzzled I could not distinguish anything around me. I was confused at the presentiment that my name would be called and . . . But after Gesner, after Orélie, after all of them, the overseer did not shout my name.

Stunned by disappointment, I did not dare raise my head. Then, indignant, I ran to find M'man Tine to tell her that the overseer had given piles of money to all the others who went to work with their parents and that I hadn't been given anything. Why?

Here again, I was in for a stinging retort.

"L'il wretch!" cried my grandmother, "you want me to put you' tail in the petites bandes, eh! That's what you were after when you caused me all that trouble in the habitation? Well, I should've really sent you to collect Guinea grass or spread guano, the way the others did! That's what you need to make you know what real misery is and to make you learn how to behave yourself."

And she kept on and on, talking, fretting, grumbling! I heard her pour scorn on the parents of my friends who had sent their children into the petites bandes, calling them shameless niggers who did not know how to do anything properly.

"Tell me! how will it all end if the blasted fathers place their sons in those things, in the same misfortune? Well! If I didn't put your mother in one, I'm not going to put you."

She cursed Mr. Gabriel who, according to her, had forbidden children from running about Shack Alley, so they could swell the ranks of the petites bandes. I heard her utter words of anger against mulattoes (Mr. Gabriel was one) who, as she would repeat at the slightest opportunity, were always quick to flatter the békés and betray the blacks.

Then, talking, fretting, grumbling, she brought up the question of my mother once again; she gave her two weeks to come for me, otherwise . . .

I ended up having a vague hunch that it was for my own good that M'man Tine did not send me into the *petites bandes,* but I wasn't altogether proud of this because of my mates.

Every week, at pay time, I had the distinct impression that the latter were separated from me, that they had grown up; at any rate, they were on the road to becoming adults, whereas I lagged behind. But the way they looked at me, even when they had collected their pay, did not seem to betray any superiority, any pride on their part.

We therefore no longer saw one another as often and in total freedom. But we were not of the age when one complained of one's lot. And then, what was there to complain about? Weren't we equal to one another and to all those around us?

Did we not represent, our parents and ourselves, in our own eyes, a beginning and an end?

In the long run I enjoyed my new mode of living.

I found it advantageous and occasionally charming. In the mango season, M'man Tine had shaken a few branches of a mango tree that grew in a small valley near to the field and stored a certain number of green mangoes in the cane straw. The result was that, for quite a while, every midday a copious and succulent dessert rounded off our lunch. Similarly, some evenings after her work, she would go down into the small valley to fetch a breadfruit; and I enjoyed it all the more since I could be of some use. For example, I helped M'man Tine pick out the breadfruits that were already full; and while she knocked them down with a rod she would say to me: "Make sure you see where they fall." For, the bushes being thick and intertwined under the trees, the breadfruit, having fallen, would at times roll very far, right to the furthest reaches of the bushes. But my instinct for finding it was keen, a fact that always surprised M'man Tine.

Then there was the harvest. That period had always seemed to us one of festivity.

We children could then suck pieces of sugar cane for the whole day. We would go looking for them in the fields. Our parents brought some back for us. We would suck so many that the juice would be running down from our mouths, soaking our clothes and leaving a glaze on the naked bellies of my friends.

But on that occasion I didn't have to bother to go anywhere to look for sugar canes. I didn't even have to ask permission to take any. I was with my grandmother in the field itself.

From early morning I partook of the first canes cut and without uttering a word—for I was a quiet, sly child—and while I played with a bit of straw, a piece of the cane peeling, lacquered and gaily painted, or anything at all, I listened to the songs by which the cutters and reapers gave vigor and grace to their movements.

I followed them, got to the depths of their every movement. Everything was admirable: their black or tanned half-nakedness, their grimy rags, revived by the light, the sweat that bathed them from head to foot, leaving along their backs and on their chests reflections mirroring the flash of the cutlasses each time they brandished their arms; the kind of background music built up by the straw being trampled, the 'tying lines' thrown backwards and caught by the women to tie the ten canes that formed one bundle, the stowing of ten bundles into a pile; those endless songs, punctuated every now and then by a grunt or a shrill whistle escaping from a chest in the throes of effort.

That vast music that thus engulfed the screeching of the carts, the trot of the mules, the swearing of the mule—and cart-drivers; those complicated songs, those unending, monotonous chants cast a spell over me, overpowering me so much that, in order not to stifle, I too joined in the singing:

> Last bag a man will pack
> is to go to work
> on Ti-Mo'ne.

But the entire field continued to work diligently and to go over, in quickened rhythm, the same words, following the same tune.

The workers seemed to like harvest time. They said that they earned more money during that period. I too liked the harvest, because on Saturday nights there would be more people selling things near the office and on Shack Alley, and the festivity went further into the night.

There were also dice and card games out in the open around a tray and a torch. These often degenerated into frightening battles: *laghias* of death.

In point of fact, apart from that, nothing would change during harvest. And nothing was changed afterwards . . .

In the off-season my greatest joy was to be with M'man Tine in a field crossed by a river. It was rather a quiet stream, growing wider and deeper at intervals, almost disappearing at times under the tall grass that grew on its edges. I didn't know where it came from nor where it went; furthermore, I'd never known that a river came from somewhere and went somewhere, like someone on a trip. For me, a river had neither beginning nor end. It was just something that flowed.

I asked M'man Tine whether there weren't any crayfish. She

explained that there were some no doubt, but they couldn't be caught by hand as was the case at the Gazelle, for the bottom of that stream was muddy. She then made me a fish-hook with a pin, took some sewing thread which she tied to a bamboo rod, added a round bit of dried cane to the thread, and I thus learned to catch shrimp by line.

It was splendid. The breathless attention with which I watched the line, the intense emotion in my heart when there was the faintest movement on the float. Then, the tug of the shrimp at the end of the line, at the end of my arm! The intoxicating effort to get it out of the water!

I would catch up to ten or twelve per day, and M'man Tine would say that I could catch even more with more patience and skill.

Even more splendid was the world of shrimps such as I pictured it in my mind's eye: hills, pathways and traces, fields, shacks. All in clear water. Therein lived the translucent shrimps, the papa-shrimps, the mamans, the children, who spoke a water language. When I caught a big one, that was possibly a papa or a mama returning from work. And I would think of the pain this would cause their children who would cry uncontrollably, the tears possibly causing the river to swell. Whenever it was a little one I would conjure up the despair of the parents, a despair similar to that of the birds whose young ones we would pluck from their nests and who remained grief-stricken the entire day and even the following day. And I would regret all the more not catching those that got away, since I feared they would go and warn the others to beware my hook handing there innocently, looking like an appetizing earthworm.

In short, thanks to all those amusements, I did not suffer at all.

One Sunday, M'man Tine donned a new dress, dressed me in a pair of breeches which were much too tight—it had been so long since I'd worn any—and decided we would go to Saint-Esprit.

"What for?"

"None of your business."

But as she continued to rail at my indiscretion she could not prevent herself from indirectly supplying the explanation she'd refused to give me.

My mother had replied to her letter, informing her that she couldn't come as yet, because "her business wasn't straight as yet;" but she sent some money.

The rest had escaped me.

M'man Tine took her basket and we set off. She walked at a brisk pace and I followed trotting behind. The hem of her dress was starched, stiff and, at every step, her heels, coming into contact with it, made a dull drumming sound.

In this fashion, we made our way down the path that circled the hill from top to bottom; then we took the main road of white tuff filled with women in flowered dresses, men in white, neatly-ironed trousers, donkeys loaded with heavy-looking bags and baskets full of vegetables and fruits.

M'man Tine met some people she knew.

"Like you're in a hurry?" they said.

"Oh, yes," she replied, "I want to reach early so I can be in time for part of the mass."

We left the main road. We walked for a long time along paths that went through stalks of sugar cane, then under tall trees; then along a railway and on bridges without parapets. But I ran as hard as I could, all to no avail for the distance between M'man Tine and myself kept getting greater and greater; and I even thought that she was going to leave me and that I'd be lost in the open country. There was no one else about, and M'man Tine just kept on walking and walking, apparently oblivious of my safety, talking to herself in a low voice, leaving behind her the tambourine-like music of her heels beating against her long dress.

I stopped, out of breath, and shouted: "M'man Tine!" and I burst into tears.

My grandmother turned around and came to a halt, surprised by my shout and my tears, as if it hadn't even occurred to her that I was following her. Shamefaced, I rejoined her.

She then bent down and took me on her shoulders. In this way our journey continued and ended on a much more pleasant note.

*

The porch of the church was crowded with people who had come mostly from the country, like M'man Tine. They were most all bare-footed. The women wore dresses similar to M'man Tine's and had placed their baskets on the steps. I couldn't see a thing inside the church. From inside came the ringing of bells and voices singing as if they were crying. At a certain time I heard quite nearby, in front of me, the soft sound of coins being thrown one by one. M'man Tine leaned towards me to tell me that it was the Abbot taking up the offering.

"He'll come and present a small box for you to put a cent into," she explained in a whisper, "but all you have to do is bow your head. And above all, don't be afraid."

When the full peal of bells was unleashed to let out all who had crammed inside the church, we went in, M'man Tine pulling me by the hand. My grandmother bent over and genuflected lightly on one knee, in front of each of the life-sized figures, sitting on some sort of shelf or table laden with flowers that looked as if they smelled good.

Sometimes she knelt down completely, whispered to me to do the same and said her prayers, her lips moving in silence. She did this in front of three or four of those statues, no doubt those she preferred, but which were not exactly my taste. For the one that struck me most was the one nailed to a huge cross of hard wood, nailed hand and foot—the way we would transfix, on the fences to the shacks, the small lizards we caught—left there bleeding. He had a beard, lots of hair and was almost naked; and you could see his ribs under his skin. He reminded me of Mr. Médouze, lying with his tattered loin-cloth on his hard plank in the center of his hut. And his tragic position there, on the cross, seemed to me as incomprehensible as Mr. Médouze's. And yet, *he* wasn't black . . .

M'man Tine went several times around the open market.

The entire area was congested with a helter-skelter array of bags, baskets, mountains of vegetables and fruits, and it was teeming and buzzing with people. She would take a pinch out of every bag of cassava flour, taste it, bargain and would move on. She tasted quite a few before buying her two cups of flour. Then, continuing on her way, she would touch and weigh the yams, hesitate, ponder awhile, then finally buy one. The same procedure for the avocado pears. The same procedure for *toloman* starch, for cassava starch; the same, no doubt. for the roots of *choux caraibes*.

But I no longer followed her. She had put her basket down under one of the trees lining the square and had made me sit beside it to watch it and to take a rest. She came with a bunch of onions, counted what money she had left, pondered a bit and set off again. She returned with a hand of bananas, counted, pondered and set off once more.

She finished her shopping with a quarter pound of meat and bones for the weekly soup, some salt codfish, sugar and a 'leaf' of three *graisses*.

Finally, she brought me a piece of hot pudding and a slice of bread. I was starved, and it was good. She didn't eat anything although, as was her custom, she'd drunk only a cup of coffee since morning.

While I was having my meal, she went off again and after some time returned, carrying under her arm a parcel looking like a large piece of bread wrapped in paper. And she told me bluntly:

"You're finished picking up bad habits on the plantation. You're going to school to get some education in your head and learn to sign your name. For the Good Lord allowed me not to spend the few coins your maman sent for you; I've bought you a li'l suit."

It was a clear, pleasant afternoon.

M'man Tine, basket on her head, walked slowly and, as always, spoke of all she had done and all she was going to do. The main concern was to place me in school. I followed her, sheltered from the sun by her shadow. My mind was on the horse-shaped candy bought for me which she carried, there, in a corner of her basket and which she'd promised to give me as soon as we reached the shack.

. . . Oh! yes, it was a beautiful day, and a fine journey!

Then there were Mondays at the river, the following days in the fields, Saturdays, Sundays at Saint-Esprit for quite some time still.

At times I would hear M'man Tine in her soliloquies complaining about a certain Mam'zelle Léonie from the village who was taking too long to finish my suit.

Certain days she would say that I was too much trouble for her in the sugar cane patches; for it was the period of continuous rains and she didn't know where to put me. When we were in a field of tall canes, she made a sort of nest with her basket, some straw, intermingled with leaves, and that more or less sheltered me. But if we were in young canes, there was no way to protect me. At such times she would grow angry. She would stop working, turn the basket over her head like a big hat, cover it with leaves and hold me close to her, murmuring in a voice that made me cry.

I believe I'd have preferred to remain in the rain, to play in the ditches, to mold the wet earth with my hands, as I used to in Shack Alley, there with all my friends. But M'man Tine was so bewildered, so unhappy on my account on rainy days that it was distressing for me as well.

She would never seek any shelter for herself and worked all the more quickly as a result. When night had fallen, her old straw hat looked like a cap made of manure, the ragged material covering it was soaked and stuck to her skull. And with her feet all muddy and swollen like stale bread in water, her veins oxidized, M'man Tine, the best and most beautiful of the grandmothers, suddenly became a frightful sight, who did not in any way resemble a maman, an old woman, a black woman, nor even a human being.

M'man Tine every night would talk about school and about that matter of the suit Mam'zelle Léonie was in no hurry to finish. That did not inspire in me any emotion, any dream. I hadn't even asked her any questions on that score.

I'd talked to Mr. Médouze about it and he had explained that school was a place where intelligent children were sent. (What, pray tell, was an intelligent child?) At any rate, in order to go to school one had to be fully and properly dressed, and speak French there. These latter details had made a pleasant impression on me. But that was all.

During all those rainy spells, I could not go out at night. We would return, all soaked and shivering, to Shack Alley, nothing but a regular mud-hole, so much did the ground appear rotten to the core. This did not prevent my wanting to go round to Médouze's shack, but M'man Tine always reminded me that "well brought-up children stay in their parents' house when it's raining."

But no sooner had good weather reappeared, I was once more a regular visitor to Médouze. Our evenings together were always the same—a few errands, the fire, the long preliminary bouts of silence, the riddles and tales interrupted, alas! by M'man Tine's voice calling me home.

*

One night, it was beginning to get late and Médouze hadn't returned home. I had already made a couple of trips to his shack. The situation was tricky, for, most probably, M'man Tine wasn't going to let me go yet another time, and her *canari* was bubbling with such effervescence that dinner could be ready in a short while.

I dashed off once more. Again I found Médouze's hut closed—from the outside, with the hank of rope he used to roll and knot around two nails, one on the door, the other on the door frame. I then decided to wait, for if I returned to M'man Tine's, it was no more coming out. I therefore sat right there, on the front step of the shack, not quite on the threshold, not in the spot where Médouze would sit. No, beside it, for children were not supposed to sit in seats regularly taken by adults, so as not to catch all their weariness and pain.

Time went by and then there came what I was afraid of: the call of M'man Tine—and Mr. Médouze was not yet back. But I did not reply and remained where I was. Shortly afterwards, no doubt since she did not see me come running, M'man Tine called me again. Several times in succession and for a long time. Her voice trembled at the end as if she was becoming angry. Finally I gave in, and in order to calm her down and assure her that I was coming right away, I shouted: "M'man-an-an!" But in fact, I was moving slowly, closely peering toward the end of the road already engulfed in darkness, trying to discern any shadow that resembled Médouze's body.

"So, when you're enjoying yourself over there with Mr. Médouze, the conversation is so interesting you forget you have a maman? You even forget there's a time to come for a bite to put in your stomach? It's Mr. Médouze's *zombi* stories that full your belly? What was Mr. Médouze telling you that was so fascinating that I had to make myself hoarse calling you?"

"Mr. Médouze is not there, m'man."

"So, what were you doing there? You weren't at his place?"

"Yes, m'man, in front of his door."

"So, you prefer to remain alone in front of Mr. Médouze's door, in the darkness, rather than keep your maman's company like a well-bred child?"

She practically threw my plate into my hands and, while eating, continued grumbling about the bad habits I was picking up in the *habitation* and called on God to be her witness, and asked Him when on earth Mam'zelle Léonie was going to make up her mind to deliver my little suit.

When our meal was finished and M'man Tine had stopped talking, I repeated, fearing that I would again be brushed off:

"Mr. Médouze hadn't returned, M'man Tine."

"And what you want me to do for that? Mr. Médouze is not the one who puts food in your mouth, is he?"

She was doing the dishes. Then, in my despair to make myself understood, I burst out sobbing.

"What's wrong with you?" M'man Tine asked.

"Mr. Médouze wasn't . . .

"You're going to leave me in peace, yes or no?"

But I couldn't stop myself from crying aloud. Suddenly, M'man Tine rushed outside. I immediately dried my tears, for no doubt she had gone for a branch off a tree behind the shack to beat me.

She took a long while to return. I was alone in the shack with the kerosine lamp which, humble and motionless on the table, lit up a part of the room. In the darkness outside, M'man Tine must be looking for a rather large one! At any rate, I thoroughly dried my tears and tried to choke off my crying.

As it turned out, M'man Tine was not behind the shack as I thought, but rather much further; for suddenly there came the sound of her voice:

"He's not home."

Whom was she telling that I was crying because Mr. Médouze hadn't yet returned?

Then I heard Gesner's father saying:

"I thought he was in bed. You're quite sure he's not lying there, in his shack?"

"No," M'man Tine replied, "his door is closed from outside. And José, who was there since I came back, would have seen him."

The voice of M'man Tine called Mam'zelle Valérine, and by now there were numerous voices talking in the night, saying to one another and repeating that Mr. Médouze had not returned from work, that nobody had seen him, that he was late and that that was strange.

I burned with contentment at having been responsible for alerting so many people and I felt like getting up from my little bench and dashing outside to tell everyone myself how I had come to notice Mr.

Médouze's absence. But at the same time, the concern the incident was apparently raising reached me in a hum which only increased the fear in my heart.

M'man Tine was still not back and I could feel the whole of Shack Alley already in the grips of excitement and anxiety!

Finally, I got up and ventured a few cautious steps towards the door which I pushed open lightly so I could take a quick look out.

Doors were opened, stabbing the darkness with violent rays of light. Voices called out to one another and spoke with such feverishness that I could hardly make out what they were saying.

I thought they had already been up to the 'house' to enquire in what field Médouze was working. It seemed they were talking about going to see for themselves.

Someone said: "We can't let the night go by without knowing."

"If you've made up your mind, I'm ready," someone else replied.

Then they remained quite some time without saying a word and all of a sudden I noticed, at the lower end of Shack Alley, torches that in the darkness made a large spot of light, filled with men bearing cutlasses and sticks. and moving away.

By this time the great excitement seemed to have died down into a few, almost imperceptible, murmurs.

M'man Tine had returned. She asked me if I'd been afraid to remain all alone for so long. She was out of breath and appeared to have forgotten the little scene we had had.

"They've gone to see," she told me.

Her voice was a quiver with her inner turmoil.

"Dear God!" she said, "don't . . . "

She could barely keep still. She touched one thing, stopped, touched another, listened . . .

Outside, the talking had started up again.

"If I left you again for a while, you'll be afraid?" she asked me.

Possibly not; but I preferred her to take me with her.

"Yes," I said timidly.

"O.K., get your hat and come with me."

*

At about the same spot from which men with the torches had just departed, stood Gesner holding aloft a piece of wood with its end aflame, lighting up, like a huge match stick, a small group of men and women sitting on the ground, some in the full light, others scarcely touched by the glow.

I could make out Mr. Saint-Louis' voice saying:

"Several times already, I've told Médouze that the work is too strenuous for him and that he should join the *petites bandes*. But he doesn't want to, saying that those young ragamuffins wouldn't show him any respect."

Everyone said something about Mr. Médouze. Some even finished their piece in a burst of laughter and concluded:

"Poor devil!"

They remained a long time without speaking, then started up again. And this time everybody spoke, But it was no longer about Médouze. They spoke about everyday matters and things I didn't understand very well.

Consequently, I much more enjoyed watching the torch that Gesner swished down once in a while to put new life in the flame; that flame which was blue at the base where it emanated from the bit of wood, and which turned yellow and red only to flicker away into fugitive cloud of smoke that seemed to further blacken the darkness.

The light reached up to the branches and leaves of the trees above our heads. The brilliant resin oozed from the wood and sometimes dripped on the hand or feet of Gesner who, with a grimace, let out little cries.

I did not dare speak. I was anxious to hear all that was being said about Médouze, to know why he hadn't returned, and I feared I knew not what for those men who had gone off to look for him, although they were armed as if on their way to battle. As for me, I had a vague feeling that Médouze had left for one of those countries he would talk about in his tales.

I would have been so happy if such were the case!

Why?

Perhaps through some indescribable desire to see Médouze become simply the hero of an adventure similar to those with which he had often captured my imagination.

I also thought that finding myself in the night in such a situation spurred my mind all the more into conceptions of the fantastic.

Suddenly, a shout.

"There they are!"

A muddle of voices echoed this shout and at the same time the whole group (Gesner in the lead), carrying me along with it, moved towards the road.

Far away in the depth of the night, a bright light, a group of advancing torches.

"My God, Lord, Virgin Mary!" the women whispered all about me.

My heart began to pound and I sought refuge near to M'man Tine who mechanically murmured imperceptible words.

"They wouldn't be coming back if they hadn't found Médouze," replied M'man Tine.

"Médouze must be with them," said another; "see how they keep stopping every now and then. You can't see?"

"Yes, because of him no doubt," Mr. Saint-Louis concluded.

Then the convoy came into view at the lower end of the road. We kept pressing forward and soon there were distinct silhouettes in the clear evening.

"They're carrying something!"

"Good Lord!"

"Of course, look at the way they're walking."

Thereupon, a feverishness more intense than that which preceded the departure of the men pervaded the group and everybody began to talk at the same time. Some said that Médouze must have been stricken with epilepsy, others insinuated that he hadn't eaten anything the night before and a worm had bitten him in the stomach. For some, he must have had too much water to drink, since he was covered with sweat. There followed a torrent of words that scared me and prevented me from realizing what was happening.

But in fact four or five men were carrying together a thing black, long, bony and half-dressed in rags, something resembling Mr. Médouze.

And it was indeed Mr. Médouze.

"If we hadn't gone to look for him the mongooses would've feasted on him!" Mr. Horace exclaimed.

They were all out of breath and dripping with perspiration. Some had walked so briskly that they stumbled under the weight of the old man, and as their voices were nothing more than a mere whisper one could hardly hear as they said:

"Had we known, we'd have carried a hammock; for when he was all alone, he looked like a bit of straw, but with death in his belly, he's as heavy as misfortune."

And it was amidst the loud burst of laughter set off by a quip from Carmélien that the body of Médouze arrived in Black Shack Alley and entered his hut.

So many people were around the body that it was in vain that I tried to see it. I did not pay any attention to the snatches of what those who discovered it were relating; but there was such a mixture of commiseration, lamentations, sighs, laughter and jokes, that I couldn't exactly tell whether it was a sad event or a mundane occurrence of little consequence. The whole scene vaguely resembled a fête, but a few persons, M'man Tine among them, had expressions on their faces that precluded my feeling in a gay mood.

People were coming and going. M'man Tine had told me not to

move from where I was, then she went outside. Many women also went outside. I then slipped in among the few people who where gathered around Mr. Médouze.

He was lying on his back, dressed in his skin-colored loincloth and stretched out in a manner across the full length of his narrow black plank. His eyes were half-open as if he wasn't sleeping; those very eyes that had reflected on other nights the flow of the fires that we used to light.

And in the middle of his scorched, woolly beard of greyish white, his mouth showed rust-colored teeth with large spaces between them and his stiff smile made him look as if he found it amusing that so many people were gathered around him. A smile that reminded one of a dead rat in the middle of a road.

At first I didn't find anything odd, even in his features; but after contemplating them for a while, I felt my heart growing heavier and heavier in my chest and I felt like shouting, "Mr. Médouze," the way I would sometimes do when he was asleep and hadn't heard me enter his hut.

But the rigidity of his pose and the fixed nature of his expression somehow made me recognize the face of death.

Many things happened that night.

Women brought rum to the men who had brought back the body so as to quench their thirst.

M'man Tine returned with a small glass filled with water in which there was a small green branch, and placed it near Mr. Médouze's head. Mam'zelle Valérine entered with a candle which she lit beside the small glass. Then other people arrived from Shack Alley who, till then, had not shown themselves.

"Well, Ole Médouze wanted to leave us just like that, eh!"

"Oh, yes, it's because his bed was too narrow, he couldn't die on it."

"What d'you expect? It's the canes that killed him, it's in the canes he wanted to leave his skin and his bones."

A heavy silence ensued, broken only by a murmur of compassion or a sudden quip. A little, discreet laughter, followed by a deep sigh . . .

Little by little, a new buzz of voices arose outside, and I was quite surprised to find, sitting on the ground in the darkness in front of the shack, some men whom I could scarcely make out and whose voices I couldn't recognise.

Suddenly a slow, drawling song rose from the ground, from the spot where those invisible people were sitting, filling me straightway with a violent fear.

But the song continued rising in a slow, enchanting fashion, calming my anxiety, carrying me off, so to speak, in its flight in the night, towards the summit of darkness. Without breaking off, it curved upwards, continuing its mournful climb.

Then, having mysteriously wandered for a long time throughout the night, it slowly descended to the ground and made its way deep into the hearts of those present.

Thereupon a sharp voice launched into another monotonous song of harsh sonority and vigorous rhythm; and all the others responded to it by a brief lament, the bodies swaying heavily in the darkness.

When this was finished another man's voice shouted:

"Eh, *cric!* . . ."

And the entire crowd replied in a loud voice:

"Eh, and so! . . ."

I found myself in the same preamble to the tales Mr. Médouze used to tell me.

Many a tale was told that night!

There was a man—the master storyteller—who told the tales standing, holding a stick with the help of which he mimed the stance of all the beasts, the carriage of all sorts of people: old women, hunchbacks, cripples. And his tales rolled along to the accompaniment of songs which, with great gestures of his stick, he had the audience sing until it was all out of breath.

From time to time, between two tales, someone would get up and say a few words about Médouze that made everyone fall into interminable laughter.

"Médouze is dead," he said in a tone befitting the occasion. "That's the painful bit of news it is my sad duty to inform you, *messieurs-dames.* As far as I can see, what is most distressing to us is the fact that Médouze died and did not want us present in his hour of agony. But do not feel sorry for Médouze, *messieurs-dames;* Médouze went to hide to die because . . . Imagine Médouze's evil plan! Because Médouze didn't want us, his brothers in drinking and in disappointment, to inherit his cane field in Grand-Etang."

"His old cracked *canari,*" added one voice.

"His old baggy trousers," came another voice.

"His old pipe and his broken *coui.*"

"And his sleeping plank planed smooth by his bones."

"And the gold and silver the *béké* used to give him on Saturday evenings . . . "

And everybody repeated with a laugh:

"And, continuing the game in opposite fashion, a woman got up, praising Médouze's generosity, and summoned each one present to declare one after the other what Médouze had left him. For this one, his old *bakoua,* for the other his loincloth full of holes and his worn-out hoe, and for everybody, all the gold and silver the *béké* used to give him on Saturday evenings . . .

"Eh, *cric!* . . ."

In the shack women, standing, were looking at the body without uttering a word, or were whispering.

M'man Tine was kneeling at Mr. Médouze's feet.

Then she came and asked me if I still did not feel like going to bed. But despite its length and complicated nature, this wake kept me up so much that in the long run, even in the darkness, I could make out all the traits in the face and all the expressions of the master storyteller, carried away by his feelings into the magical domain to which he lifted up his enraptured audience.

And each time that he raised the hymns to their most intoxicating fullness, I expected to see the body of the old black man, lying stiff on its too-narrow plank, also rise up in the night and set off for Guinea.

Part Two

It was nevertheless fairly easy for me to get over the loss of my old friend Médouze. The big event that M'man Tine kept announcing every day finally took place. Mam'zelle Léonie had completed my suit, and one Monday, instead of taking me to the river as usual, M'man Tine donned her pretty dress, decked me out in new clothes (a pair of breeches and a shirt of grey calico with fine black stripes, and a small straw hat, bought the day before in Saint-Esprit) and we set out for Petit-Bourg.

M'man Tine often went to Petit-Bourg, even at nights after her work; for she avoided as much as possible having to buy anything at the 'house'. But although this village was the nearest one to Petit-Morne, I had never seen it except from a distance.

It comprised a narrow alley lined by small wooden houses, dotted with public standpipes and I enjoyed watching the clear water fall upon the wide worn-down stones.

The school, a low house roofed with galvanized sheets and surrounded by a veranda, was on a hillock next to the little village church. So close in fact that the church's courtyard also served as the yard of the school. All the children played in the yard under the church porch. Cavorting in all directions, they shouted gleefully making me feel like joining in right away in their games, although I was a bit shy. Many of the kids were wearing shoes; but most of them were barefooted—like me. And they were all very clean, just as Mr. Médouze had told me.

Making her way through this noisy swarm of brats, M'man Tine went in search of a copper-skinned woman who was walking under the veranda. She had a pretty dress, fine shoes and her hair was parted in two long black plaits that started at the nape of her neck and her temples, falling on both sides of her neck onto her chest, right down to her waist. She spoke pleasantly with M'man Tine and smiled at me. I expected to be questioned by her, for along the way M'man Tine had instructed me that if she asked me: "What's your name?" I should reply: "José Hassam"; if she asked: "How old are you?" I was to reply: "Seven years old, Madame," and that every time she spoke to me I was to say: "Yes, Madame, no madame" very politely. But such was not the case.

M'man Tine urged me to be good and left. For a long while I watched the children at play, then at the lady. She went to one end of the veranda, pulled the chain of a bell just like the one that signalled the time for lunch and for work to start again in Petit-Morne. The ringing caused all the children to assemble under the veranda.

The large room I entered with the pupils was unlike anything I had ever imagined. And I felt a deep sense of well-being as I sat on a bench like the other children (both girls and boys, all about my age), admiring all that was stuck, written and hanging on the walls, and looking at, rather than listening to, the lady with the soft, pleasant voice, who drew fine things in white on a wide black board.

At eleven o'clock, at the sound of the bell, I went over to the lady's house to which M'man Tine had taken me for the morning: Mme Léonce.

Mme Léonce was a woman of approximately the same complexion as M'man Tine, but very fat, her head tied with a *madras,* and dressed in a long, shapeless dress, from beneath which as she moved about came the sound of old slippers.

Mme Léonce had never seen me but seemed nevertheless to know me, since my mother Délia had been a servant at her house before I was born.

She handed me the little cretonne bag my grandmother had brought that morning with my lunch in it: a small bowl containing two slices of yam and a piece of cooked cod with some oil on it. And she told me, showing me the corridor: "Go and eat over there. Don't spill any grease on the floor. When you're finished, you'll drink some water: the standpipe is near the road, opposite. Then, sit in front of the door, over there. When you see the school children coming out, follow them."

Mme Léonce and the other people living with her were moving to and fro deep inside the house which to me looked mysterious, impenetrable. I could hear them talking but couldn't see them.

I ate my lunch with all the precautions as instructed, and without making any noise, so I wouldn't even let anybody know I was there. My meal finished, I went to the standpipe to quench my thirst, freshen up my face and wash my feet and legs.

Then I settled down next to the entrance to watch the people go by and wait for the first pupils.

After class that night at the top of the village, on leaving the other children who, themselves separated from one another to go off towards other parts of the country, and on taking by myself the road to Petit-Morne, I was a completely different child. I had just been through a day full of new faces, new things and new feelings which had left me very excited, and to my love of Black Shack Alley and everything in it was added the love of what was for me a new world.

I found M'man Tine in front of our hut. She did not kiss me; she almost never kissed me. But I was not insensitive to all the tenderness and satisfaction that showed in her eyes as she greeted me.

"How did you spend your day?"

Actually, she had never spoken to me in such a pleasant tone.

I gave her all the details. Already I had learned the names of many new objects: the class, the desk, the board; the chalk, the slate, the ink, the inkwell . . . I knew new expressions such as: "Fold your arms;" "keep quiet;" "line up," "dismiss."

Nor had I ever been so talkative. M'man Tine followed my speech with a face that was more rested and radiant than when she was smoking her pipe and with eyes that seemed to find me really changed indeed.

M'man Tine woke me up early in the morning, made me take my cup of coffee with cream and my bowl of cassava flour, and after carefully checking the corners of my eyes, ears, my nostrils, my nose and my neck, I got dressed. Finally, I took my little cretonne lunch bag and left, while she continued wishing me a good day and pestering me with do's and don'ts.

At the foot of the hill I nearly always met friends from Courbaril or Fonds Masson and we would walk together all the way to the school.

Each day would bring me some new emotion. The mistress would make me read, or in turn, go through all by myself and in my child's sing-song, the days of the week. Or I'd make one more friend. Or I'd fight with a wicked boy. Or the mistress had beaten me with that little bamboo switch she used both when showing us the letters to read on the board and when correcting those not paying attention or talking in class.

The only thing I didn't really enjoy was going to have lunch in Mme Léonce's corridor. It was probably a case of my pride being hurt; in addition, the inside of that house, of which I'd never seen any more than the corridor and the dark room I barely entered to leave my little bag, inspired in me an indescribable revulsion because of the lack of attention paid to me in it. I had the distinct impression that in the corridor I was considered as being completely outside and that from the very first day, despite her pleasant promise to M'man Tine to welcome me at midday, Mme Léonce had kept me out of her house in a way I couldn't fully understand.

On Thursdays M'man Tine would take me with her to the fields. That holiday was pleasant for me, especially during the time when sugar canes were being planted in the new fields. My greatest pleasure was to suck the pieces remaining in a pile around those cutting the cane for planting.

I had also made progress in my shrimp catching and it was not without a touch of pride that, all the while enjoying myself, I supplied M'man Tine with what she needed to make the gravy for our evening meal.

Those Thursdays spent with M'man Tine filled me with a joy I'd never experienced before. And it was with even more happiness that, the following day, I returned to the village and my school.

On Sundays I would always accompany M'man Tine to Saint-Esprit; but on Mondays I lost the privilege of going to the river with her.

*

I had discovered, not long before, that opposite Mme Léonce's, behind the standpipe, lived Raphael, one of my class mates. He too had singled me out and, ever since then, we would leave the school together. It was he who, after lunch, would give me, from the other side of the alley, the departure signal.

Raphael was one of the bigger pupils, for the class was divided into big children and small children. He wrote on a copybook whereas I had just received my first slate. That, plus the fact that he was born in the village and lived there, gave him a certain superiority over me, but didn't prevent us from becoming bosom pals.

Raphael was of a lighter complexion that I; his hair was smooth and black and always stuck neatly to his skull. But he dressed more or less like me and also went to school without shoes, just like me. He had a bigger brother at another school in the village (for there was our school at one end of the village and a larger one at the other) and a small sister who was not yet at school.

His maman was a huge woman like Mme Léonce, but did not wear a *madras,* and her rope-colored hair formed a large knot atop her head. She made coconut rock-cakes and other cakes which she sold from a small tray on the sill of her window.

After lunch, when I went to have a drink of water and wash my hands and legs at the standpipe, I had only to linger awhile. Raphael would come out to do likewise and we would chat at the side of the alley. In the long run, I ventured as far as the front step of Raphael's mother's house and we played some relatively silent games until his mother shouted to him that it was time to go back to school.

As a result, I cut short as much as possible the time I took for my lunch so I could go and play with Raphael; in the end, the uneasiness I felt at middays when I had to remain in the corridor or in front of Mme Léonce's house gradually disappeared.

However, I was afraid of Raphael's mother. Was it because she resembled Mme Léonce? Possibly, also, because she had never paid any attention to me either and because the rare occasions on which she had looked at me while I was outside with Raphael, her eyes seemed harsh and mistrustful?

But Raphael apparently loved her very much. He called her M'man Nini, which led me to believe she was his grandmother and the insinuation was that she couldn't be a bad person. Furthermore, Raphael himself became very attached to me, very nice, to the point of saying:

"Pity! You're not here on Sundays; M'man Nini makes pastry and lets us lick and wash all the bowls and pots in which she's made the cakes and sweets. Sugar, syrup! Talk about tasting good!"

At times his grandmother also gave him some of the cakes that hadn't been sold and he'd promised to remember me whenever that happened.

Raphael also taught me many things: the game of marbles, how to trundle a hoop, play hopscotch, open cashew nuts.

Extraordinary! that was the word for his knowledge of games and his ability to organise them. At school, during the recess, everybody wanted to play only with Raphael. Everyone wanted to be on Raphael's team. He ran faster than we did whenever we plays 'police and thief' and never seemed to hurt himself when he fell. And, what authority he had over us!

Therefore, how painful it was to me each time the mistress beat him. For Raphael was extremely fidgety, talkative and inattentive in class; and whether it was reading, arithmetic or writing, the mistress always had some reason to scold or punish him, beating him with a bamboo cane on his legs, or a ruler in the palm of his hand. Brave as he was, Raphael couldn't help writhing hideously and bursting into tears. It just broke my heart.

Still, it never entered my mind to tell Raphael to behave himself better. Similarly, I never once felt any hostility whatsoever toward the mistress.

No, at such times I suffered for Raphael. I felt with painful sympathy the blows he received; and while he wept on his bench, his bowed head tightly clutched in his arms, I followed the soothing of his grief and wished within my heart that he wouldn't do it again, or that at least the mistress would never catch him again.

But when Raphael once more raised his head, his cheeks were barely wet, his eyes barely red. His cheerfulness shone forth once more and I then felt relieved, cured along with him.

One day as I was having lunch in the corridor, I heard the sound of Mme Léonce's sandals approaching. I was seized with panic; I looked about me frantically to see whether I'd possibly dropped some crumbs without realising it.

"Here you are," Mme Léonce said to me.

She handed me a small aluminum plate which I stood up to receive from her hand.

"Thank you, Madame Léonce."

It was a dish of red beans and a piece of meat. Surprised at first, somewhat upset, I began eating immediately. But no sooner had Mme Léonce turned her back that I stopped. It was good all the same, the beans and meat, but that unfriendly look that accompanied Mme Léonce's gesture! . . .

Suddenly I had the suspicion that the food must not in fact be good. Ever since the first day she had shown me my place in the corridor and on the threshold of the door, every time Mme Léonce appeared, I felt like a little dog in front of her. No, I wouldn't continue eating those beans and that meat.

I quickly stuffed down my boiled green bananas, my piece of codfish, then taking Mme Léonce's aluminum plate, I ran across the road and splash! I poured the contents in the water flowing from the standpipe. I washed it properly and returned it to Mme Léonce.

"You even washed the plate," she cried, visibly astonished and satisfied, "but that's just beautiful: you're a very enterprising young man."

"Well," she continued in a soft voice, "you can tell your grandmother it's no point having you bring your lunch, I'll give you something to eat at lunch-time."

Had I been wrong then? Mme Léonce was a nice person after all. And there I was afraid of her! It was quite silly of me not to have enjoyed her beans and above all that lovely slice of meat!

That proposition delighted me all afternoon. It wasn't so much the prospect of eating other dishes of beans and meat, rather the thought of the joy and relief that this show of generosity would bring to M'man Tine.

I was more than anxious to reach Shack Alley to relay this excellent bit of news to her.

Then too, the kindness that had pushed Mme Léonce to make me that offer had touched me, had spread in me, had given me a warm sensation of the affectionate scaling down of the world around me.

No, M'man Tine did not want to believe me.

According to her, I had misunderstood. Mme Léonce, already doing her the great favor of allowing me to take my lunch at her place, could not simply have taken me in hand like that. This bit of news tormented her more than it pleased her.

She finally said as she put me to bed. "You didn't ask Mme Léonce for anything whatsoever?"

"No, m'man."

"Quite sure?"

"Yes, m'man."

"Because I give you enough to eat, not so?"

"Yes, m'man."

"If it's not enough, all you have to do is say so."

"Always enough, m'man."

And in fact I would often eat at four o'clock what was left over from midday.

To make a long story short, M'man Tine decided that, the following week, she would go down to the village to see Mme Léonce to find out what had happened and, accordingly, to apologize to her or to thank her.

And she put the whole affair at the mercy of God's will.

All the same, the following morning, she wanted to make me carry my lunch as usual. The night didn't seem to have rid her of her doubts.

At midday, on my return from school, I went and stood in the corridor, waiting for Mme Léonce to bring me the aluminum plate. I was too uneasy to try to guess what would probably be on it. Uneasy, almost in anguish, I didn't know why, and couldn't even guess.

It wasn't long before I heard the sound of her sandals and Mme Léonce's head, appearing through the door, said to me:

"You're here? Do come in, come and eat."

I crossed a small room I'd been in the day I'd come with M'man Tine; on the table, its only furniture, I used to place my little lunch bag every morning. I then followed Mme Léonce into a small adjoining room, quite dark, which was obviously the kitchen, since it contained a brick stove, a table, saucepans hanging on the walls, a thick smell of roasted onions, of rancid, burnt grease, of cooked vegetables. Mme Léonce put me to sit on a stool near the table cluttered with dishes and other dirty utensils. On the stove she uncovered two or three saucepans from which she dipped carefully with a spoon one after the other. She handed me the same small plate as the previous day and said:

"Here you are, eat."

She immediately moved to an adjoining room, where, as she half-opened the door, I thought I saw it was even darker than in the kitchen.

That must have been where she ate, for I heard the tinkle of forks and plates, and certainly with her husband, for I could hear her voice and a man's.

I would never see Mr. Léonce. No doubt he used to return from the factory before I arrived and leave after me.

I didn't like the kitchen at all. It was too dark. I much preferred to be like a small dog in the corridor. I felt like I was in a prison! I dared not eat.

I suddenly felt like running away, but I was immediately afraid to do so.

All of a sudden I thought I heard a chair move and I attacked the yams and fish on my plate using the fork to put them quickly into my mouth. Nobody entered but I just kept on eating.

Once finished, I got the idea to go and wash my plate at the standpipe so I could see the sun again, fill my lungs with fresh air, play with Raphael, free for a while my heart and my entire body from that oppression I'd been suffering for the past few instants. But I hesitated and suddenly once more a chair moved, sandals were heard being dragged across the floor and Mme Léonce, plate in hand, entered and said to me:

"Finished? Well! you're going to do me a li'l favor, eh, *mon petit nègre?*

"Yes, Madame," I said obediently.

"Well," she continued, "you're going to give me a li'l hand with the dishes."

"Yes, Madame."

"Come," she said.

We returned to the small room next to the kitchen and there Mme Léonce opened a door looking onto a small paved yard where one's eyes immediately came upon a wall covered with moss and patches of dampness. The leaves and shade from a lime tree, below which were piles of fowl droppings, filled this narrow space. Five or six hens, which had been separated from the rest, obviously thinking that they were being brought something to eat, darted toward us.

In one corner of the yard water was running from a tap into a red basin and the overflow spilled over into another small basin, which itself emptied into a gutter.

Mme Léonce put the dirty plates, pans, glasses, spoons and forks in a small shallow basin and showed me what to do: begin with the glasses. You pass two fingers on the soap the put them into each glass, turning it around to scrub it properly. Then you rinse them in the water from the overflow and hold them up to the light to make sure they're properly cleaned. Afterwards, the forks, spoons and knives. Then the plates. Finally the pots—give them a good scrubbing with a rag dipped in ashes.

I tried real hard and was relieved when Mme Léonce, after checking my work, told me that it was good and that I was a really interesting little boy.

I must have spent a long time at it, for when I left that damp yard and those small dark rooms to go out into the alley, Raphael had already left and though I ran quickly, I still reached school late.

That night when I told M'man Tine that Mme Léonce was indeed giving me lunch, my grandmother was beside herself with joy and invoked heaven's most divine blessings for this charitable woman.

*

I had never been prevented from playing. As a result, the time I spent each day in Mme Léonce's dark kitchen and yard was for me a horrible experience. It was impossible for me to get rid of that sensation of being shut up deep inside the earth, from which I'd possibly never escape. Mme Léonce and her always invisible husband seemed to me capable of doing me any possible evil. I didn't know why. In spite of all the food they gave me! Furthermore, frankly speaking, I'd never been treated badly in that house; but nothing inspired any feeling of assurance in me. I was constantly afraid of Mme Léonce whom, without wishing it, I detested because of the unending humiliation I underwent at her house. I was constantly horrified by the kitchen. I would be full of mistrust as I ate or be afraid that I would betray my repugnance. And that chore of doing the dishes, preventing me from meeting Raphael, was the most mortifying of all.

*

Mme Léonce's face remained for me one without kindness and persuaded me that all she told me or had me do could not be of any good. At times I felt like telling someone about her . . . A big policeman, for example!

Whenever there weren't many plates to wash or I had finished quickly, she would give me some men's shoes to clean and polish. Two pairs, three pairs of large shoes, boots with long rows of buttons and pointed tips.

The first time she initiated me to this work, I told M'man Tine, showing how distressed I was, but being very careful, not yet daring to betray my disgust and indignation.

"That's very good," she replied, "Mme Léonce is nice to you, you must also do her a li'l favor now and then."

And once again she invoked the blessing of God and all the saints on this good woman.

What a defeat for me!

Polishing shoes . . . I preferred doing dishes a thousand times to doing that. Perhaps it was mostly because it kept me from going to play with Raphael for the few minutes I had left after doing the dishes. I had grown accustomed, despite everything, to look upon the dish-washing chore as the logical task to follow the meal; whereas polishing shoes after lunch upset my digestion, made me drunk. And it made me reach school late every afternoon.

Added to all that, for some time now, Mme Léonce urged me to come quickly after the evening class, without loitering along the way so I could run a few errands for her in the stores in the district before going back to Petit-Morne. This further robbed me of the opportunity of walking with those of my friends who were going to Fonds-Masson, to Courbaril, to Lemberton.

I began to detest running errands even more than polishing shoes.

I had by then come to like the morning class above all, as I could take it all in without ever being scolded by the mistress for late-coming. Those morning classes were as beautiful as a spectacle, as a game. In her dress, flowered or white, both protected and enhanced by a pretty apron, and with her two long plaits she sometimes allowed to fall on her chest or threw back on her shoulders, the mistress formed huge letters on the black board. Then pointing at them with her long bamboo cane, she plainly articulated each letter or syllable, making her lips move with her teeth and her tongue. Finally, looking down at the entire class, she motioned us to repeat.

Then, together, our voices repeated, once. The mistress continued and we once more repeated after her. And so it went, she repeating and we doing likewise.

I began by looking at that woman's mouth, trying to break down the charming grimace that accompanied the sound she emitted. Then as she made us repeat, her face progressively beamed with the satisfaction of hearing from all the mouths the exact sound. And from then on, it was the white signs, implacably formed on the black of the board, and projected at the end of her bamboo cane that we strove to have sink into our heads, looking steadfastly at them, while our loud voices, echoing the authoritative, inspiring voice of that woman, created a chorus that I thoroughly and eagerly enjoyed.

I also enjoyed the delightful sternness with which we went from reading to writing.

Having gone over our work with us, the mistress would disappear into her flat adjoining the classroom, not without threatening with the most cruel bout of licks the first one to open his mouth to talk.

I liked the thrill that ran through the class as we heard the sound of the returning mistress' footsteps.

I liked to hear her say: "Tidy up your things" so we could say together: "In class, we must not be la...zy."

I liked recess.

The girls would play under the veranda while we boys were allowed to go everywhere, and as far as we wanted, under the mango trees and near the gardens of the people living around the school. We could go into the church to admire the statues and see the humming-birds which had made their nests on the small chains from which hung the red lamp of the Eternal Father.

Some even went as far as to rip off the golden fringes that lined the top of the altars.

We would play long tag in a cane field behind the church.

And everywhere there were woods, thickets, bushes, lending themselves to all our games; they were good for echoing our shouts as well as for hiding us or giving us, to our eyes, the illusion of being policemen, thieves, run-away blacks, chickens, mongooses, dogs and opossums.

There was a period when we ran about like young animals enjoying their freedom, making havoc of those wild surroundings. Then without realising that there was a transition or any change, we found ourselves at various games, assembled on the raised, flat area outside the church near to the school. Games which, though less tumultuous, less furious, were just as passionate, just as full of shouts, queries, protests and quarrels.

And here again, Raphael was the master.

*

But once I had set foot in Mme Léonce's place at midday, the rest of my day was spoilt.

How long was this torture going to last?

I could do nothing to get accustomed to it nor to put an end to it.

*

One afternoon I had reached school later than usual because, after the dishwashing and shoe-polishing chore, I had had to sweep the yard. I had complained to Mme Léonce with tears of anger, which placed the responsibility on her. But Mme Léonce had seized the opportunity to scold me for wasting too much time in those minor tasks she gave me to do.

One evening I arrived quite late in Petit-Morne because I had stayed behind to run a series of errands for Mme Léonce and M'man Tine didn't want to hear anything, accusing me of loitering along the way. And, as a result, I had to remain outside on my knees until dinner time.

How much more misery was this detestable woman going to cause me? One day, Mme Léonce had just given me my lunch and gone into the dining room when she returned to the kitchen with an earthen pitcher in her hand, and said to me:

"Here, go quickly and fill this from the tap."

She had hardly finished talking when I sprang up to do what she had asked. Holding the pitcher by its handle, I dipped it halfway into the water in the basin, leaving the neck above the water and under the tap. I then withdrew the pitcher from the basin to hurry over to Mme Léonce who was waiting for me in the kitchen. But as I raised my foot to leave: "splash", the pitcher crashed onto the ground in the yard. It hadn't slipped from my fingers, however my hand hadn't opened. Nothing had bounced against it. My fingers remained clenched on a fragment of the handle.

Still very much in a daze as a result of the noise of the pottery broken at my feet, with the splash of water on my clothes, I immediately heard the voice of Mme Léonce shouting:

"You broke it?"

. . . And I couldn't make out anything, neither with my eyes, nor with my ears, neither with my hands, nor with my feet.

I was out of the house. I ran and ran. Mme Léonce, Mr. Léonce, dogs, perhaps everybody else as well was running after me. I ran straight ahead in the alley without looking at the people who saw me running, without looking back to see those who must have been trying to catch me.

I didn't know how long I'd been running. I didn't know where I was going nor how far I would reach.

I would have crossed any obstacle as I ran: flames, burning coals, a river, a sugar cane field.

Besides, it wasn't on my own that I ran. I was a ball of fire hurled into space.

However, little by little, my chest grew hard, like a fist being clenched, and grew heavy with a load that reached down to my knees, to my calves, and gave my bare feet the sensation of running over jagged stones.

I felt like a load about the crash to the ground. I couldn't run any further; I was lost; they were going to hold me. I couldn't hold out any longer; I was about to scream! I turned around, terrified—nobody.

Nobody was chasing me.

I had escaped. I was saved!

But I still couldn't stop; my noisy irregular breath carried me along and I continued walking, irresistably turning around every now and then.

I continued until the houses, the people, the alley regained their clarity, their reality, not hostile to my eyes, and until only the pounding of my heart in my chest, the tiredness of my legs and the cutting of the stones into the soles of my feet made me think of seeking a refuge.

I thereupon mechanically took the road to the school.

The school was closed, the veranda empty. I was obviously the first to arrive. I sat outside the classroom and tried to compose myself in my disarray.

I wanted simply to appear to have been the first to arrive. But my breeches were wet with water to the front and, as my hand reached out to touch it, I found in my still tightly-clenched fist a piece of pottery, a piece of the handle of the pitcher!

Dull anger rose up in me with such violence that tears sprang to my eyes.

"It wasn't me who broke the pitcher. It fell by itself." And Mme Léonce accused me there and then: "You broke it." And that's not true. And I would never be able to say how it happened. I don't know.

"Mme Léonce thinks I did it. She'll beat me, she'll consider me less than a puppy. She'll hate me so much she'll do me all sorts of wicked things."

I would weep aloud, so great was my anger and so deep was the ache in my heart.

But the mistress was going to hear me, perhaps. Perhaps I didn't even have the right to arrive at school so early.

I dried my eyes with the sleeve of my shirt and went and threw into a nearby bush the old piece of pottery. I then returned to where I'd been sitting, my heart still heavy, my head light, unable to find anything to help me pass the time.

Finally a small group of pupils arrived and at the same time the door opened, the mistress came out and went and pulled the chain for the first bell.

Perhaps I did not appear sad that afternoon; I played as usual.

From time to time, the memory of what had happened suddenly came back, making my heart jump, then the reading, singing and playing chased it away and reassured me that I was in school, in other words in the most pleasant, the most hospitable of the houses.

That evening after the class, I had to resolve a burning question which, alas! I hadn't thought about.

How could I get to Petit-Morne without passing in front of Mme Léonce's house? The village had but one alley and Mme Léonce lived right along the path I had to take.

There was absolutely no way I could pass in front of that abominable house, even if I ran, without running the risk of being seen, if not caught. Mme Léonce must surely have been watching for my return from school and I knew that if she saw me and called, I would not be able to flee: I would surrender.

I was the last to leave the school yard. But I made a bold decision.

The village's only alley ran at the foot of the hill like a river, and the houses were clustered at its edges. But to the side of the hill were scattered some shacks, among some canes, mango trees and tall breadfruit trees, forming an area called Haut-Morne.

There had to be, under those trees, paths joining the shacks to one another and linking them from one end of the village to the other. Consequently, it should be possible to go around the entire village by going through Haut-Morne.

So, taking the paths we used to roam in around the school, I penetrated the thick foliage of Haut-Morne. I needed much instinct to guide me, but I managed to make it myself and when a track brought me right behind the standpipe where I would wash my feet every morning as I entered the village, I felt with relief, with pride, that I was getting the better of my terrible misadventure.

That didn't prevent my being afraid as I returned to M'man Tine.

As I saw her, I suddenly felt that she was somehow aware of what had happened. Didn't parents know everything? Then again, no; she didn't mention a word about it. She didn't know anything. And I tried my best to appear calm and confident.

My God, was I hungry!

Although I hadn't eaten any lunch, I hadn't felt hungry at any time in the afteroon, but that night, as soon as M'man Tine lit the fire, my stomach was put to as painful a torment as were the soles of my feet on the jagged stones in the road.

While my fears had been allayed, the sensation of hunger rose to my head to the point where I'd have fainted if I didn't take hold of myself. I suffered so much that the hunger I felt did not seem to be the lack of anything whatsoever, but something too heavy, too acute, too voluminous that invaded and overpowered me.

The following day I was fine and calm.

I set out for school.

What was I going to do? Never again pass in front of Mme Léonce's house either on my way to or from school. Take the Haut-Morne road every day from now on. Forego lunch at midday. Roam about around the school between eleven o'clock and one o'clock. Of course, she would find out one day.

One day she'd go to Petit-Bourg, she'd see Mme Léonce. But in the meanwhile such was my resolution.

However, this attitude quickly turned out to be less ascetic than I had envisaged.

Despite my efforts to ignore it, to mask it, by drinking my stomach full of water at the standpipe, hunger forced me to walk about Haut-

Morne and in this area, every midday, some windfall would come my way, as if by magic. Someone, seeing me pass by, would send me to the store on a few errands, and as a reward would give me a couple of cents. Or I would come upon a guava tree laden with fruits, a wild cherry-tree all red with cherries. I ended up finding all the fruit trees in the surrounding areas and, when they were fairly far from the shacks, I helped myself without fear or remorse. If they were near the shacks, I carefully picked my moments and stole the fruits. I would steal oranges from Mam'zelle Edouarzine, mangoes from Mr. Ténor, grenadines from Mme Sequédan, caimites from Mme Uphodor.

Harvest time began. From then on, there was no longer any need for me to use any stratagem or trick to eat lunch. All around Petit-Bourg, nearby as well as in the distance, fields of sugar cane were given over to the violent cutlasses of the "cutters," and like so many flies attracted by the sweet juice, children would go and quench their thirst with all the canes they could suck.

At such times, I wouldn't have given my lunch of sugar canes for the most beautiful fish or the biggest piece of meat from Mme Léonce's.

Oh what infinite happiness—no longer being at that woman's house! I'd now have been prevented from going every midday to nibble on the canes. I'd have died.

I filled myself with so much sugar cane juice that, at the school's first bell, when I ran from the field, my full stomach resounded with a noise of liquid being shaken, like a huge bell—a noise similar to that made by the belly of a trotting horse that has just finished drinking.

Nothing worried me at that time; no more fear of Mme Léonce. The way I took via Haut-Morne was pretty much safe and every day I would find my lunch with ridiculous ease.

I really was not difficult to please.

And all of this went on completely unknown to my grandmother, the school mistress, my friends, even Raphael himself who, for some time now, saw me only at school.

That was my secret. I was able to keep it closely guarded, or rather, it was able to keep me. It happened however that it caused me some grief. I was in fact hungry at times and was tempted to open up to a friend. But every time, tear, shyness or some indescribable modesty would stop me.

*

Finally there came a time when the recess breaks became very long and the games wilder and more passionate. In class itself, we did more singing than reading.

I knew and understood, I can't say how, that school was about to finish and that for quite a while–longer than we'd done on two or three occasions before–the children were going to remain at their parents' homes.

That was why the mistress would have us sing over half a dozen times a day:

> Long live the holidays,
> the holidays,
> the holi . . . days!

That was why, one morning, M'man Tine had started carrying me to the fields with her once more.

I enjoyed spending Thursdays in the cane fields with my grandmother just as much as I hated following her once again every morning to all those fields that bored me and that I began to detest.

At first I was filled with pain and nostalgia for the school. Although I was certain that for the time being school was closed and that I'd be returning as soon as it reopened, my presence in the canes filled me with apprehension and remorse.

It was painful to me to spend days on end without reading aloud and in unison with other children. It was strange not hearing the school bell; and the one on the plantation at midday made my heart heavy. I felt like seeing and hearing the mistress.

I suffered as a result of not running among the swarm of school mates and of not shouting myself deaf and hoarse.

I often thought about Raphael.

Remaining silent beside M'man Tine in the field where the only noise I would hear was the uneven scraping of the hoe on the crust of the earth, and the rustle of wind in the leaves, having nothing else to do but sit down, stand up, cut blades of grass into little pieces . . . At times, I would spend hours attacking and decimating long lines of ants . . . I was bored.

Now, all games, save those I could play on my own, had become something of a rarity for me since the incident that had separated me from my friends in Shack Alley; and since I'd begun attending school there was almost no more contact between them and me. Almost no more friendship.

We were mutually touchy about frequenting each other. We were, it seemed to me, both suffering from a sort of inferiority complex. We no longer gave vent to our tyrannical whims in Shack Alley. No more games, no more pilfering, no more expeditions to far-off 'traces,' no more massive incursions into deep woods, entwined with lianas, that frightened us by the multiple echoes of our voices.

Be that as it may, I did not relish going everyday to the fields. Furthermore, the whole thing lasted too long, in my opinion, and I had this vaguely nagging fear that I would no longer be going back to school.

As some degree of consolation, every night I organised a class in M'man Tine's hut, tracing on the wall with charcoal the letters I knew, pointing at them with a bamboo rod, playing both mistress and pupil at the same time. And I rounded everything off with a boisterous medley of all the songs learned at school until M'man Tine, charmed and proud at the outset, shouted to me in a suddenly irritated voice: " 'is night time, enough singing!"

M'man Tine had once more started to talk about writing to my mother.

The time for resumption of classes was fast approaching and I had to get a new suit. Every Sunday, on her return from Saint-Esprit, M'man Tine would keep talking to herself about the various bits of fabric she had bargained over in order to buy me a new suit. This perspective should have sufficed to make my heart able to bear my days in the fields if, at that same time, the awful rainy season hadn't arrived. Had I become more sensitive to those heavy downpours, with the frightful noise of storms? Was that season exceptionally violent? The fact remained that I could no longer allow myself to be drenched as passively as before.

For M'man Tine, I felt the same pity, the same desolation that tormented her for my sake. I wouldn't have wanted her to allow herself to get soaked. But she only worked herself all the more to death pulling on her hoe.

My grief became so intense that in the end the sugar cane fields seemed a danger to me—that danger had killed Mr. Médouze without anyone seeing how and which could at any moment, especially on a stormy day, also kill my grandmother under my very eyes.

When the sun began to set and M'man Tine persisted in uprooting those stubborn clumps of Guinea grass, a feeling of great panic spread through me.

I had finally understood that Médouze had died from fatigue, that it was the stalks of cane, the clumps of Guinea grass, the showers, storms, sunstrokes which, once evening had fallen, had struck him down. Now it was M'man Tine's turn to undergo all of that: sun, storms, weeds, cane stalks, cane leaves.

It was quite clear that school must have been about to re-open, for M'man Tine was still mulling over whether to write to my mother, and my returning to school was the daily subject of her debate and interdiction. That's the way M'man Tine was when she had anything to do: she would begin by talking about it—to herself alone, and never to another soul on this earth—once, twice, over and over; then she would go over her projects with impassioned fervor and finally, with the same thrust, she would move on to carrying them out.

Thus leaving work earlier than usual, M'man Tine went down to Petit-Bourg to see Mam'zelle Charlotte and have her write a letter to my mother. That decision filled me with sudden joy that made me see my return to school as a triumph and the end to those sad, wretched days on the plantation.

But M'man Tine returned from the village that night thoroughly upset.

"When you went to school, where did you eat at midday, José?" she asked me point blank.

I didn't know her voice to be so calm, so deep when she was scolding me. Her tone as she addressed me was so serious and heart-felt that I asked myself before replying whether it was the start of a set of questions which, as usual, would lead to a spanking or whether it was some bit of grief that was responsible for that quivering in my grandmother's voice, which she tried her best to control.

I hadn't yet replied to her question.

With regard to what I was guilty of, the question, to my mind, was badly put. I could not answer.

Why hadn't she asked me whether or not I'd broken the pitcher? Or why I had done it? Or why had I run from Mme Léonce's? Since she was obviously leading up to that, wasn't she?

Unless, perhaps, that ole Mme Léonce had told her things about me I couldn't even imagine.

"Eh!" M'man Tine pursued, "where did you have lunch when you were going to school?"

"Nowhere, M'man."

"How you mean, nowhere?"

"No, m'man."

"What did you eat then?"

"Nothing, m'man."

"And why didn't you tell me you weren't going to Mme Léonce's anymore?"

I didn't reply to any other question. Besides, M'man Tine didn't insist. She didn't mention a word about the broken pitcher. But never had I seen her so heart-broken and despondent.

As if she had become almost dazed, she started moaning profusely:

"The poor child! Remaining like that without lunch. A worm could have bitten his heart. They could've brought this child home dead, starved to death! How shameful for me! And what would Délia have said? What explanation would I have given her? And no one would've believed how ignorant, how innocent I was in all this. The law would possibly have put me in chains, dragged me away, like a grandmother who sent her grandson off to school with an empty stomach. God above, do you really believe I wouldn't have given this child even a speck of flour? . . ."

I couldn't understand this reaction on the part of M'man Tine. She hadn't administered the most stinging of spankings—I couldn't get over it! That sort of tenderness seemed abnormal to me. Mme Léonce hadn't told her that I'd broken the pitcher then? And wasn't I guilty of having fled, of having constantly given the impression that I was still having lunch at Mme Léonce's, of having gone roaming about the village every midday?

No, the whole thing left me completely baffled.

For most of the following day M'man Tine still spoke to me in the field with that sad, grief-stricken voice, and that accent which little by little made a lump stick in my throat.

For a whole week, M'man Tine went down to the village almost every night, which did not put me out in any way since on each occasion she would bring me back either a sweet, or a bit of bread which I ate—one and the other—as dessert after my dish of vegetables and gravy.

One day she began to take things off her shelves, the way she would do whenever she cleaned the shack from top to bottom. But instead of washing her cups, glasses and plates only to put them back where they had been, she wrapped them in rags and put them in her bamboo basket. In similar fashion, she gathered together everything in the shack.

It was a visit from our neighbor, Mam'zelle Valérine, that finally made me understand what was happening.

"So, you're leaving us, it seems?" she asked.

"Oh, yes," replied M'man Tine. "Mam'zelle Charlotte is a person who doesn't like children; it's no point my asking her to allow José to take lunch at her place at midday. Mme Léonce was the one to do me that favor and see what . . . So, that's all I could do—school re-opens next week."

"When are you going to move? I'd like to give you a li'l hand."

M'man Tine was leaving Black Shack Alley. She was going to live in Petit-Bourg!

*

I would be returning to school and at midday I'd be going home to M'man Tine's; I would eating at her place. I would become a child of the village.

And this was done a few days afterwards.

To my eyes everything took place with an ease that, once again, reinforced my conviction that parents sometimes held prodigious powers that children would never understand.

Everything was done as if M'man Tine had been one of those old women Mr. Médouze used to talk about in his tales, whenever a nice person was unhappy, would appear to deliver him and carry out his wishes.

Hadn't M'man Tine really been the fairy who made my dream come true?

Everything was arranged in an order such as my brain could not have created and which held me spellbound.

We were living at Cour Fusil.

Two long parallel sets of barracks covered with tiles, divided into units, looking onto a narrow blind alley with a rough, uneven surface.

The entire area bore the name of the great local aristocrat who owned it: Fusil.

*

My mother had certainly sent the money, for I had a new suit and I had returned to school.

Every morning, M'man Tine would do exactly as she had done when we used to live at Petit-Morne: coffee, my cup of coffee with cream along with cassava flour; vegetables for lunch; the packing of her bamboo basket; her usual bits of advice:

"Don't get your clothes all torn, don't rip off your buttons to play marbles with, don't run too fast and fall and bruise your knees, don't interfere with anything in the bedroom. Don't do anything to make me mad."

She would then light her pipe, settle her basket on her head, put herself in God's hands and set off for Petit-Morne.

For she remained attached to it, as did most of the people of the village besides who went to work on the neighboring plantations.

At midday I returned, at my lunch, searched the room from top to bottom, found the sugar tin and skillfully took my dessert from it.

Then I went roaming about in search of fruits until the school's first bell sounded.

On evenings I stayed behind with some friends in front of the school, then returned to Cour Fusil after making sure that I wasn't guilty of anything extraordinary. At times I would go to a standpipe at the side of the alley to wash my face, hands and feet and, while waiting for M'man Tine to return home, would remain at the entrance to the yard so I could look at the people: the factory workers, the travellers on their way back from Fort-de-France on a little steam boat which, via Rivière-Salée, linked the village to the sea and the entire region to the town.

It was also the time when the other residents of Cour Fusil were returning from work. Most of them probably worked at the factory not far from the village, since many of them went home for lunch at midday.

I didn't know them all. M'man Tine scarcely paid any visits to her neighbors.

I knew Mam'zelle Délice since I'd heard her call and above all because she had aroused my curiosity in particular—a small, old woman, short and upright, with a tiny face, but who was endowed with the biggest foot you ever saw.

From under her crumpled skirt there extended one leg and one foot that were just like the naked foot and leg extending from the crumpled skirt of any old black woman; but next to that, the other leg, from the knee down, was swollen, rounded out evenly and puffed up to bursting point, looking like a huge, black sausage, then growing narrower as it met her instep which, yielding to the same movement and in the same proportion, imitated the form of an overturned half-calabash. She had huge warts for toes and they each made me think of a stone, so much so that I was just as surprised not to hear this foot make any noise as I was at the ease with which Mam'zelle Délice walked.

I had nevertheless seen cases of erysipelas and of lymphadenitis in Shack Alley, I can assure you! But that elephantiasis seemed to be the most horrible monster.

It was, I was to learn subsequently, a case of *quimboisement,* an evil spell that a former jilted lover, his pride wounded, had cast on Mam'zelle Délice.

I also knew Man'zelle Mézélie, whose room was immediately adjacent to ours. A tall woman who, once home, was always dressed in a simple smock and who would always send me to buy rum whenever there was a man inside with her.

Then there was Mr. Toussaint who, for his part, must have worked on a plantation—on his trousers he wore the sack cloth apron like the workers in Petit-Morne.

There was a woman whose breasts bobbed about like two calabashes in her dress. She had an infant who kept crying almost the entire day because he had to remain alone while his maman was at work.

The most pleasant person, and the most important to my eyes, was Mr. Assionis, storyteller, singer and a drummer by profession. His wife, Ti-Louise, though hardly younger than my grandmother, had a brilliant reputation as a dancer of *bel-air.*

He did not work at the factory nor on any plantation. He remained at home during the day, and almost every day people would come to fetch him to go and 'sing' at the wake of some dead person, either close by or far away. Then almost every night, he would put his drum on his back, take his stick and, together with Ti-Louise, would set off.

His presence would sometimes be required in several places at the same time. People would beg him, promise him left and right vast sums and all sorts of good things to eat and drink during the night. He would become angry, show everybody out and, later on, go off with the most persistent of his customers.

On Saturday nights he would go to play and sing on the plantations; and it was there, between two *laghias* of death, that Ti-Louise would dance the *bel-air* like a woman who had sold her soul to the devil, according to the bystanders.

Mme Popo was also nice—she sold *corrosol* and made ginger beer.

Finally, Cour Fusil's inhabitants comprised other people whom I heard laughing, talking, quarrelling, and whom I'd seen very little of until that time.

I had never visited the other rooms in Cour Fusil but, seeing them from the outside, I imagined that they were similar to the one M'man Tine occupied: somewhat small, somewhat dark, with a flooring of long, disjointed, shaky boards, that made everything dance about at every movement made and every step taken; infested as well with roaches, mice and rats, and pervious to rain and sunlight.

In one corner M'man Tine had mounted the bed—the same four boxes as at Shack Alley, with the planks, the straw mattress and the rags. On another box placed at the head of the bed, she had put her basket containing our good clothes. Her table, her shelves, her kitchen utensils, everything else had been set up the way it was in the 'front room' when we lived at Black Shack Alley.

From what I could see whenever I glanced into the other inhabitants' homes as I passed by, the room was divided in two by a screen of printed cotton, wallpaper or newspaper. The forward portion was the 'front room' and the section behind the screen was the bedroom.

For a long time I wondered why M'man Tine hadn't done likewise. In the end I came to the conclusion—I knew not how—that it was the women who had a man with them who hid their beds with a screen.

*

Something had changed in my way of life. On Thursdays, instead of following M'man Tine to the sugar cane fields, I would remain in the village. I no longer went to Petit-Morne.

Like the majority of the children in the village, I spent my Thursdays walking about the bank of the Rivière-Salée. Along with other friends, I enjoyed catching, so we could play with them and mutilate them afterwards, tiny crabs whose holes dotted the bank, and launching onto the water bits of wood under the guise of racing boats, and also fishing for shrimp.

I had learned to swim by watching the bigger ones jump into the water and cross over to the other bank, wildly beating their arms and feet in the process.

The number of my friends had increased considerably. In particular, I was friendly with Michel, a huge lad, whom we called Paunch because of his big belly. He was strong and never cried. Michel had a brother, Ernest, by contrast frail and very cowardly, and a younger sister, Hortense.

The three were always seen together.

I knew Sosso, one whom we respected a lot because he was a good swimmer and made things unbearable for us in the water when we didn't obey him.

There was also Camille, whose breeches just refused to be mastered by any suspenders or any belt, and would slide down from his belly at the most unexpected moments and in the most inappropriate places.

Raphael was still my good friend but we only saw each other at school. He lived somewhat far from M'man Tine's and, furthermore, his grandmother would always give him petty domestic chores to do after class.

Michel, Ernest, Hortense, Camille, I appreciated them all, in particular out of school, near the river, for example. And Raphael was almost exclusively my school mate.

I had another friend who in class used to sit right next to me: Vireil. The mistress beat him often, accusing him of being 'as lazy as a louse' and 'as talkative as a parrot'. In spite of everything, Vireil was a boy who astonished me.

Of tanned complexion, his skin and hair (long, black and soft) shone as if he bathed every morning in coconut oil. His suit was too tight across his shoulders, his chest and his legs. His breeches always seemed about to burst in the area of his behind, for he was thickset and stocky. He spoke in a voice that made everyone turn around and which the mistress always heard, even when he tried his best to whisper. The fact was, his voice was already that of a man, a big man already working, riding on horseback, smoking and talking to women. And, like a man, he had long, stiff hair on the back of his hands and on his huge calves. Vireil was one of the rare pupils who wore shoes to school. He was the son of a manager, the one at Digues, I was made to understand.

We all liked Vireil and it was a great stroke of fortune to be sitting next to him. Vireil knew lots of things and told us sparkling, captivating tales that delighted us, held us in suspense and made us shudder.

Stories about *gens-gagés* for example—people who, at night, would turn into any beast, sometimes even into plants and who, in that form, did evil things to others, to Christians, on orders from the devil.

Vireil had already heard about *bâtons-volants—gens-gagés* in the form of sticks with wings who at night flew over the countryside with a noise of wind that seemed to talk and spread sickness, misfortune and death even in the shacks.

As such, he had advised us to erect a wooden cross on the roof of our parents' houses since, according to him, that was the only weapon that killed the *bâtons-volants*.

The animal whose form the *gens-gagés* assumed more often than not was the hare. One night you are returning from some fête, for example, and suddenly something white leaps across your path: a rabbit! a *gens-gagés*. Make the sign of the cross.

Gens-gagés also sometimes assumed the form of huge dogs that you would come across at night, at a crossroad, its eyes projecting blinding light, its mouth all aflame.

How upset we all were then, the day Vireil informed us that every night there was a horse with only three legs running up and down, from one end of the village to the other. When there was absolute silence, it seemed, all the people in the village could hear the footsteps of that hideous animal.

Vireil cited names of people in the village reputed to be *gagés*-people to whom one had to be respectful, whom one had to be careful not to laugh at or to make fun of, people like Mr. Julios, Mme Boroff, Mr. Godisart, Mam'zelle Tica.

He gave us recipes for protecting ourselves from the evils done by *zombis:* always wear around your waist next to your skin, just as he did, a string of *mahot*.

Confirming what Mr. Médouze had told me, Vireil informed us that all *békés,* all the rich folks, were thieves who were *gagés*.

In addition to those real-life adventures, those personal testimonies, Vireil also told us stories. But the way he told them, the stories weren't in any way different from reality.

*

"There was a little boy without a maman who used to live with his godmother. In the country, of course. A place like Courbaril. The godmother was a wicked, wicked woman and she used to beat him. Polo was the little boy's name. At nights after dinner, the godmother and her godson would put on their night clothes and go to bed. As there was only one very small room, the godmother did not make a separate bed for Polo and they both slept in the same bed. Besides, she didn't

have a husband. Then she would blow out the lamp and Polo would
soon be asleep. Polo was a very sound sleeper, but a very early riser. He
would be awake at the first crowing of the cocks. As there was no place
for him to go, he would remain in bed but could hear all the noises of
the new day as it began. And as soon as the light had filtered through
the cracks in the partition, he could make out everything in the room.
So that, on one occasion, as Polo opened his eyes he noticed that his
godmother was no longer lying beside him. She couldn't possibly be
elsewhere in the room either. There was no light, no noise. That hadn't
frightened him, but he was no less puzzled by this occurrence when, all
of sudden, he heard 'woo-woo'—something flying above the roof of the
shack. Then the noise stopped and at the same time Polo felt as if a
huge bird had alighted on the shack.

"That time, his heart began to pound.

"Thereupon he heard the door open and someone came into the
room."

"His godmother!" Raphael exclaimed.

"But she was without her skin," Vireil continued.

"Good heavens! . . . "

"Bundled up like a rabbit, she entered quietly. Polo did not stir. The
godmother went behind the door, unhooked something: her skin! She
put it on the way you put on a jacket and a pair of trousers, shook
herself a bit to adjust it and became herself once more.

"Naturally, the day did not go by without Polo receiving a flogging.
She was a wicked woman, I tell you."

"Since that time, Polo would not be sleeping when his godmother
blew out the lamp. Shortly afterwards, he would hear her get up, light
the lamp once more. Then she would take off all her clothes, remaining
stark naked; then she would make some gestures, like this and this,
murmur a few words, prayers no doubt, and her skin would fall off,
exactly like a piece of clothing. She would pick it up, hang it on a nail
behind the door and 'woo-woo-woo,' she would fly off into the air
above the shack."

"So she was a bâton-volant!"

"Polo didn't like that woman at all and ever since he realised that
she was gagée, hated her all the more.

"Now, one day she beat him so badly with a strip of liana that she
made blood flow from his bruised skin. And that night, as she was about
to go to bed, she said to Polo:

" 'Let me put a little medicine on your sore.'

"In her hand she held a basin full of a liquid with which she washed
the child's sore. Good God! It was brine. Imagine how the poor little
fellow ached, how he hollered with pain, how he cried!

"But when he was in bed an idea came to him.

"He waited for his godmother to take off her skin for her diabolical expeditions through the air and no sooner had she flown off than he got up, looked for the basin with the rest of the brine, took the skin, dipped it in it, spreading it all over the inside, then carefully hung it back in place.

"At dawn 'woo-woo-woo,' the godmother returned as usual, went behind the door, took her skin, but: 'oh-yo-yo-ee! oh-yo-yo-ee,' she wailed, 'oh-yo-yo-ee!' every time she tried to put the skin on her flesh.

"Oh-yo-yo-ee," Vireil imitated.

And his grimacing, his wincing and his twisting were so impressive, so suggestive, that the godmother's torment made us squirm while sympathy for Polo roused us, made us burst out both with vengeful horror and in a laugh of triumph. But, there came the mistress bearing down on us!

By the time we moved away, bending backwards with our arms held up to shield us and shouting: 'not me, madame,' the bamboo cane had broken the spell. And the entire group, down to Vireil himself, sobbed with pain.

But nothing was going to prevent us from hearing the end of that fascinating story.

Shortly afterwards Vireil got back to his task and whispered to us, one hand before his mouth:

"The godmother was unable to put her skin back on. When day finally broke, she died, for sunlight kills *gens-gagés*. Since she had a fine shack and a large property, Polo inherited them. He bought a beautiful horse and married an adorable woman."

Vireil, what an extraordinary pupil! What a wonderful friend! So extraordinary and so wonderful to us in fact that though the mistress would constantly repeat, all to no avail. that he was the worst pupil, our admiration for him always remained nothing short of complete.

The school was mixed but we could not play with the girls during recess, since they would remain under the veranda under the watchful eyes of the mistress. In class there were benches for girls and benches for boys, so much so that, not being able to have fun with them, we would play jokes on them, tease them and call them all sorts of ugly names.

Warmer still was my friendship with George Roc. He had a brown, round face, with course hair, sticking to his skull like a cap, large black eyes, always veiled with melancholy, and heavy, drooping lips. George Roc was bigger than I. He was possibly fatter but could not have been stronger, at any rate. He was always clean, changing clothes on

Mondays and Fridays and, just like Vireil, wore boots which, again just like Vireil, he took off so he could run about more easily during recess.

It wasn't at school that I'd met him. His parents lived not far from Cour Fusil and whenever I was passing by in the street, sometimes at midday and every night, I would see him sitting under a veranda.

One day, having noticed that we attended the same school, we struck up a conversation. Was it he who spoke first, or I? Since then, although I didn't specifically look for him at school, every midday and every night I would go to meet him under the veranda to chat.

The house in which George Roc's parents lived was much more beautiful than the other surrounding houses. Painted in bright colors, the facade contained many windows with venetian blinds. I had never seen George Roc's maman nor his papa.

She was always inside, it seemed, and he, Mr. Justin Roc, came on evenings in his car; and from as far off as George could hear the horn, or even the noise of the engine, he would shout, cutting short any conversation.

"My papa! Off with you!"

My going to chat with George Roc seemed to involve an element of risk for him or for me. At any rate, my friend, though insisting that I keep on coming, appeared to be infringing some ban!

Yet I had become very attached to George Roc. I liked him, not for the joy of playing with him, not for some talent that made him stand out from the rest, not even for his kindness; above all, I liked him because he was always sad and because the things he told me caused me some degree of pain.

I had never felt any sadness for any friend. George Roc was the first being I'd met who saw and felt himself unhappy.

In my seven-year old infant heart, he had secured a special place, the most sensitive and the most gloomy.

Every day George Roc would have some misfortune. Every day he had been crying and when on evenings, about six or seven o'clock, I went to meet him, it was his misfortunes that he spoke about.

Mam'zelle Mélie had complained to his mother about him and the latter had beaten him. Mam'zelle Mélie was an old black woman in a black dress and with dried legs, whom, in my mind, I associated with a crow because of her silhouette and her name. In Mr. Justin Roc's house, she appeared to be a maid with great esteem which conferred on her even a certain authority over George.

He had either dirtied this or dropped that, hadn't done such and such a thing, had said something or the other, as a result of which he had been beaten or scolded.

As for me, I used to do as much without being punished in most instances. Whereas everything he did led to blows—the cat whose tail he would sometimes pull; his shoes which he wore down too much or which he hadn't polished properly; his clothes that he would soil or rip apart; his teeth he hadn't brushed; his finger nails he hadn't cleaned; his fork that he would hold incorrectly at table. The result was that George was in a perpetual state of chagrin and when, later on, following the confidences and revelations each of his outpourings brought me, I learned his story, George Roc became for me the object of greatest pity.

How could I have imagined that one could have a maman who was always in the shade and freshness of such a lovely house, and a father who was in charge of the factory, with a car, and not be the happiest boy in the world?

I had to hear George Roc, sitting on the ground beside me, under the veranda, relate his sad story for himself in a low voice.

At home he was called Jojo, but for all that received no special favors. His father, a tall mulatto, had a moustache and wore a Panama hat. But Mme Justin Roc, whose footsteps and voice I could sometimes hear behind the venetian blinds, was not his mother.

Imagine my amazement when Jojo confessed to me that his real mother was Mam'zelle Gracieuse, that woman who lived not far from Cour Fusil, not far from Mr. Justin Roc's house, whom I saw every day and for whom I'd even run some errands on occasions.

Why was Jojo not living with his mother? Why had I never seen him at her place? Why didn't he go there very often?

"Why don't you go there right now, for example, now that that woman who's not your maman has just beaten you?"

Jojo's explanation was even more frightening and pitiful.

Mr. Justin Roc was the bastard son of an old *béké*. Before taking over the factory, Mr. Justin had been manager of the Reprise plantation.

Mam'zelle Gracieuse was a worker on the plantation and as nothing was easier for the managers and overseers than to do what they wanted at the whim of their desires, tastes and appetites, both with the young girls, their breasts barely beginning to show, as well as with the soft, musky-fleshed women, their backs bent over in the fields, Gracieuse had had a child for Mr. Justin.

Since she was a young, plump, beautiful octoroon with an amber-colored complexion, Mr. Justin had made her his mistress and acknowledged the child. They had come to live in the village when Mr. Justin had been promoted to foreman. In a small three-room dwelling Gracieuse had continued living with him, at the same time loving, respectful and obedient, passing in the eyes of her former friends for a woman who had been lucky enough to be chosen as the mistress of a mulatto, of a foreman, and in fact finding herself in the situation of a maid who slept with her master.

Thus Jojo lived. I was no doubt still at Petit-Morne. And he was never beaten, never wanted anything and was spoilt by his papa. He was as free, as happy with everything as all the boys of the village.

Then one day everything changed.

Mr. Justin Roc had built this lovely house, had outfitted it with new furniture; there was a function, with many cars, many mulattoes, a few békés and ladies in formal dresses. Mr. Justin had gotten married.

He had brought Jojo to live in the lovely house with the new wife who was called Mme Justin. His mother had remained alone in one room instead of three and whenever Jojo went to see her, would embrace him with tears in her eyes.

To my way of looking at things, it was regrettable, but I couldn't yet see what there was in that change to make Jojo himself so unhappy.

"I cried a bit, too," Jojo told me, "since I saw maman crying; but I used to go to see her often and didn't feel the change very much. I would pass to give her a kiss every morning on my way to school, at eleven o'clock on my way back, after lunch on my return to school and at four o'clock I would spend a longer time with her, eating the afternoon snack she'd left me and playing in front of her door.

"But, I don't know why, one day maman Yaya—that's how papa told me to address his lady—told me she didn't want me spending so much time with my maman. So I cut short my visit after the evening class; but as soon as I was alone under the veranda I would run over—after all, it was just for a minute—to see maman 'cause I couldn't remain alone like that, under the veranda, while she was right there, just a stone's throw away.

"Well, fairly often, while I was over there, Mam'zelle Mélie ('twas maman Yaya who had brought her) would come and fetch me and on every occasion maman Yaya would scold me.

"This went on every day until one night, following a complaint from maman Yaya, papa gave me a licking with a wide leather belt: 'Since you're so disobedient,' he shouted, 'I forbid you to go and see maman Gracieuse without my permission.'

"The following morning, on my way to school, I told m'man Gracieuse what had happened, and that night when my father returned home, maman Yaya told him how that morning, like a true black woman from the plantation, m'man Gracieuse had come to the front of the house and had called her out and insulted her.

"She then turned on my papa, telling him that if he hadn't been such a damn' scamp before his marriage, running around with those dirty, vulgar black girls, I wouldn't have existed to come and cause her so much scandal. And that night I received a few slaps. Since then, Mam'zelle Mélie was given the job to accompany me to school, way past my maman's place to make sure I didn't stop in at all.

"One day m'man Gracieuse had a fight with Mam'zelle Mélie. Another time, she came here to abuse and curse my papa's wife.

"Nonetheless, every time I found the opportunity, I ran over to see my maman. But Mam'zelle Mélie kept spying on me and did not fail to carry tales to maman Yaya and my papa. Then they took everything out on me—there was always something to reproach me for so they could beat me or have my papa do so."

As a result Jojo could not go beyond the limits of the veranda to go and play elsewhere with the other boys of the village. He was always worried, always trembling, urging me to run off or to hide every time he heard his maman Yaya stir, Mam'zelle Mélie talk or his father's car approach. He begged me every day to return that evening, since I enjoyed the freedom of being able to play awhile in the neighborhood after dinner, as opposed to him, who was only allowed to remain squatting under the veranda until his father's car returned.

Jojo did not tell me all of that in one go. Each one of his outpourings brought out secrets that made my friend's misfortune impossible to fathom.

At times I would have wanted to indulge in noisy, devilish games, as was my custom. But he was a boy bound and condemned to silence. He found that I always spoke too loudly, and that I laughed too heartily.

Jojo was to my eyes all the more worthy of pity because, since I'd come to live in the village, M'man Tine almost never beat me any more. Every now and then I would receive one or two boxes on my ears for having ripped buttons from my clothes to play at marbles with Raphael, who always beat me—he would beat almost everybody—or for having pinched some sugar when I felt for some. Furthermore, M'man Tine though not showering me with any more affection than before, still paid a lot of attention to me. On certain evenings she would question me about what was being taught to me in class and would ask me to read her a little story, a fable or a song. Occasionally she would give me a piece of printed paper in which had been wrapped two cents worth of sugar or one cent's worth of pepper, and would ask me to read what was on it for her. On more than one evening, while in the glow of our kerosine lamp, I was struggling valiantly with one of those bits of paper, I thought for a minute that I detected in M'man Tine's eyes a look of deepest tenderness, enhanced by the most touching admiration.

*

My life was beginning to assume a routine nature. I already knew the village, its houses, all its woods, the slightest little path in the surrounding area. I no longer feared approaching Mme Léonce's house. The people who were the most noticeable for one reason or another were as familiar to me as the most laden of fruit trees.

There was nothing left for me to discover.

Time went by, impassively, or rather seemed not to go by at all. People, things, my friends remained the same.

And if at school we learned new things, that was not sufficient to make me feel that I was changing or that anything or the other was undergoing any shake-up.

Some things were so quietly incorporated into the string of events that they had appeared quite natural to me, almost worthless—my moving from Mme Saint-Brix' class to the bigger children's school, at the top of the village, my entrance into the catechism class, the disappearance of certain of my mates, among them Vireil who, it was widely held, had become so badly-behaved that he had made a girl from the country pregnant.

Nothing seemed to make the time go by any more.

First of all, M'man Tine had told me that she was sending me to school to learn my alphabet and how to write my name.

Later, when I could write my name in full and spell a few words, she told me that, with that knowledge, I was sure I wouldn't have to go to work on the plantations and that I had a chance to become a factory worker.

I was already quite proud of this new light on things, though I'd never yet seen what a factory was like—hence my impatience to grow up.

And now she was telling me I had to continue up to the examination class—a proposition that was much less attractive for me, I must confess, for I did not know, for I couldn't see how I could get out of it.

The fact of the matter was, though, that I was still all too happy to be at school. I still had my good friends and gaiety and joy abounded therein.

*

Catechism, however, was a bit boring and sad.

Ever since, one Sunday after mass, M'man Tine had gone and given my name to the village priest, every evening after class I had to go to Mam'zelle Fanny's to learn catechism.

Mam'zelle Fanny, the 'instruction mistress,' was a woman feared by all the children and respected by all the adults.

She had, it seemed, the power to save or destroy with her tongue anybody she saw fit; to transform herself into angel or devil. When speaking to the priest she was holier than the Virgin Mary. When speaking to the Mayor or a school master she was more sophisticated than a marchioness—such as I'd seen in the reading books. But whenever she abused someone in the street or when she was angry or when she was beating us, she was worse and more awful than one of the *gens-gagés*.

As for me, she made me wish night and day that she were dead and I had sworn a long time to burn her alive when I grew up.

I didn't know why it was Mam'zelle Fanny who was the one to look after the souls of the children in the village—she who picked those who were about the age of reason to place them in the catechism class when the parents themselves hadn't done so.

I was therefore part of Mam'zelle Fanny's class along with Jojo, Michel-Paunch, Nanise and a score of others.

Raphael was not one of the group because his maman Nini could read and taught him the catechism herself.

From that time on, every evening after class I would make a flying visit to M'man Tine's and set off again to meet my friends who gathered in the street, in front of the door to Mam'zelle Fanny's house.

Normally she would not be in at that moment, for though she did not work either on a plantation or in a factory, Mam'zelle Fanny seemed to have pursuits that were as numerous as they were far-flung. But on her arrival, we had to be all there. Failing that, the slightest bit of tardiness required precise excuses and caused long, painful bouts on our knees.

We had to look out for her arrival from as far as we could see, so we could halt our games, fold our arms and shut up, without the slightest sound.

Mam'zelle Fanny was so irritable!

So profound a silence reigned among us that, without doubt, those colleagues standing in this respectful trance felt, like I did, tempted to fall on their knees or to make a sign of the cross to greet Mam'zelle Fanny.

But we only managed to intone altogether and in as angelic a voice as possible: "Good evening, Godmother Fanny." For, in appreciation of the unanimous affection we were supposed to have for her, Mam'zelle Fanny had insisted on that form of greeting from us.

Our arms firmly folded, we gathered around in a circle on a sort of terrace which was between the roadway and the threshold of the door.

Godmother Fanny would go inside to put down all she was carrying, then reappear a transformed being, a picture of recollection and with a gracious, almost pure gesture, would make a touching sign of the cross and start prayers.

That part was not very difficult. Some of us knew that particular prayer and since the recitation was done aloud, those who weren't too sure of the words had only to keep up the rhythm, for Godmother Fanny, despite her profoundly inspired air, did not fail to exercise extraordinary vigilance, following the movements of our lips and being able to detect automatically the slightest error.

Following that, opening a small book she carried in her dress, she would begin the catechism lesson.

She would read a question and have us repeat it. Then she'd read the answer, would go over it, making us repeat it word by word. Altogether, we would repeat.

"Again!"

Once, twice.

"Again!"

Three times, four times . . .

And we repeated aloud, altogether and at the same rhythm; so much so that by dint of constant repetition, we ended up twisting the sentence into a sing-song rhythm which, on its own, tirelessly dragged us along. I then noticed that Mam'zelle Fanny had disappeared like a real saint, and it was from way inside her bedroom or her kitchen that she kept shouting: "Again," and repeated along with us to stimulate us.

During that time she was no doubt lighting a fire, peeling some vegetables, ironing her clothes.

Soon afterwards, she had reappeared. She would move on to another question in the same fashion and, having asked it, would go back inside to her domestic chores.

In the alley, the passers-by looked at us with the same respect paid to the front of a church one passed, if not to a funeral one crossed. I suppose that spectacle must have enhanced all the more Mam'zelle Fanny's reputation in the entire village, even making her position more fearsome and more enviable at the same time.

The lesson dragged on until it was too dark for Mam'zelle Fanny to see to read. Then to close, she would again assume her place in the circle and lead the long evening prayer whose composition must have been, to my mind, comparable to that of a copious menu, with its pleasant preamble, the different sections of varying length and, for me, varying difficulty, varying consistency. And the final litanies were a real dessert, having even the effect of liqueurs.

*

But it was the following evening that everything changed.

Having done her lesson the previous evening and having taken great pains to make us repeat the answers over and over again, Mam'zelle Fanny now moved to the stage of asking questions. And that evening she appeared with whip in hand. Apart from the fact that, already, we had forgotten everything we'd repeated in our sing-song way the evening before, the frightening look on Mam'zelle Fanny's face, as well as our obsession with the inevitable licking, made any effort at remembering anything virtually impossible.

For example, when asked about penitence, I began by: "Penitence is a sacrament which . . . ," repeating those words every time the ensuing silence seemed to make me dizzy, waiting to receive the fatal blow on my head, on my back, even wishing it would land as quickly as possible, since the anguish and torment that took hold of my tortured body while I was searching or pretending to search for the answer were even more painful than having my skin whipped.

That saved me, for Mam'zelle Fanny, tapping it out on my shoulders with her whip, supplied the answer and I repeated after her some fifty times. Then she moved to the following pupil.

None of us escaped.

*

And the evening after that we fared no better.

All the same, I wasn't one of the more unfortunate ones in this catechism class. Certain pupils, whose memories were poor and who had been recommended to Mam'zelle Fanny by their parents, would sometimes leave with their legs bleeding.

Jojo was one of those.

As catechism pupils, we had to attend common prayer at church every Friday during Lent. As a result, instead of going to Mam'zelle Fanny we gathered in front of the little church. Mainly women came— nearly all those from Cour Fusil. M'man Tine never missed a day. She would come in her work clothes, having however, for the sake of decency, loosened the waist of her dress and thrown a scarf over her shoulders.

Prayers began at six o'clock but the priest did not take part in those. The staunch members sat in the first pews and right in front of the holy table were three *prie-dieu* occupied by old Mr. Popol, who assisted the priest on Sundays, Mam'zelle Fanny and Mme Léonce. For the latter, from all appearances, was also very strong in prayer and had a fine reputation in the village.

Those were, moreover, the only times I ever saw her.

We catechism pupils did not sit on the seats reserved for us every Sunday, but as the congregation was nowhere near the crowd that came on Sundays we sat in the regular pews.

Mr. Popol began the prayers. At times he would read from a book that was not very big, but very thick; at others, he would recite, hands clasped, eyes firmly shut. Kneeling, everyone listened, hands clasped, head bowed. I listened to the slow, endless murmur of his voice which, gradually, began to sink in and form in my head visions of heavenly life with angels playing trumpets, flocks of soft, white lambs, processions of saints in long robes of blue, red, yellow and gold . . .

Then came Mme Léonce's turn.

Well! when her turn came it was already beginning to get dark. One candle alone placed near her along with the flame of the Eternal Father emitted a subdued glow in the middle of the church. In addition, the effort we had made to remain quiet during the first part of the service was starting to show signs of flagging.

Furthermore, Mme Léonce would read in a voice that made us laugh. "A voice like a mad goat," said Michel-Paunch. Or rather, according to Nanise, "a voice like a hen that has just laid an egg."

At the same time as well, most of the staunch members, their bodies worn out by the hardship of a long day's work, and for some time now kept silent and immobile, began to nod, drowsy with sleep.

Then in the darkness, we began to have this uncontrollable urge to laugh, and without exchanging a single word, we felt just about to burst out laughing. But with all my strength, with all my will, I kept it in, clenching my fists, biting my lips, holding my body together till it felt like my bones would break.

Suddenly the tone of the prayer changed and, with Mme Léonce's voice coming to a halt, the congregation continued in a dull, monotonous murmur which, because it had surprised us and because it was deep enough to allow us to take the chance, was increased by our unbridled giggling.

From then on it was impossible to control ourselves; we laughed at anything, but in a way that neither the fear of being heard nor the terror of all the saints who must surely be looking down on us (despite the darkness and despite the color of our skins) could restrain.

At times, in a supreme effort not to let out the hearty laugh that convulsed him, one of us would let out a fart, and it was the breaking of that barrier that deafened the outburst of all our sniggering.

But our ensuing punishment was swift and violent. Mam'zelle Fanny, who hadn't forgotten to bring her whip, lashed out in the darkness with blows on our backs and even on our faces if we hadn't had time to bend down. And she would lead two victims away by their ears, putting them to kneel down in front of the Holy Table.

Finally it was she, Mam'zelle Fanny, who brought the service to an end.

She muttered a few words in haste and launched into a long list of objects such as: Ivory Tower, House of Gold, Star of the Morning; names of animals and saints, especially female ones. She knew more saints than there were inhabitants of Petit-Bourg. After each name, in the same murmur of black voices that covered our silly laughter so well, everybody responded: "Pray for us."

Some time after that, as I left catechism class one night, I found M'man Tine's bedroom full of women from the surrounding houses. On her bed of rags, M'man Tine, in her old work dress, her feet all covered with dried mud, was stretched out with her eyes closed. At intervals, she uttered a sigh of pain.

"You take the cake as a bad little fellow," Mam'zelle Délice said to me. "Your maman comes back dying and you weren't even here . . ."

My explaining that I'd been to catechism class was to no avail, everybody accused me of staying behind to play.

But what was wrong with M'man Tine? She was being given a tisane and there was talk of wrapping her in wool blankets and of giving her hot infusions to make her sweat like the cover of a *canari*. I was sent to buy some rum and soft candle. On my return people were still coming and going, carrying cups, bowls, jars, medicinal leaves and flowers.-

A fire was lit, water was heated, and I was made to go outside so they could take off M'man Tine's dirty dress and put on a white smock found in the clothes basket. Then the lamp was lit.

Later, Mam'zelle Délice brought me something for dinner.

*

When everyone had left, I was finally able to get close enough to M'man Tine to tell her: "Goodnight, m'man." Although she seemed to be in a sound sleep, she groaned, opened her eyes and asked:

"Did you eat?"

"Yes, M'man Tine . . . You're sick?"

"Yes, my son," she said, "your maman's body is not so good any more. Your maman's body has only old, weary bones."

I couldn't find anything else to say to her and I remained leaning on the foot of the bed for a long time, looking at M'man Tine's chest heave up and down and examining her face which bore no sign of suffering, but which seemed to be simply hollow and lifeless.

The kerosine lamp lit up the table, surrounding it with smoke, and the silence between M'man Tine's sighs seemed about to overwhelm me. I couldn't tell whether she had really slept soundly or whether she had just dozed off for a long while, but opening her eyes all of a sudden and seeing me at her feet, M'man Tine said:

"You're still here? Go and wash your feet and get ready for bed."

That night I was afraid to go outside. I didn't wash my feet. I took my rags, bundled in the corner where I put them every morning, spread them on the floor and was perhaps about to get right down to bed just as I was, when M'man Tine's voice reminded me:

"Take off your clothes, put on your night things and don't forget to say your prayers . . . "

The following morning my grandmother did not get up. The women came back with cups of coffee and bowls of tisane. M'man Tine didn't feel capable of going to work.

I began to feel somewhat puzzled, embarrassed and even annoyed, for Mam'zelle Délice (with her big foot, she was the most zealous of all the women) sent me to ask everyone for medicines with difficult names and when the first school bell sounded and I was about to leave, she pointed out that my grandmother was sick and told me I should remain at home with her.

For several days I didn't go to school. I spent my days in the bedroom next to M'man Tine, always ready to bring the cup of tisane nearer when her hands groped out in search of it on the box that had been placed at the head of her bed, to receive the mug from her hand when she had finished drinking and to hand her the first object she asked me for.

If she seemed to be asleep, I slipped stealthily out, remaining sufficiently close to the door so I could hear her faintest call, and there I frittered away my time, the way I would do in the sugar cane fields.

In the morning, at midday and again at night, M'man Tine would receive visits and care from the neighbors. They would always come loaded with all sorts of plants and sometimes there would be a lively discussion on the tisane or the brew to be made.

Mam'zelle Délice always brought me my meals along with the bowls of pap for my grandmother.

In the end, a few days later, Mam'zelle Délice who, to all appearances, had been given something rather important to do, returned to give an account to all those women gathered near M'man Tine's bed, that the *Séancier* had "seen" that my grandmother had drunk cold water while her body was still hot and had caught pleurisy as a result.

Everybody looked discouraged. Mam'zelle Délice suggested writing to my mother in town, but M'man Tine would have none of it, on the grounds that my mother had sent her some money not too long before and that my mother was going to find her indiscreet; or that she was going to waste her time leaving where she was to come to see her; she preferred to wait a bit.

M'man Tine groaned all night long. Already, for several days now, she no longer smoked her pipe and shouted that she was stifling.

Mam'zelle Délice proposed that she be cupped and Mr. Assionis, who was no doubt the most skillful person in Petit-Bourg at cupping, after cutting M'man Tine's skin and applying his little calabashes to her side, declared that her blood had already turned to water.

After a day of feverish activity in the bedroom and of long

conversations, the women brought men who carried a long bamboo
pole with a hammock. They wrapped my grandmother who kept
moaning and crying.

"You must go, dear friend," Mam'zelle Délice said to her, "you'll be
all right."

She was placed in the hammock while each end of the bamboo pole
rested on a man's shoulder; she was covered with a sheet thrown over
the bamboo, the flaps of which fluttered from side to side.

At that moment M'man Tine called out, weeping aloud:

"José, José . . . "

"José!" someone shouted, "come and tell your maman good'bye."

The flap of the sheet was raised and M'man Tine took my head in
her cold hands, pressed my cheek against her icy, tear-streaked face.

And with no more attention being paid to me, a cortège gathered
around the hammock, proceeded into the yard and into the alley.

I remained in front of the door and didn't even think of going to see
in which direction my grandmother was being taken.

So she was dead. Yet, Mr. Médouze . . . Perhaps there were several
ways you could die . . . Was she going to return? Would I ever see her
again? Mam'zelle Délice had said she would be all right. Ah! . . .

Mam'zelle Mézélie, who was perhaps the only one to remain in the
yard, seeing me there, came to me and said, placing her hand on my
head:

"José, poor child!"

I cuddled up close to her and began to sob.

She took me to her house and gave me a glass of cold water and
some bread.

"Next week, your maman is going to be back; they've taken her to
hospital for treatment. She'll come back all cured."

                                        *

When Mam'zelle Délice returned, hardly able to move her foot
which seemed to pull her down from her temples, she explained that
M'man Tine was at the Saint-Esprit hospital.

Mam'zelle Délice washed and tidied up everything in the shack, fed
me and that night asked me if I wanted to sleep at her place or alone in
M'man Tine's. I opted for the second proposal.

"Won't be afraid?" she asked me.

No; my fear that M'man Tine was dead having passed, I was no
longer afraid of anything and it was with a heart full of tenderness that I
went and snuggled up on the bed of rags in her place.

Mam'zelle Délice took care of me, gave me my meals, made me
change my clothes, washed the dirty ones, cajoled me from time to time

and scolded me as well when I dirtied my things or when she didn't find me in the yard on her return from work. From the very day after M'man Tine's departure, she had made me return to school.

Jojo was the only one I told my troubles to and I wondered whether I didn't experience a certain pride at being his equal as a result of the misfortune that had thus befallen me.

But I soon realised that M'man Tine's absence was lasting a long time.

I even began to suffer for I somehow suddenly felt that the people in the yard were looking at me as if I were something unpleasant. None of them could see me pass by without sending me to run errands; they even took advantage of my kindness and it seemed that the more that happened, the less consideration they had for me.

No longer did I change my clothes on Fridays and before the end of the week, I was disgustingly filthy, ashamed of myself. In addition to that, I was constantly hungry—a hunger that knew no end. At night after my dinner, I could still have eaten two or three times what I'd just finished. Luckily, sleep would come to take all hunger from my mind. But on mornings I would wake up with even more demanding pangs of hunger. I no longer had my cup of coffee with cream, well sweetened, with cassava flour, only a bit of coffee at the bottom of a tin cup, a bit of vegetable cooked the night before and roasted on the charcoal embers in the morning. As it happened, especially on mornings, I didn't have the time to run about Haut-Morne looking for fruits.

No sooner did I enter class that I was gripped by intense hunger; I felt like feasting myself on enormous cups of sweetened coffee with huge amounts of cassava flour.

And it was precisely at that time that the mistress would come to have her breakfast.

For after the reading exercise, she would give us a bit of written work and while we were thus occupied, she'd go to her place and return with a large porcelain bowl and a huge piece of bread on a waiter.

The mistress broke the bread into small pieces in the bowl. The bread was a golden brown and crunched under her fingers, dropping little crumbs that I felt like avidly snatching up to eat. Then, dipping the little silver spoon into the bowl, the mistress carried to her mouth pieces of bread covered with a brown, milky, oily liquid that smelled of vanilla and must have been sweet and delicious.

I did not write. I looked at the mistress. The hand in which she held the beautiful spoon was fine and clean. Her hair was well done. Her face was of a clear complexion, made velvety by a touch of powder, her eyes shone with pure, quiet brilliance and her mouth, which she half-opened as the spoon passed, was at the same time the most beautiful and the most cruel thing to behold.

Then too, that bowl of white porcelain with pink and blue flowers, that silver spoon, that waiter of polished mahogany, how it all must have served to enhance and complete the taste of that meal! How it all added to my torture!

Did I really feel like tasting that milk chocolate? I'd never eaten any, but I dearly longed for some. Perhaps I wasn't good enough for such a meal? Sometimes M'man Tine made plain chocolate with water and raw cocoa and thickened it with a pap of starch, or soaked my cup of cassava flour with it.

But my stomach, my entire chest hurt me and my hand trembled, unable to write. I was dizzy.

The sight of the mistress' milk chocolate tortured me so much that I felt only suffering, no desire, so much so that, in point of fact, I had the distinct sensation of being less starved once, having finished her meal, she took the waiter back inside and returned to her chair.

"Bring your books up for correction," she exclaimed.

But when, a little later, the pangs of hunger again gripped me, it was under the appearance of a large bowl of milk chocolate, smelling of vanilla, with golden bread, that the mirage of supreme relief presented itself.

I couldn't have the slightest grudge against Mam'zelle Délice. I had fully understood that she lacked the means to give me more. I liked her a lot. I had become so attached to her that I didn't even notice her hideous foot any more.

About that same time a grave misfortune befell Jojo, making me forget my sorry plight for several days. Mam'zelle Gracieuse had left the village going off with a man who had large gardens of yams and sweet potatoes in Chassin, on the other side of Petit-Bourg.

His stepmother forbade him to cry.

One afternoon he had hidden himself in a little corner of the house so he could cry and Mam'zelle Mélie, having surprised him, had shouted:

"But what's wrong with this Jojo? How come he's crying?"

Thereupon Mme Justin Roc had put him in punishment until his father came home.

Jojo's maman had thus also gone far away, like someone who had died or gone to hospital . . .

And to think that on certain nights despite our grief, we took delight in dreaming aloud!

"When I'm big," Jojo said, "papa and maman Yaya will be dead. I'll be foreman at the factory. I'm going to buy a prettier car than papa's, and I'll go for m'man Gracieuse and I'll build a beautiful house to live with her. But I'm not marrying a wicked woman like m'man Yaya. I prefer to remain with maman."

As for me, I'd have a large property, as big as the whole countryside around us. I wouldn't plant any sugar cane, except a few stalks for my dessert. But I'd have many people cultivating vegetables and fruits along with me, rearing hens, rabbits, but even to go to work, they'd put on trousers and shirts that were not torn, they'd wear fine suits on Sundays, and their children would all go to school. M'man Tine would not be dead; she'd take care of the hens, gather the eggs. M'man Délia would look after the housework.

I was really dreaming when Jojo, bringing me back to everyday reality, said to me, without any malice:

"But you couldn't have all that—you're not white, you're not a béké."

"Makes no difference."

"But your workers, then, they'll be almost as well fed and lodged as the békés! Then, there'll be no more niggers; and what are the békés going to do!"

I remained confused, ashamed, somewhat sad.

*

I was at school the day M'man Tine returned from hospital. She had come out by herself, on foot. I found her at midday. Sitting on her bed, looking tired but radiant at the same time. I was surprised. I exclaimed: "M'man Tine!" and remained standing at the entrance, unable to go a step further.

"Come," she said.

Then, confused and overcome with joy, I went close to her, weeping aloud, tears streaming uncontrollably down my face.

*

I did not take my First Communion that year owing to M'man Tine's illness. I resigned myself readily to this fact but not without the painful impression, in spite of everything, that those of my mates, such as Jojo and Raphael, who took theirs had left me behind.

Furthermore, I learned very quickly how to abstain from many a fête and ceremony destined for children, and always for the same reasons: no fine suits, no shoes. In particular no shoes, since I hadn't taken my First Communion which, for all the kids like me, was the occasion to christen their first pair of shoes.

It was an entirely different picture the day I was forced to stop going to play with Jojo. One evening we were under the veranda, chatting quietly as usual. Seeing Mam'zelle Mélie approaching from the road, we remained quiet and still, the way, to be on the safe side, we always did, our heads down so she could go inside.

On that occasion when she was close to us, she stopped and asked Jojo:

"What were you talking about, for you to jump like that when you saw me?"

"Nothing," Jojo replied, trembling already.

"Nothing?" Mam'zelle Mélie said threateningly; "every night you' talking for hours with this little black boy (Mam'zelle Mélie, as I said, was to my eyes black like me, if not like a crow) and tonight you weren't saying anything. Well, you'll explain that to Madame."

No sooner was she inside than the voice of Mme Justin called Jojo.

Jojo knew, alas! what was waiting for him and with tears in his eyes he dashed off.

He had hardly left me, indeed, before I heard the jerky outbursts of his cries, so agonizing that, myself filled with anger and fright, I left the veranda and went into the alley, straight across from the house, in an attempt to catch a glimpse of what was going on inside and in the hope that, perhaps, after his spanking Jojo would return.

Luckily I had gotten up. Mam'zelle burst out from the corridor with a basin in her hands and, seeing me in the road, shouted to me:

"You' lucky. I'd have bathed you down . . . that'll teach you to remain in your mother's shack instead of coming here to teach other people's children vices."

I had to wait till the next day at school for Jojo to tell me what that awful woman had said about us.

"She said that I speak only créole with you and that you're teaching me bad words."

Jojo had always told me that Mme Justin had forbidden him to speak patois and as he couldn't resist doing so, we had agreed to speak as softly as possible in order to go against his stepmother's prohibition.

Now, Mam'zelle Mélie spoke nothing else but patois and I was surprised that she disowned us with such scorn. With respect to the foul words she accused us of uttering—a pure invention—Mam'zelle Mélie then seemed to me more odious than M'man Tine had said she was and I firmly believed that adults never told lies.

Thereafter Jojo was forbidden to play with me. He was greatly perturbed at no longer having a single school mate. At first I was concerned for him, even very embarrassed. But I had no end of friends. All my original buddies, and new ones too. Like Audney, for instance.

He lived at Haut-Morne and his father had a horse.

One of the chores Audney had to do after class was to take the horse to drink at middays from a pond at the foot of the other side of the hill, and, on evenings, to go and cut grass for it along the "traces."

I had become his companion and helper.

As we carried it to drink, we both rode on the back of the animal and, on evenings, as we cut the grass, we found guavas and other wild fruits.

But the most pleasant part of the caring for the horse was bathing him on Sunday mornings. We had to rise early, get astride the animal and take it to the little lake in Génipa. The sun had already risen, but it wasn't very hot as yet.

That was the day that nearly all the men working on the Poirier plantation came for their baths and to bathe the horses belonging to the managers and overseers. Some took the opportunity to wash their old work clothes. They all took off all their clothes. Each one mounted his horse and made it enter the water. The animal moved deeper in, disappeared in the water, swam around, head held high. And the man's body emerged, evoking that half-man, half-horse figure that I saw on the packets of vermicelli.

The animal then came back to the bank, the man alighted and, with a wisp of straw, rubbed it down energetically, returning to the water afterwards to rinse off the creature. We did likewise with our mount.

It was pleasant being carried into the water by the horse, snorting as it swam. The water, in the rays of the rising sun, felt heavenly on our skins.

And I'd never seen anything so simple and so beautiful as big black men in the nude, standing beside stalwart horses, their reflections mirrored in the water of a lake.

*

I was now in Class I, the toughest in the school. And we no longer had a mistress, but a master.

This was a source of joy for the inhabitants as well, for this master was a son of the commune who, after serving just about everywhere in the island, had just been appointed Principal of the Petit-Bourg school.

The word had spread quickly among the pupils that he was a teacher who 'explained' well and beat severely.

He didn't hit with a bamboo cane nor did he beat you with a ruler in the palm of your hand; he didn't wring your ears. He beat with his bare hands. He boxed you on your ears!

He was as impressive as a school principal could be in the eyes of little eleven-year-old country children, which we were.

He sported a tanned complexion, was tall and wore black shoes with shiny, pointed tips. His trousers were of white drill with two arrow-straight creases running down the front and his jacket was of the same material, its little upper pocket bedecked with a heavy gold watch chain. His head, which he kept high and rigid, was distinguished by two gold teeth nestled among his large white teeth, a black moustache, a pair of *pince-nez* and a straw hat.

Mr. Stephen Roc had long, thick, powerful hands with fingernails hard like ducks' beaks; he kept constantly breaking the chalk as he wrote on the blackboard.

Yes, a box on the ears from hands like that must have really hurt!

Already, the mere sound of his voice coming from his chest, even if it were very faint, always seemed to be shouting at us to be careful.

However, our first feeling towards Mr. Roc was one of respectful as well as affectionate admiration. For us, who had now become the 'bigger ones' in the school, proud as we were to have such a master, it was at the same time very pleasant to feel afraid of him. Everything he taught us presented itself in a fascinating, alluring way, even when there were difficulties.

But this was perhaps not so for everybody after a few days. Mr. Roc had no doubt sounded each one of us out and what had been heard about him the morning school opened began to manifest itself.

We were already being boxed on our ears. I had had my share over the agreement of the past participle. Michel-Paunch, who was strong in problems, received clouts every day for spelling. Raphael, always for the same reason: talking in class; and Jojo, for everything. The master made him recite each lesson, questioned him, endlessly examined his exercise books—the entire proceedings unfolding not without his clouting him a few times on the back of his neck or his ears. Jojo would shake without stopping.

It seemed to me, nevertheless, that Jojo was not the weakest or the laziest pupil in the school; but the master called him a blockhead at his slightest lapse and flogged him with his hands that were ever ready to strike.

I came to the conclusion, without any logical justification, that it was because he was related to Jojo that he beat him so much.

I wasn't mistaken. Subsequently, Jojo himself admitted that his father and stepmother had recommended to his uncle, the school master, that the latter make him work a lot, and above all, that he beat him when his work was not correct.

Be that as it may, Jojo, by reason of the constant and terrible amount of care on the part of the master, seemed to me once again more worthy of pity than of envy.

If we could have seen each other at nights the way we did before, perhaps he would have told me about all the suffering he underwent between his father's house where he led an unhappy life, constantly likely to be flogged, and the classroom where every day he was boxed about the ears at least a good dozen times or more. But our relationship at school did not have the intimate character of our conversations under his father's veranda and either we played as madly as possible during the recess breaks or we spent entire days pretending to be indifferent to each other. Furthermore, was it children's nature to speak about sad things when frolicking and games were beckoning to them? There were even times when I laughed or smiled as Jojo, caught in some pitfall, burst out sobbing after the heavy hand of his uncle had rained a few clouts on his head.

Frankly speaking, our life had changed. You might say that the very presence of our school master had made it assume a somewhat manly air. We had lessons to learn. We had many exercise books, all of which we had to keep very tidy. We had many books belonging to the *Caisse des Ecoles,* which we had to avoid destroying. Everything we did was governed by the fear of receiving a box on the ears from Mr. Roc and by the concern that he and our parents drummed into us ever since school had reopened: that of the examination for the *Certificat d'Etudes Primaires.*

As far as I was concerned, there was also something else to worry about: my First Communion.

I had resolutely quit Mam'zelle Fanny's catechism class. Raphael, who had taken his First Communion the year before and who was now a choir boy, had lent me his catechism book and I studied alone, reading aloud and late into the night near the kerosine lamp, so as to reassure M'man Tine who doubted that I could manage on my own.

The rest had not changed.

We had not given up any of our amusements and remained fondly attached to everything we had liked. Not without the attendant penalties. Hadn't we once been condemned to put up and pay for tiles we'd broken while throwing stones at a mango tree near Mme Sequéran's house? Hadn't we, Michel-Paunch, Ernest, Audney and I, been surprised one day by a manager as we were cutting sugar canes in a field, when it was not even time for the canes to be cut, making our parents pay a fine of fifteen francs for each of us? And that same Michel, didn't he sport, for months on end, a wound he'd received on his foot as he went for some *pommes-lianes* in a patch of bushes?

We did so many things that delighted us and caused us to be banned or beaten and we felt life so full of things to do around us!

On beautiful evenings we would play in the moonlight.

Moonlight nights meant a sort of nocturnal fête in the village.

After dinner everyone would sit in front of the houses, some on chairs, others on the front step itself. Those in groups chatted, told stories, gave *timtims.* Those by themselves sang or hummed. Couples went for walks in the road.

The children would assemble and swarm in noisy games all over the places that could serve as play areas.

As such, late into the night the village would still be celebrating the moonlight. There were things, it seemed to me, that people said only on moonlight nights, games that were played, that could only have been played on moonlight nights and not in broad daylight, nor in the pitch-black darkness of night.

At times also, the sound of a flute, the source of which was impossible to pinpoint (did it come from the direction of Mr. Toi in Haut-Morne? or from Mr. Mamès on the other side of Cour Fusil?), would penetrate the still air like a silver thread, or would float limply over everything like a long sigh from the moon itself. Never had any sound seemed to be so closely identified with the moonlight as that one emanating from those rustic flutes played for the night in festive yet pensive mood by some little black boy sitting on the front step of a shack that was difficult to imagine.

I was part of the noisier ones, part of those who could not remain dreaming near their maman, watching the moon sail by in a periwinkle sky and pass, from time to time, without rolling or pitching, through huge waves of clouds.

I belonged to the frenzied band of those who met in front of the church near the school for the 'little ones,' our former school. Whenever there were many girls among us, we would dance and sing in a circle—one of those outsized circles—well-sealed by our hands. And we would sing in one innumerable voice, light as the flight of small birds, songs we had never learned, but were being sung because it was a moonlit night and because there were a lot us and we were happy.

Then we would play 'eel' in order to feel out the shadows sleeping under the bushes, 'gauntlet' so we could sit very closely next to one another, hide and seek so we could run about a little, 'my bag' for the pleasure of hitting one another with a cloth-filled bag.

For certain, we'd have gone on playing until daybreak if, all of a sudden, our parents' voices didn't call us one after the other. And, still playing and singing, we would run to the standpipes to wash the dust from our feet and retire home.

Meanwhile, the time was fast approaching for me to take my First Communion and, although not part of Mam'zelle Fanny's class, I still knew my lessons.

M'man Tine spoke to me about that forthcoming First Communion with the zeal she injected into her soliloquies, as she made plans for things that she set her heart on. She never stopped making up in her mind and evaluating aloud the outfits I would need: a white suit for the retreat, another for when I received absolution from my sins; underpants, white socks, handkerchiefs. And above all, the communicant's dress: a white piqué suit, silk arm-band, white straw hat, gloves, candle, shoes. All items white and brand new. That was compulsory, indispensable in order to taste the white host.

So many things, so much clothes, so many suits for me! It was enough to make me die with longing and impatience. But I couldn't see how M'man Tine would manage to procure all that for me. It was true that those whom I'd already seen take their First Communion had not been dressed in anything else, although their parents were field or factory workers.

It was true that M'man Tine was talking not only of writing, but of actually going to Fort-de-France to find M'man Délia to talk to her and make her understand that it was time for me to take my First Communion. It was equally true that she had been praying a great deal for some time now in order to obtain the grace to have me take that First Communion, and that she seemed certain that God would help her to do so.

Well! It really looked as if that category of women as represented by the old black, unfortunate mothers did possess in their hearts, beating under their rags, some sort of power to change dirt into gold, to dream and to wish for something so ardently that, from their earth-stained, sweating, empty hands, could appear the most palpable, the most immaculate and the most precious of realities. For already, every Sunday on her return from Saint-Esprit, M'man Tine would bring back either a remnant of material or a pair of socks.

And after talking about doing so for a long time in advance, of course, M'man Tine decided to take me to see my godmother. A child did not take his First Communion without going to embrace his godmother, no matter how far she lived.

I had never seen my godmother. I knew that her name was Mme Amélius and that she lived in a country district called Croix-Rivail on the other side of the village of Trou-aux-Chats.

We set off one morning during the Easter vacation. Whenever she had such a trip to make, M'man Tine would avoid, and prevent me from, talking about it the night before so that evil spirits wouldn't make her oversleep. We therefore set out early. Through paths wet with dew, we crossed savannahs where oxen still lay sleeping. We climbed several hills. We passed several *habitations* where dogs barked and cocks crowed. Without uttering a word, M'man Tine walked on, her skirt tucked up on account of the wet grass, while I trotted bare-footed behind her.

When the sun beamed down on us M'man Tine began to talk,

evoking memories of my godmother whom she hadn't seen in years and whom she'd probably met only twice since the day I was christened. She also mentioned the names of quite a few inhabitants of Croix-Rivail whom she doubted she would see again as it had been so long since she'd heard anything about them.

We kept walking like that all morning and I was, perhaps, just about to collapse. I was hungry and thirsty, my legs couldn't make it any more. We arrived at a place where the land was divided into small gardens surrounding shacks sheltered by mango trees. That was Croix-Rivail.

Groups of children stood in front of the shacks. Every now and then we met a man or a woman whom M'man Tine asked the way to Mme Amélius. On each occasion she was assured it wasn't far again; she was shown the way and we set off again. But after covering some distance in this fashion and jumping over a ravine, after climbing a hill and passing through the damp shade of a large cacao plantation, we had to ask for directions once more before continuing our journey.

My godmother was an old, thin, black woman.

She didn't spoil me as much as I had been led to believe she would by M'man Tine's laudatory soliloquies. She kissed me, found that I had grown, upbraided M'man Tine for not bringing me before. She offered us lunch: yams, codfish with oil and okras—and to think I detested okras!—and spoke all the time about her sorrows.

Since the last time she had seen M'man Tine, she had lost her husband, her eldest daughter and her brother, Gildéus. She took all the time in the world relating their ailments, her successive bouts of grief, and the confusion that ensued over the things each one left.

When it was M'man Tine's turn to tell her that I was about to take my First Communion, she greeted the news with a cry, as if it were a climax to her frustrations:

"But, Amantine, why did you wait so long to tell me? How unfortunate! Here I was wanting to give my godson such a nice gift—his First Communion suit for example—and it's only today you bring him. Only two weeks before!"

In that regard, there was hardly a reproach that was not leveled at M'man Tine who, moreover, was more or less all apologetic.

In the end she couldn't see what she could rightly offer me. She was heart-broken.

When M'man Tine wanted to leave, my godmother put a handful of seeds in a tin, went outside, shook it, thus calling together her numerous fowls in front of her house and, with an agile movement of her hand, grabbed a tall chicken. She stroked it, still saying in her pitiful voice:

"I have nothing, nothing to give my fine godson, Tine, my dear; I'm going to give him this chicken. If you don't make a fricassee with it for the Communion lunch, it'll become a fine hen, a good layer; and if José is lucky with me, it could in the long run bring him as much money as an ox."

She uprooted a tuft of wild grass which she twisted and with which she tied the two feet of the chicken. Still looking around for some possible gift, she found a coconut and asked M'man Tine to make some jam for me with it. Then some cassava starch she had made herself, so my clothes would be good and stiff.

I was, I believed, very happy. Besides, despite the tiredness I felt as a result, I was always very happy to make journeys of that sort with my grandmother. M'man Tine seemed content as well. Was it the trip or was it the fact that she'd seen my godmother again? Was it the presents? . . .

To make me happy, she let me hold the hen under one arm and the coconut in my other hand; and she put the little packet of cassava starch in her pocket.

We walked quickly on our return. M'man Tine kept looking at the sun and repeating:

"Before it reaches the crest of the hill over there, we must be in Belle-Plaine."

We were going along a path at the side of a hill bordered by a cane field. The joy of carrying my presents gave me courage to walk. At a certain time, my fingers, weary from holding the coconut, slackened their grip no doubt and the fruit went pelting down in the grass towards the foot of the hill.

Seeing how upset I was, M'man Tine assured me that I was going to find it and told me:

"All you have to do is go down and look for it there, in the bushes."

I rid my other hand of the tied-up chicken which I laid on the side of the path, while my grandmother stood waiting for me, and I got ready to go down into the bushes where my coconut had rolled. But immediately, M'man Tine gave a shout, threw her arms into the air and started to prance about: the chicken had escaped!

The grass holding its feet together had come loose, and it had fled away with a cackle right in front of M'man Tine who, in her bewilderment, tried to block it in all directions.

Retracing my steps, I too began to run after it. But thereupon, the bird reached the cane field and disappeared.

M'man Tine spent a long time searching for it and I myself almost got lost. We didn't give a second thought to the coconut.

We returned to the village; it was dark.

That incident had been too much for M'man Tine and that night she brooded aloud over it almost to the point of tears, saying that I was a poor little black boy who didn't have any luck at all, none whatsoever.

Personally, I viewed the whole episode with absolute indifference, bordering on insensibility.

The following morning the first thing M'man Tine noticed was that, during the night, rats had gnawed at the pocket of her dress in order to eat the little packet of starch which she had forgotten in it. Struck dumb with amazement, she hardly uttered a word.

Oh! what a memory I was going to have of my First Communion!

When I related this trip to my school mates, one of them immediately shouted!

" 'Bet your godmother is a *gagée!*"

"That was their unanimous opinion. It was mine as well. My godmother remained for a long time in my mind under that diabolical aspect. She died, I think, without my ever seeing her again.

*

That first Sunday of the patronal festival of Petit-Bourg was not alas! to go by without another traumatic experience, this time even more brutal for me and all the pupils of our class.

As early as the Saturday night, as happened every year, a rickety, noisy truck had arrived with wooden horses. In the afternoon, the merry-go-round (the same little merry-go-round with squared, stiff horses patched up with bits of planks and nails, bedecked with gawdy garlands, which between appearances had gone all over the island from village to village) had been set up there in the market square, topped by its pointed hat of sail canvas, in the midst of the bubbling excitement of all the brats in the village. And as was done every year, that Saturday night, on the eve of the festival, the merry-go-round had offered three free rides to the children.

Our need for money was far more pressing than any I had ever experienced hitherto, on a Saturday night, in Black Shack Alley; for, from the Saturday night before the festivity, you had to be sure you had the necessary sums—at least fifteen to twenty cents—for two or three rides on the merry-go-round. That year, with my First Communion coming up, counting on M'man Tine's generosity was out of the question. Now, I had more of a problem than my friends, since I didn't have a bigger brother, nor an uncle, nor an aunt, nor a godfather, nor a godmother who could help me out. But as I did so many favors for everybody, I hoped to receive the rewards already promised by several kind people.

Friends, like Michel-Paunch, Raphael, were even boasting that they had saved up some money—from the shrimp they'd caught or the land crabs they sometimes sold. I would never have any savings. I used to spend all my money on macaroons, cakes and other sweets like everybody else, and above all on my one luxury: school supplies. I loved fine exercise books to copy the poems and songs we learned in class. I bought fine sheets of blotting paper—one for each exercise book—red ink and green ink for the titles of the poems, colored crayons to illustrate the songs, compasses to make rosettes, erasers. M'man Tine had never had to worry about my school supplies.

Furthermore, since M'man Tine had definitely forbidden it, I couldn't ask adults for money the way most of my friends did, and at certain times, I found myself in the most agonizing of situations.

I awoke on the Sunday morning with the sole five-cent piece M'man Tine had given me for collection and which, in compliance with the orders given by my friends, for that period, I was careful to keep.

Later my grandmother asked me:

"How much money do you have?"

"None, M'man."

To save me from despair she gave me a cent, saying:

"I don't have any money to give you, you know, for the wooden horses . . .Look, take this, to get some barley sugar . . . "

A bit later on one or two other coins were added upon a chance meeting or out of sheer luck. At the advice of my friends, I roamed about the game tables and the little tents that had sprung up in the market square next to the merry-go-round. Didn't the more experienced among my friends claim that people, while playing or drinking themsleves drunk, sometimes inadvertently dropped coins? Many boys had already found in this way ten cent pieces, even as much as two francs. But I never found anything. Nothing, except empty peanut shells and bottle caps. So I stopped in front of a game—one of the many trays forming so many islands of players standing in that ocean of people who were strolling about in every direction.

My favorite games were *rouge et noir, entonnoir* and *pataclac*. I saw people winning and met Raphael or Michel-Paunch—always very lucky, they were—who were winning or had already accumulated eighteen cents or a franc, whereas they had come with no more than two cents. With a confident heart (for the luckier ones had willingly told us their secret for winning: do not hesitate, do not be afraid), I bet a cent, lost it, then another cent, but which (was it because, in those ups and downs, my heart had begun to pound somewhat heavily?) ended up giving in and disappearing.

Apart from the free ride on the merry-go-round the night before, I hadn't yet been on it once, whereas the wooden horses had been turning round and round since morning after mass, and it was already past midday.

The orchestra accompanying the merry-go-round enthralled the entire village. From afar only the beat of the drums reached us, keeping the time of the waltz to whose rhythm the merry-go-round turned. But they only seemed like strokes of a gong inviting people to enjoy themselves and were like blows to my entrails. To the pain of my alarming and almost desperate situation when money didn't come my way, and like a constantly coaxing voice and an irresistable, evil force, they brought us all back to the market square. As you drew closer, you could hear the rhythmical sticks and the maracas and, just as the swivelling roof with gaily colored banners came into sight, the sound of the clarinet burst forth in my head, in my belly, took hold of me, drew me forward more quickly.

Then, from seeing women walking by under the effect of the music, rolling their shoulders and shaking their behinds and men with waists rolling strangely up and down; from seeing, close up, the wooden horses spin around with children astride in white dresses with red bows, children in new suits, children in polished shoes, black children, with clear, infectious laughter; and from feeling deep in my soul the convulsion of the drum beats, loud and sweet like thick blood, I remained in a sort of trance from which I took a long time coming out.

When night fell the high society came out in full dress; the little tents were lit and everything that went to make up the festival and everything around it took on a brilliance and resonance that were even more disturbing, and still not a cent had fallen into my hand. If the Devil himself (the one in my catechism) were to offer me ten cents for my soul, which the coming First Communion was going to cleanse from sin, I would not have refused.

That year I was to invent, in order to ride on the merry-go-round, a means I hadn't thought about in previous years.

The merry-go-round was operated by two men who, running around, from inside, pulled the circular floor with the horses. But some insignificant little brats, with whom we did not play, were pushing along with the two men.

This voluntary help afforded them, by way of reward, the advantage of getting up onto the merry-go-round without paying, for once the impetus given to the turning floor had attained its climax, they would spring on its and, crouching or standing, find themselves enjoying the ride as much as if they were on the finest horses of the merry-go-round.

Suppose I too were to join in! . . . It seemed a bit difficult because you no doubt had to push hard—both men were sweating and their bare feet dug a path all around. It seemed to require great skill to be able to jump onto the floor once the merry-go-round was started, to

heavy drumming, at such a speed that, from the horses, you couldn't
look at the crowd which, standing on the ground, could not make out
those who were going around. But I felt myself capable. At the end of
that ride, all I would have to do was climb onto the floor, cross it and
take up my place as a pusher on the inside.

However, my feet couldn't yet make up their minds to take that
simple step. Scruples, scruples . . . If M'man Tine . . . For sure, she would
beat me lame if she were to catch me; but apart from the fact that there
was every likelihood she wouldn't see me—since, at that hour,
M'man Tine was in Cour Fusil—no formal ban had been imposed on
me as yet with respect to going to push wooden horses. That was a
great advantage vis-à-vis my conscience and my grandmother. Still, all
the same . . .

Suddenly, I turned around. Someone had placed his hand on my
shoulder. Oh! was it possible? Jojo! Jojo, about whom I couldn't have
been thinking at that time! Jojo all alone in the festival, not
accompanied by his distinguished parents or chaperoned by Mam'zelle
Mélie. And without his blue velvet breeches, his white silk jacket with
the sailor collar, his shoes with ankle-straps and his white socks with
designs on the side. Jojo, in school clothes, dressed like me, almost,
with coarse shoes to boot. How come? Why?

"Been looking for you," he exclaimed.

Jojo's eyes shone with triumphant brilliance.

He did not answer my questions; he showed me discreetly, but with
a thrill of joy, a note of one hundred cents crumpled up in the palm of
his hand.

"I found it," he said.

"Where?"

"At home, in the dining room. It was possibly maman Yaya or papa
who dropped it without even noticing."

What luck, all the same, for Jojo! Finding money at home!

"This morning, I found it. So I hid it in my room, and as I knew they
weren't going to bring me to the festival because of the zero on my
exercise book, when everybody went to sleep, I gently opened the
window and . . . "

Good heavens! Could Jojo really be so brave, so bold!

But the important thing right then was to spend the five francs as
quickly as possible so Jojo could return home in the same manner he
had left.

First of all, we would buy some cakes. But which one of the two of us
was going to confront Mam'zelle Choute, the woman selling them, with
that large note of hundred cents? Jojo, of course, since it belonged to
him. No, he was afraid. Mam'zelle Choute would probably notice him

and would say something to Mam'zelle Mélie. Jojo was full of mistrust. Adults talked about children so much!

Thus, I had to go. My fear, on the other hand, was that Mam'zelle Choute would suspect me of having stolen that money. People were so suspicious of black children! I too was afraid. I spurred Jojo on and the desire to stuff ourselves with everything that tempted us was to end up getting the better of him.

We chose cakes with coconut jam, bits of barley sugar shaped like men, flat cassava flour cakes, cornets of peanuts.

While munching away at our goodies, we sprang onto the wooden horses. One ride, two rides, three consecutive rides. Oh! liberating intoxication of my childish escapades! Then we bought a bottle of aerated lemonade which we went into the shade to empty, leaning against the gable of a house and pouring it into our mouths from the bottle held above our heads.

We tried our luck at several games, giving up at the loss of the first cent, or calling it quits after winning the first cent. We stopped outside a dance to listen to songs, enhanced by strains of the accordion, composed in the village itself, which well-bred children only sang when they were far from school and out of earshot of their parents. Men and women were dancing with the disturbing mimicry of dances of love and of joy.

We saw with our own eyes two men quarrelling in the middle of a crowd of people unable to quiet them and actually saw one of them slit the flesh of the other with a swift, violent stroke of a razor.

Finally, with the last ten cents, we each had a last ride on the merry-go-round and, the games, the crowd, the merry-go-round having now become less attractive, we went down to the bottom of the village to go to sleep.

At the entrance to Cour Fusil, I took leave of Jojo.

Having found M'man Tine's room, I had only to lean against the door, for only a huge stone on the inside kept it closed.

Imagine my disappointment when I didn't see Jojo in class the next day! Not only did I have my heart set on hearing how he managed to make it back into his room, but I was dying to get together with him again to relive our previous evening out.

For my part I was delighted. All the others told me about their festival Sunday caused me no envy or regret. What a pity Jojo wasn't there.

He did not turn up in the afternoon either, and to my impatience to see him again was added the budding feeling of concern. Jojo never missed school.

That evening, at my own risk and peril, I went roaming about in front of Mr. Justin Roc's house. But not once did Jojo come outside. I dared not believe some misfortune had befallen him. Could it be he was caught as he returned home and was beaten so much he couldn't walk? We'd have heard about that at school. None of us ever received a spanking from our parents without, by our cries, betraying the fact to a friend in the neighborhood, who willingly saw it as his duty to broadcast the news in class.

Well, there was indeed a bit of news the following morning at school:

Jojo had run away.

Could I believe it?

Jojo had fled from his father's home like a runaway slave; he had gone off into the woods . . . It was a topic of heated discussion in the entire school.

I was the only one left thunderstruck by it. I was afraid. I was completely lost. I couldn't understand how Jojo could have run off on his own. And at what time? After leaving me, not having gone back to his papa's house, or after being caught and flogged? Had he fled to escape the blows or did his maman Yaya throw him out?

Nobody knew for sure at school. Everyone just kept repeating, only too happy to spread the news:

"Georges Roc's run away. Georges Roc's run away!"

The explanation I sought was brought to me at Cour Fusil by Mam'zelle Délice, a close friend of Mam'zelle Mélie, as she related to the tenants that incident that set the tongues a-wagging in the village.

In the middle of the night, Mme Justin heard a noise of something falling. Fearing it might be a burglar, she woke her husband. Mr. Justin went to have a look and found Jojo, who hadn't had time to close the window behind him and who was now slipping into bed.

"Say, it's you, Jojo? Where are you now coming from?" the father asked. "Eh, where on earth you just come from?"

Jojo, who was supposed to be in his night shirt and asleep in his bed, was dressed in his school clothes that he wore last week, with his socks on his feet and his shoes on the floor.

Was he about to leave? Did he just come back?

"You were out? Fine," said Mr. Justin. "Tomorrow morning, we'll see about all that."

The following morning, no Jojo.

"He must have gone back to his mother," Mam'zelle Délice hinted.

And that hypothesis determined my ideas and dispelled my worry.

Ever since then, Jojo, for as long as I remembered him, was to remain in mind as a little prisoner, a stolen child who, one morning at dawn, escaped like a runaway slave to find his mother and freedom. But a deep feeling of sadness and true remorse often came over me.

I missed that evening of festivity spent almost clandestinely with Jojo. If only I could also have been his accomplice when. out of sheer despair, he fled into the high woods and vast sugar cane fields.

And in my head, Jojo was running with tears in his eyes, in turn lost through fear and guided by instinct; and in my heart, there weighed the feeling of guilt at having shared the cakes, the sweets, the merry-go-round rides he'd offered me with the five francs concealed from his father, without enduring any of his misadventure.

And now, was he happy or unhappy that he had run away? Had he found his mother? Was he at school? Would he be taking the *Certificat d'Etudes?*

I also imagined him still wandering about, starving and naked. But every time I met Mam'zelle Mélie and thought about Mme Justin, everything led me to believe that Jojo was happy with his real mother.

Jojo's absence had greatly changed the atmosphere in class. Mr. Roc would now do a whole lesson without stopping to clout anybody at all about the ears. Jojo was missed when the time came to correct the dictation and, in particular, the problems, and during every lesson at that, for everything used to start with him. Indeed, the class seemed strangely quiet for a few days. Then it became restless and austere.

The master would keep us in on evenings after four o'clock to prepare for the examination—difficult dictations, tough problems, names of rivers and mountains, names of battles, dates of victories.

There were ten of us being groomed in this way. Ten whom, according to the saying prevalent among the inhabitants of the village, Mr. Roc was going to send to Saint-Esprit. The master filled our heads to such an extent that the four or five days away from school for the ceremonies surrounding my First Communion and the new sacrament had hardly detracted me from the worries of that supreme examination.

Not only did Mr. Roc relentlessly make us go over our books again and again, he preached morning, noon and night about the virtues of the *Certificat d'Etudes,* which was most indispensable to the humblest of men, without which you could not write other examinations nor do any lucrative work. Without the *Certificat d'Etudes,* we would all end up in the *petites-bandes* and all our parents' sacrifices would have been to no avail.

Did Mr. Roc himself believe in the effectiveness of his sermons on us? If not, did he notice all their effect? However, there was no doubt that, warmed up and urged on in that fashion, it was in a state of veritable heroism that we lived until that day of the examination.

The day before, a Sunday, all the girls and many of the boys had taken communion—except me, and to my shame. For, so as not to confess to the priest that, through a crack in the partition, I had seen our neighbor Mam'zelle Mézélie stark naked on her bed with a man who was touching her, I had already stopped going for communion.

Then in the afternoon, Mam'zelle Fanny had gathered them altogether in front of her door, the way they did for catechism.

Because I hadn't taken communion and because I had broken off with that spiritual godmother a long time before, I couldn't be part of the group. So, curious to know what was going to happen, I went and stood in a clump of bushes on the other side of the alley. I should have known: it was so they could meet and pray. Standing in a semi-circle, facing Mam'zelle Fanny, herself standing in the doorway with arms folded, they prayed aloud for success in the examination they were about to sit.

At first I felt a tinge of regret at not being with them—wasn't that a chance for success that I was losing? They invoked all the saints I knew to be reputed for their kindness towards examination candidates: Saint Expédit, Saint Michael, Saint Anthony.

Mam'zelle Fanny, hands together, eyes raised to heaven, let flow from her mouth a stream of stirring prayers.

And I would be the only one not to benefit from all the grace which, right then, through Mam'zelle Fanny's intervention, came down and spread over my friends to lighten their spirits, sharpen their intelligence and make them successful. But I quickly consoled myself. That morning M'man Tine had taken communion on my behalf and experience had already proven on many occasions that everything M'man Tine requested of God she would receive. So, half envious, half contemptuous, I let them shout themselves out of breath reciting litanies thus in public, and I returned to Cour Fusil because the master had recommended that we get plenty of rest that day.

I fell asleep while M'man Tine was preparing all I would need the following day.

Spurred on by a devotion that, to my eyes, magnified the importance of the event I was about to experience, she had ironed my First Communion suit, brushed my black boots that I had only worn some five or six times. Sleep took hold of me as she was frying the codfish to make sandwiches for me to carry.

After she woke me, very early, she gave me a mug of very strong coffee and when I was dressed and armed with my supplies, I set out in the morning twilight. Mr. Roc had summoned us all to be in front of his house for five o'clock.

We had always appreciated Mr. Roc, despite the stinging clouts to Jojo's skull and his slaps that made our ears ring. But I don't think our feelings ever attained such a degree of affection as there was in us that morning as we walked alone on the road beside that man, that sort of shepherd who relentlessly showered us with bits of advice that betrayed to what extent, more than we, he was concerned and moved.

*

The day went by with the disappearance of all our fears, an exaltation of our hopes.

Our school master was satisfied with the overall accounts of our dictation, the scrap work from our problems and our composition. He had even found new faith in Germé, the girl who was incurably obsessed with the mania of putting an 's' at the end of every word, and in Louisy who got all puzzled up at the slightest rule of three.

It was evening and in the darkness of the Saint-Esprit school yard we awaited proclamation of the results.

We remained literally tied together in the crowd of pupils and parents filling the yard.

Only Mr. Roc left us and returned. We constantly heard children spelling, in the surrounding clamor, such and such a word from the dictation, or giving the results of the problems.

We were hardly tired from remaining standing in one place for so long, but some, like me, complained that their feet were hurting them. As such, taking advantage of the darkness, I was among the first to relieve myself by taking off my boots. I had tied the laces together and held them tightly so as not to lose them.

The later it became, the more an ill-contained state of nervousness took hold of us, manifesting itself in some by endless chattering, plunging others into a silence bordering on a daze.

Suddenly, there was a confusion of voices, the crowd lurched forward, then silence. A window on the first floor had been opened and its rectangle of light formed a frame, against this light, around the busts of two men. One of them immediately began to announce names of pupils.

As these were called out, shudders, muffled outbursts and stifled exclamations shook the crowd. I did not move. My blood, my entrails had been crushed together by the appearance of those two men and I remained riveted, hanging on to the voice from the magic window calling out names that floated down on the pupils like a shower of stars. There was an endless constellation of them and the more the names came, the more I moved away from the crowd which was already bursting about me.

I could see only the lighted frame of the window and could hear only the lone voice of the man reading the results . . . Hassam José!

That name, coming from the man's lips, hit me full in the chest with enough violence to blow me to bits.

Never had I heard my name pronounced in so solemn a tone. Never had I felt with such acuteness everything that bound my being to those four syllables. But if that name hadn't been called I'd no doubt have turned into stone.

My friends were hugging one another, hugging me.

"We all passed! All ten of us!" they shouted.

I didn't jump, I didn't shout, I just allowed myself to be carried along, smiling, not finding anything to say Mr. Roc was very excited and almost submerged by the pupils' show of joy. He kept on repeating with a smile that looked rather like a grimace: "That's good, that's good," and looked at us with sparkling eyes behind his spectacles. He turned around constantly, starting a sentence, interrupting himself, turning around once more, shouting:

"It's late, children, hurry up."

Under the glow of the street lamps all the streets of Saint-Esprit were swarming with pupils and in an uproar.

Mr. Roc took us to a garage owner and hired a taxi into which piled all ten of us along with him.

M'man Tine, like all the people in Cour Fusil, was already in bed when I reached Petit-Bourg. She was not asleep; no sooner did I touch the door, held shut as usual by a stone place behind it on the floor, than she had lit her lamp and asked me:

"José, how did you do, son?"

I threw my hands into the air and danced.

"Ah, thank God!" said M'man Tine, clasping her hands together over her heart.

That was all. She went back to bed, told me that my dinner was covered in a plate on the table and that my bedding must be quite nice, since she had put it out to sun for the entire day.

The following week, when classes were practically finished and our activities at school consisted of more games than work, Mr. Roc gave me a letter to post, explaining that it was an application for another examination I was to sit shortly afterwards: the Scholarship Examination.

Of the ten I was the only one who was successful in the *Certificat d'Etudes*, the others being above the required age. This competitive examination was to be held in Fort-de-France. If I were successful, I would be going to a school in Fort-de-France, to the *lycée*. Mr. Roc told me all of that without betraying any emotion, without smiling, but with an air of seriousness beneath which I could sense a certain indescribable feeling of anticipated joy, whose warmth made all the more impressive the prospect he was presenting me.

As far as I was concerned, I did not even have the faintest idea how all the school master was talking about could come to pass. Consequently, it was not my application to sit the Scholarship Examination that took up a lot of my time during the succeeding days.

When we stopped playing, it was to make plans for the future, only it was an immediate future.

Raphael would be going to the *Cours Supérieur* in Saint-Esprit, where his brother Roger was already a student, to prepare for the *Brevet Elémentaire*.

Mérinda, lucky girl she was! said that the Post Mistress would take her on in the office to teach her to operate the telephone.

Two others, from among the girls, were going to learn to sew in Rivière-Salée. There was only Laurette who did not have any plans— her parents were hesitant to send her to Saint-Esprit for fear that she would meet boys along the way.

Mr. Roc had shattered my own dream. For the time being, my one and only borrowed dream was to be successful in the Scholarship Examination so I could attend the *lycée*. Later on, I could be a lawyer, a doctor . . . But did I really believe that?

The fact remained that I was happy at the idea of going to sit an examination in Fort-de-France, because, at the same time, I would be able to see my dear mother, M'man Délia.

After going to see Mr. Roc about it, M'man Tine had made up her mind:

"Well! I'll have to get my petticoat with the English embroidery ready for this trip."

I had often seen the sea in the distance. From Haut-Morne one looked down onto a marshy plain crossed by a wide, lazy river, and the sea, in the distance, into which it blended. For me the sea was something visible and beautiful, but as inaccessible as its brother, the sky. Now, Lake Génipa, where I often went to bathe, though small, had given me such an idea of what the sea could be like viewed from a short distance, that I was not particularly impressed that day when, in the little steam boat that linked Fort-de-France to Petit-Bourg, I found myself on the high sea. M'man Tine accompanied me. Travelers from the country, barefooted and wearing coarse straw hats, and immaculately dressed people were talking aloud, laughing, eating, sharing bread and fried foods among themselves.

But I only had eyes for what was going on outside the boat. It was a huge bath of space. The only thing to impress me was the void between the sky and the water. Strange, too, the force with which the water moved in all directions, like a herd of blue, skinless excited beasts that barked, foamed and lashed the small boat with their soft, slimy sides, then sped away, their manes flying in the breeze, to beset and toss about the few canoes around us that seemed to be heading nowhere.

In the long run M'man Tine, no doubt noticing that I was beginning to feel upset by this perpetual motion, made me put my head on her lap and I fell asleep.

When, still stiff, we found ourselves on the wharf, I wondered whether M'man Tine would manage to find the place where the examination was being held. The town seemed to me more extensive, noisier than the deepest forests, the biggest plantations, the most awful factories I could ever imagine. What a lot of streets! What a lot of automobiles!

But M'man Tine, less disturbed than I was, took her time putting on her shoes, making sure her dress looked presentable, fixing her pettticoat, then, taking me firmly by the hand, ventured out towards the town.

We stopped at every crossing. M'man Tine asked a passer-by the way, then we set off again.

My grandmother was an amazing woman. We arrived at the girls' *lycée*—that was where the examination was being held. There was the same atmosphere as at Saint-Esprit the day of the examination for the *Certificat d'Etudes*—students milling around in the yard, with teachers and parents, the roll-call, the entrance into the classrooms.

The dictation seemed easy. As for the two problems, so easy in comparison with those Mr. Roc had trained us on, when I returned to the yard after the composition and heard the other candidates shouting the figures they had arrived at, I realised that I had done one wrong. I was immediately very much put out by this, but tried my best not to let M'man Tine see. And I hardly thought about it any more for we had to go to see my mother right away.

On my return to Petit-Bourg, I had not hidden from Mr. Roc the blunder which caused me to do my second problem badly. At first he rebuked me, then changed his mind:

"Too bad, the essential thing was the *Certificat*. Now, you've got that already."

But what was I going to do?

On more than one occasion I had heard M'man Tine ask:

"My God, how shall I manage to send this child to the *Cours Supérieur?*"

She did not know anyone who could receive me at middays. Personally, I felt capable of doing without anything. The experience I had been subjected to at Mme Léonce's probably did a lot towards this feeling of mine, and I saw myself willingly having for lunch under the school veranda the most frugal of meals, which I would have brought with me in the morning. But where I proved as stubborn as a mule was on the question of shoes. You couldn't attend the *Cours Supérieur* bare-footed. Of course, there were my First Communion boots and I could make them last longer by carrying them in my hand on the road between Petit-Bourg and Saint-Esprit, putting them on only to go into class; but, at any rate, they would still go. And afterwards? I once had the idea of going to work in the *petites-bandes* during the long vacation to earn enough to buy me a pair of shoes. Vergène and her brother, for instance, used to do that every year in order to buy a new suit for the opening of school. I couldn't bring myself to do it. It was not my fault: there was no particular liking for sugar cane fields. Despite all the pleasure I had nibbling on and sucking pieces of sugar cane, a field still represented in my eyes a damnable place where executioners, whom you couldn't even see, condemned black people from as young as eight years old, to weed, to dig, in storms that caused them to shrivel up and in the broiling sun that devoured them like mad dogs—blacks in rags, stink with sweat and dung, fed on one handful of cassava flour and two cents' worth of molasses rum, who became pitiful monsters with glassy eyes, with feet made heavy by elephantiasis, destined to collapse one night in a furrow and to breathe their last breath on a dingy plank on the ground of an empty, grimy hut.

No, no! I wanted no part of the splendor of the sun and the charm of the work songs sung in a sugar cane field. And the wild sensual delight of the love that consumed a vigorous mule-driver with a fiery black girl in the heart of a sugar cane field. For too long a time I had witnessed, helpless as I was, my grandmother dying a slow death in those fields of sugar cane.

As a result, my idea of joining the *petites-bandes* scarcely had time to take root. Furthermore, it would not have worked. M'man Tine would have objected strenuously and might even have whipped me for coming up with such a plan.

The long vacation was about to begin and the prospect of my going on outings in the country, making fishing trips, picking fruits and roaming about in the most unrestricted fashion, soon erased all worry from my mind.

*

The long vacation had hardly begun when, one night, the woman who swept the classrooms and cleaned Mr. Roc's house came on his behalf to fetch me at M'man Tine's place, to the great amazement of the latter.

When I entered, Mr. Roc was sitting at the dinner table.

"My boy," he said, swallowing a mouthful, "you're lucky, you know.

Look, I've just received this."

And taking a bit of blue paper which was lying near his plate, he unfolded it, saying to me:

"You were successful in the Scholarship Examination."

He handed me the telegram. His eyes sparkled and his half-open mouth showed the edge of his teeth—an expression that wasn't quite a smile, but one I had seen on his face at times of great joy.

And he repeated:

"You lucky boy, you!"

Part Three

I had obtained from the Colony a quarter scholarship.

In the offices of the Head of the Office of Public Instruction, where my mother Délia and I had learned the news, a young clerk had told us that with scholarships it was a question of whom you knew, and that she was surprised that by some unheard-of stroke of luck, without the intervention of anyone with some pull, or any recommendation, that partial scholarship had come my way.

In the bursary at the *lycée,* a bit later on, it was explained to us that, in order to benefit from that quarter scholarship, we still had to pay eighty-seven francs fifty per term for my schooling.

We were both crushed by this disappointment.

But what I couldn't understand was that my mother did not show any sign of discouragement or of giving up. I sensed in her a feeling of anguish even more acute than mine and yet I saw her persist in walking throughout the town, skipping from office to office, dragging me behind her, constantly enquiring what she was to do. How could I enter a *lycée* where my mother had to pay eighty-seven francs every three months, and for several years—about seven, we'd been told?

I couldn't understand, either, why my mother didn't just give up, since in the final analysis, there were the *Cours Supérieurs* and *Cours Complémentaires* that were free.

But she kept on saying:

"*They* are too wicked! It's because we're black, poor and alone in the world that *they* didn't give you a full scholarship. *They* fully realise that I'm an unfortunate woman and that I couldn't pay for you to go to the *lycée. They* know only too well that giving you a quarter scholarship is the same as not giving you anything at all. But *they* don't know what a fighting woman I am. Well! I'm not giving up this quarter scholarship. You will go to *their lycée!*

My grief stemmed not so much from my doubting her ability to do this, but from her seeing my poor mother so desperately engaged in a struggle beyond her strength, against people who seemed to be numerous and powerful as well as invisible.

Eighty-seven francs fifty! My mother counted over and over the contents of her blue cotton purse. I gave her the hundred cents M'man Tine had given me the day I left Petit-Bourg, that morning of our

125

separation, when she came to see me onto the little steam boat. My
mother counted her money again, mumbled something, thought a
while then, seeming more determined than ever to pick up the
challenge, she repeated, as if to cheer her own self up, as well as me:
"You're going!"

M'man Délia had an excellent job with some local whites in Route
Didier. She did the washing and the housework, shared with a cook, a
driver and a gardener the left-overs from the masters' meals, had a
room furnished with an iron bed, with clean, soft bedding. She made
one hundred francs a month. Very few maids, she had confided to
M'man Tine, were as well paid. Not even in Route Didier where one
found the richest white people and the best black servants.

Now, because of me, she had to begin by giving up that position,
rent a room and take in washing.

We were then living in the Sainte-Thérèse district.

A certain Dr. Guerri, who owned those lands, scarcely cleared of
trees, to the east of Fort-de-France, had cut out and rented small lots to
all who wanted to put up a shack.

A sizeable black population of workers—the overflow from the
other slum-filled, malaria and typhoid fever-infested districts of the
town—flocked to the area and, on the initiative of each person and with
epic zeal, set up a huge encampment. Five or six alleys had been traced
out, paved in any old fashion and given names whose origin or
meaning no one knew. Along those alleys, there sprang up a line of the
standard type of shacks: huge boxes, that had contained imported
American cars, set gingerly on concrete or dried stones or on mere
wooden stilts and covered with eight sheets of galvanize. Often the roof
consisted of a multitude of more or less rusty tins, smashed in, cut,
flattened and laid out like scales of a fish.

And already, many of the shacks served as groceries, as tailor and
butcher shops as well as peaceful dwellings. All around, children would
play, by no means afraid that they would knock everything over in the
frolicking. And in front, on a Sunday afternoon, a man would settle
down in a *chaise-longue* to smoke, with nothing else on his mind, or
with his wife would cultivate a few somewhat humble flowers, not too
ordinary, though, to offer as a sincere token of affection and of love.

In the middle of a wide space rose a pile of excavated dirt, behind
which a large part of the population of Sainte-Thérèse worked on the
building of a church to which we would belong.

I liked that district very much. It was not that I found it beautiful to
look at, but I was very happy to see the arrival and settlement of all
those people who, with the greatest of ease, and no doubt thinking only
of their immediate concerns, dug into those vague lands, with the force

of an act of love, their inexpugnable human roots.

A few people, who already owned more solid and more conventional dwelling places in town, built in Sainte-Thérèse shacks befitting the style of the area, that were rented by people who were not in a position to build their own. My mother was part of this latter category; but she was so contented to be in Sainte-Thérèse, so happy to see a glimmer of hope that one day she could buy a car box and six sheets of galvanize to build herself a small two-room house!

Near the district flowed the Rivière-Monsieur. It was there that, from Tuesday to Thursday, my mother went to do her washing. The other days of the week were devoted to mending and ironing.

She had large and small loads of washing. The small ones were paid for every Saturday night, on delivery, the large ones at the end of the month.

*

However, I managed to enter the *lycée*, on payment of the eighty-seven francs fifty, or rather a little before paying that sum.

At one of our visits to the bursary, the cashier had told my mother that she did not have to pay when I entered, that she could have a few days grace.

So she took me there and left me, hoping that, at any rate, she would in time muster up the necessary money.

But two weeks had gone by and the bursar had sent for me to remind me about the unpaid fees.

Then two days later, there was a further reminder and a threat of failure. So I remained in Sainte-Thérèse for two days.

In the end, after a day and a night of ironing, and a morning spent delivering laundry, my mother gave me, one Monday morning, an envelope containing some notes that she had taken pains to smoothen out with her iron. Thanks to that, I returned to the Lycée Schoelcher, making a stop at the bursar's office.

*

I found this *lycée* very big, teeming with students, well-staffed with teachers.

The most striking change from my school in Petit-Bourg was the fact that I had to be caged during classes in a room whose windows did not look out onto any trees, and to be held captive, at recess time, in a wall-enclosed yard in which, considering the amount of students, it wasn't even possible to have a good game of *barres*.

Then, too, in that crowd of students (from tiny tots from the Infant School right up to the bigger ones whom I had mistaken for teachers) I found myself as lonely as I'd ever been—there was nobody who said anything to me; nobody I'd dare share a secret with.

The first day, I was dressed in my First Communion suit with my black boots; the following week, I wore the white suit in which I had received the absolution; and little by little, I started wearing my old suits from the elementary school and a pair of rubber-soled shoes.

What a difference compared with all the other students dressed in suits that bore the mark of carefully selected wardrobes, and carrying leather schoolbags, pens with golden rings, watches!

Next to me, in the study, sat a boy wearing an identification bracelet with his first name engraved on it: "Serge." The name of a clean, fresh child, of a fair-skinned child. At any rate, not the name of a little black, unfortunate boy. The name of a nice, little boy in velvet breeches and silk jacket, with brown shoes, smooth, sweet-smelling hair, separated by a slanting part, and wearing a gold watch on his wrist.

His father brought him and picked him up by car at the school gate. And whenever it rained, the caretaker, who would look at me so unpleasantly, graciously brought him a raincoat so he could cross the yard.

There were many students like that, those in my first year class and those I saw gathered or playing together.

There was no one like me. Furthermore, nobody paid any attention to me.

Could it be I was *that* repulsive in my dress?

I think rather tht it was my self-centeredness, my lack of gaiety, in contrast to their easy-going behavior, their joy among themselves, the fact that they were at home in this *lycée,* that isolated me. Of course, if there were one who had been born in a Black Shack Alley, one whose parents wielded a spade or a cutlass, I'd have recognized him and approached him. But I was the only one of my kind.

*

During the entire first term, my relationship with my mates in year I hardly improved.

I did not talk in class. I did not have any fun during recess. It was impossible, until then, to rid myself of my complexes and regrets. For I also missed Petit-Bourg and my old school, and all that went to make one and the other. I regretted not being at the *Cours Supérieur* in Saint-Esprit where I'd have kept most of my friends.

What was I doing in that *lycée?*

My mother was told that I could leave school with enough knowledge to enable me to go to France and become a doctor, a lawyer, an engineer. While filling out my application for the Scholarship Examination, Mr. Roc had hinted that to me; but I didn't feel very much inclined to do something in that field. The others, the Serges, yes. But me . . .

It was because of that lack of incentive, no doubt, that my first term's results were so poor. I had only been on the honor roll the first month.

When, on Christmas Eve, my mother received my term report, she was plunged into the depths of despair. All my grades were mediocre. And among the unfavorable comments, there was the one made by the mathematics teacher: "Student of little interest." Me, who, with Mr. Roc, always solved both my problems!

"José," my mother said to me, "you don't see how I work my fingers to the bone scrubbing piles of dirty clothes and how dry I'm becoming from ironing day and night? You don't know it's so I can pay the eighty-seven francs fifty for your education and that you must work in class so that money doesn't go down the drain; so I don't kill myself for nothing! You've just thrown away eighty-seven francs fifty, since you don't have a single good grade for the term. Yes, it's as if you had thrown into the sea all your maman's money, along with the five francs M'man Tine had given you . . . "

My mother had never rebuked me more angrily; but if she had beaten me, I'd have detested the *lycée*, hated the teachers and all the students—they were the ones, both of them, who had prevented me from working.

Nobody bothered with me; I was not asked anything. In Petit-Bourg the schoolmasters saw to it that you learned your lessons and did your homework, otherwise you were clouted about the ears. But in this *lycée*, you did as little as you wanted.

My mother hadn't even raised her voice and, listening to her, I had the impression she was crying; as if her hands, bruised by the scrubbing of the heavy clothes, were bleeding; as if her arms, worn out by the iron, were hurting her; or as if it was I who had struck her on her bruised hands, on her painful arms . . . struck my maman!

I burst out sobbing.

I cried for my mother who had wanted to see me become a good student and whom I had disappointed and caused grief.

But when I dried my eyes, I wanted, if it were possible, to return to school immediately. I had made up my mind to work.

*

During the entire term, I had cherished the hope of returning to Petit-Bourg for the Christmas vacation. I constantly thought about my village, forever comparing my subjects of melancholy to the memory of the turbulent, carefree life I led there, and I tried my best to retain all the details of my new school life, in order to relate them to my former mates. Then, as the vacation drew near, the thought of the Christmas festivities kindled in me a feeling of joy that lasted several days. The carol-singing evening sessions at the parents of my friends, especially at

Audney's father's house; Christmas night when I would go, along with the whole band of brats, to midnight mass in Grand-Bourg, to laugh and eat sausage-rolls of minced pork, peanuts, and on the way back to Petit-Bourg, to shout in the night, at the top of our voices:

> Jesus is born to-day
> Wa-ee, ya-ee, ya-ee!

Then the following day, to go to Aunt Norbéline's house, in Courbaril. The music of the accordian and the maracas would be circulating throughout the country air and in the people, like one burning sap, and from all the shacks there would come the same aroma of roast pork, of Congo peas and yam. And those outbursts of gaiety, heightened by alcohol! I feasted mainly on that spicy pudding which, as far as I was concerned, was the best reason for having Christmas festivities.

Afterwards, there would be New Year's Day.

*

For me, that day was a gloomy one indeed!

A sunny, pleasant day, alive with the sound of trumpets, filled with balloons, colored with toys, with the scent of nougats and sugared almonds around me, while I never had anything. No trumpet, no balloon, no sugared almond; and my heart was sad and heavy.

I was not envious, but the entire scene filled me with an inevitable sadness which cut my desire to go gallivanting about the streets.

Be that as it may, I liked New Year's Day on account of that very feeling of gloom as well as the mood M'man Tine inspired in me on that day.

My grandmother would rise early, give me a white suit and put on a new dress—an end of cloth she had had put aside in a store in Saint-Esprit, and had paid for, cent by cent, throughout the better part of the year before collecting it and having a dress made with it. A dress of printed cotton with a design of peas—for prosperity—or numerous tiny flowers, its smell reminding one of the holiday preparations, and of the festivity surrounding New Year's Day.

M'man Tine would take me to the early morning mass. It would still be dark, the air fresh and actually new.

The church would always be filled to capacity, and beyond, with the faithful.

After mass, M'man Tine would kiss me. One of the rare occasions on which she would kiss me.

"Happy New Year," she would tell me; "may you grow up to be a man."

She would give me two cents and an orange.

Then she would leave me and go round from door to door to the neighbors in Cour Fusil and to her old acquaintants to wish man and woman alike a Happy New Year and give each one an orange.

She would return home around midday, laden with more oranges than she had gone to give away, and would not go out for the rest of the day.

That was one day when she did almost no talking. Almost no monologues muttered beneath her breath.

She would start preparing lunch with infinite tenderness, although it was never very substantial.

Lunch would be a little late and, in the afternoon, she would stretch out on her bed (the only time for the year, except if she were sick, that she'd lie in bed during the day) and really enjoy her pipe, whose still smoke would fill the shack with a smell that, in me, gave rise to a feeling of absolute well-being and dissipated in my heart the gloominess of the morning.

But that year my mother had kept me in Sainte-Thérèse.

She would well have liked to send me to see M'man Tine, despite my unfavorable report, for without any allusion on my part, she said to me:

"With this year coming to an end and the other about to begin, with your canvas shoes to be bought, the *lycée* to pay for, things don't look too bright. So you'll send a pretty picture post-card to M'man Tine."

I felt no grief over this for my philosophy was such that my wants did not surpass my parents' means.

My second term at the *lycée* showed a marked difference from the first. An improvement. I learned my lessons thoroughly; I gradually attained more confidence. I became aware of what was happening. From time to time, the teachers asked me questions.

And I had a friend.

We sat beside each other in nearly all the classes and in the study. His name was Bussi, Christian Bussi.

He had tried to entice me to play during recess. I had given in on one occasion. But those games looked silly to me. I found the yard too small and then, accustomed as I was to romping in the grass, I did not like running about in that paved yard.

The plain fact was that I hardly ever played. Yet, every morning, my friend and I sought each other out; we met in the yard.

It was Bussi, so to speak, who introduced me to the entire staff of the *lycée*. He already knew everybody, having been in the class below ours the year before.

In particular, he knew everyone's nickname, from Foetus, the head-master, right down to a boy in class, Cello. I was very much amused by them, but never allowed myself to be tempted into addressing a teacher or a supervisor by his nickname.

Was it shyness or some complex that led me to believe that the other students, the Serges and the Christians, could do so, but that I must not allow myself to?

Another source of rejoicing: the sale of cakes by the caretaker during each recess.

Five times a day, the crowd of students flocked around the window through which the caretaker sold her cakes, then broke up in the yard to play and walk about, all the while biting into long pieces of a type of gingerbread with jam.

And five times a day I was forced to endure this spectacle without participating in it. I never had a cent to my name. I was forced to stand in the background, and the sight of those cakes the pupils bought in a joyous uproar and devoured greedily and freely about me, overwhelmed me with passionate desire and longing; for at that time, on mornings for example, I only wanted to eat some like the others. But on evenings, during the long recess period supervised by day students, as I never had any mid-afternoon snack, the hunger that on its own already was hounding me mercilessly, tormented me even more fiercely when I saw that happy crowd stuffing itself with fine cakes, talking and laughing. My affliction was then so acute that it was not my stomach that caused me pain, but a bewildering emptiness, making my head grow heavy, transforming all around me into a nightmare, into an ignoble plot against my hunger.

Thus, I began by filling myself with water from a tap in a corner of the yard and every now and then, I returned to it, trying to drown my stomach to keep it quiet. Similarly, I tried to hide myself in the crowd to escape Bussi. I had neither the urge nor the strength to talk. It was already quite a problem looking calm, indifferent, even filled, like everybody else. But Bussi managed to find me. I saw him; he had seen me; impossible to get away. He came up to me, holding a long piece of golden brown bread, its white, foam-light inside cut in two to receive fried eggs.

He looked more impressive to me with this large loaf in his hand than Asselm, whom I had known in my childhood in Petit-Morne. I found it terrible.

But Bussi was a kind friend. Seeing that I hadn't had anything to eat, he offered me his bread in a natural gesture.

"Break it."

"No," I said, "thank you."

"Come on, break it with me."

He held out his bread to me. That golden brown and white bread, spongy and stuffed full of fried eggs, smelling good.

No, I was adamant in my refusal, and with an air of indifference; for, at his insistence, my hunger had disappeared, overcome or driven back by some indescribable pride risen up in the face of what could be a gesture of pity on the part of this boy. But he broke the break himself and handed me a piece, a large piece, all full of egg yolks.

"Come now, don't make such a fuss."

I put both my hands behind my back and with a quiet smile, I persisted with my refusal.

Then, to end it all, Bussi shrugged his shoulders, did a little pirouette, bit deep into his bread and we spoke about other things. We walked about the yard. The walk relaxed me from the struggle I had just been through.

As he spoke, Bussi kept on eating.

After a while, cutting short our conversation, he said to me:

"You didn't want to share my snack with me, and I have too much. My maman always gives me too much to eat."

Indeed, looking fully satisfied, he showed me a large hunk of his oversized sandwich and, with a gesture of disgust, dropped it, catching it before it hit the ground with a kick that propelled it towards a corner of the yard.

And I found enough control over myself to appear indifferent to his gesture and to smile foolishly as if to approve the skill with which he had booted home the bread.

But at that moment it wasn't hunger I was struggling with—rather with a sudden and wild impulse to also kick Bussi with all my strength. For, what he had just done resounded in me as if it were I who had received it, right in my behind; or as if it were a little boy, very much like me, whose behind Bussi had kicked in my presence.

Thereupon, Christian took from his trouser pocket his pretty purse and with an "excuse me" ran off towards the caretaker's stall. Then he returned greedily biting into a slice of cake two fingers thick, and this time, dispensing with the useless trouble of offering me any, once more continued our conversation which went on until the end of recess.

*

Afterwards, like everybody else, we dashed off to the urinals, then to the taps, Bussi to wash his fingers, dropping into the sink the rest of his cake; and I, to take my last fill of water.

*

In the following Easter vacation, I did not go to Petit-Bourg. For the same reasons as at Christmas. But my second term report was better than the first. My mother was happy.

Proud of my good grades, and to console myself over not seeing her, I wrote a long letter to M'man Tine—I was working a lot. Soon I'd be big, I'd be successful in my examinations and she'd not have to work in the sugar cane fields, or anywhere else.

I also wrote to Raphael, depicting the school as an establishment as huge and colossal as the Petit-Bourg factory appeared to us. I suggested a few outings and fishing trips for the long vacation.

The third term was more pleasant.

I finally had the feeling I was contributing something to the class; that made me more comfortable and gave me more self-confidence. And on their own, my complexes and my fears had vanished.

The end of the term in particular had been easy. There were frequent long hours of prep periods and as we had nothing to do, we played those little games that consisted of two partners each tracing, in turn, arabesques on a sheet of paper, according to various agreed patterns. Certain assistant masters tolerated quiet talking and, on evenings, I spent the entire study period reading.

It was Christian Bussi who had awakened and who maintained in me this taste for reading. His parents bought him books and he passed them all on to me.

From that time on, the world began to broaden around me, beyond any tangible limits.

The world, as portrayed in those works destined for young people, was divided in two: an ordinary, everyday world, brutal and unresponding to desires, and a spacious, logical world, above all kind, interesting and desirable.

Wasn't the very act of reading a pleasure more substantial than that of playing or eating, for instance, even when one was starved?

On that occasion, I had finally gone up to Petit-Bourg and my vacation began in splendid fashion.

I had once more found all my friends, except Jojo, alas! and we had once again participated in all those things that so delighted us before our separation.

But I had brought a new and magical pastime: stretching out or sitting for long hours, for entire afternoons, in the shade of huge trees, in Haut-Morne, beside the river, anywhere at all, and plunging into my reading, to the point of obliterating myself from all that surrounded me.

Books brought back from Fort-de-France, books found at my friends; very old books without their covers and their first pages, for which I had begged Mr. Roc.

To the pulsating pleasure of discovering and pursuing an adventure enclosed within the printed leaves, was added the strange joy of my actually being there, lying on my belly, my elbows dug into the grass, my head cupped between my hands, while the breeze, blowing in the countless instruments of the greenery, made the silence musical; and of my witnessing, or better, even of my participating in that adventure! . . .

In a very short time, M'man Tine's room was bulging with books: on the girders, on shelves I had put up everywhere. That was another trait that distinguished it from the other rooms in Cour Fusil.

Therefore, for the few days since thunder and rain ushered in the month of September, instead of devoting my leisure time to roaming about in gullies and hollows, I curled up on M'man Tine's old bed (I could use it with impunity now, especially since this stay, after so long an absence, gave me all the little privileges) and while the water leaking from the cracks and holes in the ceiling dripped into containers I had placed just about everywhere on the ground and on the bed, I read. And the rain, and its freshness, and its vast, extensive orchestra on the outside, and its drops musically beating down all around me, superimposed its charm upon the one captivating my imagination.

I enjoyed that feeling of being, through the book, cut in two: my body bathing in the throbbing well-being of the rain or of the silence, and my head thrust through a world that I was very often forced to transport a bit to the image of my own in order to broaden it all the more.

I preferred novels. I admired the gift, the power possessed by a man who wrote a novel.

I would really have liked to do likewise one day. But how would I manage that?

I had never frequented those people with blonde hair, blue eyes, pink cheeks, that were put in novels.

Towns, with their motorcars, their big hotels, their theaters, their salons, their crowds, the ocean liners, trains, mountains and plains, the fields, farms where novels were set, none of that I had ever seen. I was only familiar with Black Shack Alley, Petit-Bourg, Sainte-Thérèse, men, women and children, all more or less black. Now, certainly that was not the stuff novels were made of, since I had never read any of that color.

I did not know if I had settled down a lot, or if it was M'man Tine who, out of kindness, deliberately showed herself more obliging now. She did not scold me any more. She was, to me, so sweet that I wondered whether I hadn't possibly grown much more than I myself imagined and whether I wasn't in fact much closer than I thought to being a man.

Perhaps it was because of her heart, more penetrable at that time, that M'man Tine's condition became apparent to me with painful, abnormal acuteness. Abnormal and shameful, since that scene at the lycée. A teacher had asked each student his identity and the name and profession of his parents. Without any hesitation, I had naively given those of my mother, washer-woman, with my address in town; and just as naively it was the name of M'man Tine that had come from my mouth as next of kin. But, at her "profession," I had faltered. First of all, I didn't know, in French, the name of the job she held. No, it certainly did not exist in French.

"Profession!" the teacher shouted, impatient.

"Doctor, school-teacher, cabinet-maker, office worker, tailor, seamstress, pharmacist," the other students had said.

For me, impossible to find the name of the work my grandmother did. Were I to dare to say: "she works in sugar cane fields," the whole class would burst out laughing. There was nothing like such things to have those students in stitches.

"Farmer," I finally stammered out.

That word, on its own, had slipped from my mouth and I was grateful that it had come to my rescue.

Fortunately, the opportunity to give my parents' profession never again presented itself.

But this time, stronger and deeper than when I used to accompany her to the fields, a feeling of compassion came over me every time, on evenings, during that stormy month of September, M'man Tine came home, her rags and her skin weather-beaten, soaked like a sponge, and every time that, wanting to send me to the store, she looked in vain for the missing cent in every corner of the room.

Since she had first fallen ill, she was always ailing. She often complained of sharp pains in her back, and of suffocating fits. When she had been drenched by showers, I saw her get up during the night, make infusions and shiver with fever.

In addition, M'man Tine still remained an old woman very meticulous when it came to cleanliness. She liked everything to be neatly put away and well kept. Yet, her room was dirty. Now, in vain she often washed the rags from her old bed, washed the slightest utensil immediately after using it, swept the flooring every morning before setting out, the room still looked no less black, grimy, damp, smelling both of mud and rotten wood as well as, from time to time, of a frog dead under the floor—in short, of all the miasmas associated with blacks or with misery.

There was no repulsion for one or the other of those two states M'man Tine found herself in; but now, more understanding, it seemed, existed between my grandmother and me.

Thus, at an age when I felt myself naturally given to a carefree existence, all my impulses were at the same time thwarted by the constant suffering, by a sort of oppression that weighed more and more despicably on my grandmother.

The more I looked at M'man Tine, the more I felt within me that she was subjected to an unjust punishment which, at times, made her appear more frightening than pitiful.

Why? Why not live in a house, why not wear dresses without holes, why not eat bread and meat, without always having to mumble those long, sad words that stuck in my throat and strangled me?

And who forced her to be like that?

Referring to stories about misers that Vireil had related to me, I had believed for a long time that the minute you were an adult and began to work, you acquired a certain 'fortune' to buy all you needed; but there were some who used it and some, the misers, who hid everything, preferring to have terrible dwelling places, shabby clothes and poor food.

For a long time, as a result, I had thought that M'man Tine had money, perhaps bags of gold hidden somewhere under the ground, and that she refused to ever lay a finger on it. Now, how I regretted no longer believing such!

In point of fact, something seemed to me positively abnormal—not in the rather bizarre job M'man Tine did, but in those perpetual feelings of destitution, of shame and of slow death emanating from this job.

And the anguish with which those considerations gripped me abated a bit only in the earnestness of my dreams of becoming a man, so that M'man Tine wouldn't have to work anymore on the sugar cane plantations.

The re-opening of school and my return to the *lycée* took place with this determination uppermost in my mind.

*

It was also marked by a great surprise when I stopped off in the bursary; in consideration of my work and conduct during the previous year, my quarter scholarship had been made a full one and, in addition, I was to receive a half-scholarship for my upkeep. Instead of paying eighty-seven francs fifty per term, I was going to collect seventy-five francs every month.

Shortly afterwards there was yet another event.

One evening, I had just reached home, and we were having dinner at our table of white wood, which my mother had cleared of all the clothes piled on it. Suddenly, there was a knock at the door. Normally, nobody ever paid us any visits, except our neighbor who, instead of knocking, announced herself by calling out to us.

My mother opened the door and shouted joyfully:

"Elise, it's you, my dear!"

A middle-aged black woman, correctly dressed, came in and my mother said to me:

"José, come and say hello to Mam'zelle Elise."

My mother launched into countless apologies for the state of the room which was small and, above all, not in any apparent order. The bed, for example, groaned under a huge pile of clothes rolled in bundles and stacks of garments already ironed.

The visitor apologized for her late visit.

"But," she added as she sat down, "it's something important."

"Nothing serious?" my mother asked.

"No," came the reply, "it's only that I thought of you concerning a matter that will interest you perhaps."

My curiosity aroused by the Mam'zelle Elise's detailed tone, I stopped eating.

"Well! it's like this," she continued, "Firmin, you remember Firmin, the driver with the Paillys?"

"Firmin!" said my mother, "the fellow who used to come and chat with you on the road, on Sunday afternoons?"

"Same one," Mam'zelle Elise agreed. "Well, he has some good intentions where I'm concerned, and I think we're going to hit it off."

"I'm happy for you, *négresse*. He looks like a serious fellow and must certainly love you very much."

"Ah, yes, he's very nice," Mam'zelle Elise chimed in. "Now, the position is this: I'm going to live with him and I'm leaving the Lasseroux. We're going to live at L'Ermitage where we've found a room. He'll keep his job, and as I'm not too bad at sewing, he's bought me a sewing machine, and I hope I'll not waste my time. And you, how are things with, *négresse?*"

"I'm making out the best I can, doing some washing," my mother said, showing the heaps of clothes lying everywhere.

"Oh! you've got quite a bit."

"Two large and two small."

"And you manage on that?"

"The large ones at sixty francs a month, the small ones at twelve francs a week."

"But you must have a lot of work, poor girl!"

"You can say that again!" my mother said. "Here, look at my fingers. As for my arms, my shoulders, I think it's no longer flesh and bone, only rheumatism . . . What can I do? I have a growing child. Especially with him being at the *lycée!* . . .

She related to Mam'zelle Elise how difficult a time she had had during the course of the year, because of those eighty-seven francs fifty.

"And if you were to find a good job?" said Mam'zelle Elise.

"You know I can't work like that anymore, with my son to look after.
. . . And then the *békés* are becoming more and more demanding, more
and more distrustful . . ."

"That's a shame," said Mam'zelle Elise, visibly disappointed. "I had
come to propose that you take over my job. For Mr. Lasseroux didn't
want to hear about my leaving. You understand, seeing the length of
time I've worked for him. But in the end he resigned himself to the fact
on condition that I found him someone he could trust and who had her
wits about her. I don't see anyone else but you, my dear."

My mother confirmed that it was not possible.

"You'll not make less than with your washing, you know. Mr.
Lasseroux gives me two hundred francs a month in salary and for my
meals, plus one hundred francs of supplies for washing his clothes and
cleaning the house. And as he's single and takes his meals at the club,
in spite of the amount of work needed to clean his villa, I found time to
wash Firmin's clothes. So you can always do one or two small loads on
the side. Then, too, Mr. Lasseroux is not a *béké* who harasses black
people. All he wants is to have his house spick and span. It's really a job
like no other you've had. A bachelor, no wife to call you all day long, to
have you constantly hovering around her, and to turn the house upside
down every week. I think it's a job that's really tailor-made for you,
négresse."

"I can't," my mother retorted; "I'm sorry . . . I already have my room
here, with my few things in it; I have my son. Then, let's say the boss
agrees to let me come home every night, that'll be too tiresome. Route
Didier is on the other side of Sainte-Thérèse. Impossible, you see . . . "

Mam'zelle Elise stood up, somewhat upset at not having had my
mother see things her way, and left.

We started eating again. This refusal had also made me a bit uneasy.
During the discussion, I had felt like whispering in my mother's ears to
accept. After the visitor left, I was still tempted to reproach her for
having refused. But I wasn't very brave with respect to my mother. What
little familiarity there was between us made me rather shy with her.

As a result, I showed my disapproval only by sulking in silence for
the entire end of the meal and until bedtime.

The next morning, just when, as was customary every morning, my
mother handed me my cup of coffee, she asked me:

"Listen, José, you heard what the lady who came last night told
maman?"

"Yes, m'man," came my reply, "you should've accepted."

"And what about you?" said my mother, surprised by my frank
reply.

"Well! I'll sleep here, all alone. I'll not be afraid, you know."
"But what about your meals?"
"I'll prepare them myself."
My mother did not say another word and remained rapt in thought.
I, too, thought it over all morning, in class.

*

Why would I want my mother to go to Route Didier? I didn't know. I wanted her to give up taking in washing, for fear of seeing her fingers bleed, of hearing her complain about her arms, about her shoulders. She would therefore go to Route Didier, to a job where she'd be comfortable; the skin on her hands would no longer become chafed, no longer be burnt . . . On mornings, I would make my coffee, wash myself and leave for the *lycée*. At middays, since I didn't have much time, I'd eat bread and margarine for lunch. On evenings, at seven o'clock, after study, I would prepare my dinner—rice or chocolate. I would read for a while. I wouldn't stay up too late reading, so as not to use up too much kerosine. On Thursdays and Sundays, I'd go to see maman.

It wasn't very difficult and I envisaged that solution with a secret feeling of joy.

My plan had not been so bad, since it coincided with the one my mother came up with that very night, the only slight difference being that I wouldn't have to make any coffee. Our neighbor, who had also encouraged my mother to accept the job, volunteered to supply me every morning with a bowl of coffee with cream.

M'man Délia went to see Mam'zelle Elise and was quick to take the job as general maid with Mr. Lasseroux in Route Didier.

I remained alone, trying my best to be beyond reproach.

My mother had left some charcoal, some foodstuff, some small change, and I did with them exactly as she had prescribed.

Much more so than on the day when M'man Tine had taken me to see my mother, Route Didier made on me a delightful impression that first morning I went to see M'man Délia in her new job.

Just outside the town, the road became a wide strip that stretched, in one piece and moving uphill, between alternating rows of trees and hibiscus hedges, behind which, from place to place, lay bright-colored villas, large and small, surrounded by lawns and flower beds.

Cars reflecting all the colors of the countryside were moving along silently in both directions.

I walked along, my steps lightened by the feeling of calm and well-being emanating from that marriage of sun and freshness, shadows and color, silence and life.

Mr. Lasseroux's house, my mother had told me, was called "Villa

Mano," and to find it, I willingly lingered at the gate of each of those smart dwelling places. In the garden, a black man would be cutting the lawn in some, trimming the hibiscus in others, or meticulously digging up flower beds.

"Villa Mano" came into sight, surmounted with small spires, at the end of a small white walk, set in a spacious lawn blooming with roses and zinnias.

I proceeded discreetly, and not without an irrepressible feeling of mistrust, towards the servant's quarters. My mother received me in the kitchen with a display of joy that seemed at the same time that of seeing me again after a few days of separation, as well as that of welcoming me in so charming a place. The kitchen was almost twice the size of our room and was nicely painted and decorated with utensils that shone like mirrors.

The boss had already left for his office in Fort-de-France. The car was not in the garage. My mother took advantage of this to show me around the house.

Behind the house lay a square lawn, spouting water from a fountain in the middle around which grew dwarf palms and mango trees. A high, well-trimmed hibiscus hedge, compact like a wall, enclosed everything. The air and the silence were exquisitely pure.

In one corner of the lawn, leaning against the house, a bird-cage contained the multi-colored frolicking of a handful of small birds.

Mr. Lasseroux, as described by my mother, liked three things for his leisure time: his birds, his aquarium and his wireless radio set-up which he had installed in his studio. He smoked many scented cigarettes. He also liked flowers, picking them in his garden and arranging his own bouquets which he placed in the various rooms of the house. He did not particularly fancy having people around and received very few friends.

In addition to all that, M'man Délia claimed, he was a good boss, giving his orders without any hint of arrogance and was not at all fussy.

*

Nevertheless, despite my determination to blithely endure my new solitary existence in Sainte-Thérèse, the situation kept growing on me ever since my mother started to work in the suburb at the other end of the town and we saw each other only once or twice a week.

During the first days, I had been sustained by a secret pride in the fact that I could behave myself properly, that I could make out on my own, and a sense of immense relief at the thought that my mother was in a good job. But, little by little, a terrible impression of being abandoned crept into my heart. The absence of my mother tormented me with gloom in that room whose windows I didn't even bother to open any more, where everything was covered with dust, and to which I came to eat, sleep and leave again, without anyone to speak to, without anyone to guide me with gentle or even with vehement words.

Some days, armed with the thirty or forty cents that M'man Délia would give me on each of my visits, so I could buy my bread on mornings, some sugar and other commodities, I would yield to the desire to eat cakes at the *lycée,* and that financial lapse would make me go without bread on certain days, or kerosine at night—a situation in which not only did hunger gnaw at me and the darkness make me unhappy, but where I felt awfully close to a poor orphan.

Without my even realising it, a feeling of grief was taking hold of me, and also a looseness due perhaps to malnutrition. For management of the money my mother gave me, I can assure you, left much to be desired. And the times, quality and quantity of my meals felt the effects of it.

In class, I had no zeal. Time seemed to move by slowly and I no longer had that confidence in the power of the school to enable me one day to improve the lot of my parents.

I had lost my best positions in class without any regret, any reaction.

And I spent my time thus, indifferent, with no one to guide me or control me.

Often I missed class because I couldn't get out of bed in time on mornings or because, in the afternoons, it was too hot.

When I did not remain in bed in the room, I would go roaming about town, all alone, or in company with friends whom I did not hold in high esteem, but whom I was delighted to find at times such as those; especially in the mango season when you had to go on foot to the orchards situated more than two kilometres from the town.

By now, I knew Fort-de-France inside out.

My predilection was to go into the crowded districts: Bord du Canal, Terres Sainville, Port Démosthène. All those conglomerates of black barracks, tottering crookedly on marshy lands, teeming, with a disconcerting vitality, with children in rags, with noisy women, always quarreling with one another or singing songs, with bare-backed men lazing around not doing anything, which I found—which I had always found, without being able to say why—more admirable than the entire presentable and honorable section of the population.

More than anything else, I liked the port.

That was the area that had left the most lasting impression on me when I first arrived in Fort-de-France; and I was still very much attached to it.

Bord de Mer, all the same, had nothing particularly seductive about the way it looked. It comprised mainly a long strip of debris spewed up by the sea onto the black, slimy sand, mixed with the garbage from nearly all the houses in the town. Then, behind, on the other side of a curving street, stood a series of wholesale food stores, their fronts in various stages of disrepair.

But for me, the port meant, above all, boats of all sizes—steamboats and sail boats—anchored not far from the shore and off-loading in pot-bellied barges cargo from all the ports in France and the West Indies.

A crowd of traders, as arrogant as tall buildings, of attentive, zealous workers, and above all stevedores handling with astonishing rapidity the heavy cases, the huge bags, the enormous barrels that the barges, moving by means of yards, had just off-loaded on the shore.

A grandiose spectacle of men under pressure; under a broiling sun, everything was movement.

Everywhere there was the din of work, made up of the thud of cases being raised and thrown over, of the loud rolling of full barrels, of the dull thump of bags of flour, salt or cereals being piled on one another. Carts squeaked by, trucks moved along, cutting their way through with blasts of their horns.

Men, in an endless chain, carried on their heads bags weighing one hundred kilos, crushed the asphalt on the roadway at a pace that would have made one think of a heavy machine shot forward at full speed. I shuddered at the thought that the slightest false step by one of them, or my imprudent approach to where they were walking, could cause a catastrophe!

And in that port, where there was not one single quay, not one single crane, it was those Herculean black men, dressed in a sackcloth loincloth or in a pair of old breeches, dripping and steaming with sweat, who, by their zeal alone, caused those noises, did all that work, gave off all that hot air, set in motion all that titanesque trepidation, communicating to the entire district a mechanical hum, ably supported by the beating of human hearts.

It was mainly in the afternoons that I would go roaming about the seaside district of Bord de Mer. I would spend a long time looking at a cargo ship as it arrived slowly, scanning the port and the town with its surprised hawse-holes and stealthily coming to take its place among those that berthed before it; or at another that was blowing its whistle, over there, half hidden by the boats closer in, having pulled in its long anchor chain and already was clumsily turning around and beginning to move away, its sides heavy with drums of rum and bags of sugar.

I would look at the men who were using pulleys to hoist from the depths of the hatches, bags, cases, barrels, Norwegian lumber, complete trucks which, once off-loaded, sprang to life under the hand of a driver and moved off.

Admirable too, the handling of cargo by the black giants walking the length and breath of the edges of the barges, one right behind the other, their bodies leaning on long yards to give the necessary impetus. Then the barges having run onto the gravel on the shore, the frenzied rush of the black men grabbing hold of the load to carry it, roll it, pile it up in a large area that stretched between the sea and the street.

And little by little, under the heat of their efforts, they entered a trance that gave their expressions, their gestures, their movement, a frightening intensity and liveliness. At times, at the very peak of this effort, a docker would let out some crude joke that would have the entire crew laughing, injecting into the work yet another superhuman outburst.

Of my own free will, I frittered my time away in Bord de Mer until work was finished. The stores were closing. The trucks had disappeared.

Without my realising it, calm had spread throughout the district. The stevedores remained alone on the shore at the foot of the mountains of merchandise they had just off-loaded. Covered with dust and dirt, they looked like veritable bronze statues. In order to quench the burning thirst that must have been consuming them, they emptied together, and without a twinge of remorse, bottles of strong rum. Afterwards, dropping their loin-cloths or their breeches, they dived into the sea, snorting like pure-breds. Standing in the water up to their navels, they rubbed their skins to get rid of the dirt, all the while talking and laughing with voices that carried far in the silence.

The sun, after lingering a long while on the horizon, had disappeared, melted, one could say, by its own heat.

And the whole twilight belonged to those naked black men—some standing, others swimming—with the silhouettes of the cargo boats riding at anchor and the mauve hills to the back of the port.

The bathers came out of the water without bothering to hide the complete nakedness of their bodies. At that late hour, no one would be passing in that area. They dispersed behind the heap of merchandise, from which they re-emerged, one by one, dressed in white calico or blue drill trousers, fresh cotton shirts and shoes.

They went away towards the town, and the night encroached on all sides.

I had often gone without eating in order to buy a fishing rod, a line and a fish-hook and, along with a few experts at playing truant, I spent entire afternoons on the wooden landing-stage of the old careenage. That was yet another district that met my fancy.

As in Bord de Mer, under huge trees that had grown at random, there were boats and small craft. There were, above all, piles of scrap iron, of anchors and chains made stiff by rust, of ships' hulls, of buoys in the shape of tops, lying on their sides, having turned to minium; all sorts of strange debris on which one could perch, or which offered the most opportune refuge to our clandestine idleness.

The Le Carénage district was next to that of Pont Démosthène, itself less pleasant, as far as I was concerned, since the people living there had nothing that I envied. There was a row of gloomy cafés and hotels, where crew men of all colors from the boats in the port entered, waylaid by women with make-up and ill-fitting clothes, spent hours drinking in a haze of smoke, of toothless laughter, of tasteless music, went up and down the stairs, and left, either staggering or cursing.

It did not look unpleasant on mornings, when I was on my way to school, when the cafés were opening, the sides of the roadway were crowded with women selling fresh coconuts, *corossol doudou, bananes macang'ya,* and when men and women in a hurry, in their work clothes, crossed one another on their way to the town or the Transat. On the contrary, that moment gave it a vigorous, wholesome aspect that invited a close friendship.

But our favorite rendez-vous spot for playing truant was the Jardin Desclieux, the Botanic Gardens.

Everything drew us to that place—the space, the shade, the verdant complicity of its thickets, its fruit trees, especially its mango trees.

Certain lovers of playing truant preferred the Savannah, an enormous natural lawn surrounded by mango trees, whose fruits you could easily pick by throwing stones at them, and enshrining the statue of Joséphine, Empress of the French. To my way of thinking, the Savannah was particularly suited to long games of soccer.

I was one of those that appreciated Jardin Desclieux more. That place, which looked at one and the same time like a small English park, and a French garden, in addition to the lovers' rendez-vous and the places to walk babies to which it lent itself with such grace and innocence, was also marvellously made for playing truant.

There you felt secure and, according to the mood and the season, you could, away from all eyes, devote yourself to picking the mangoes that were turning yellow in the trees, admiring an old crocodile rotting away in a fenced-in pond, or two monkeys chained to little boxes perched atop posts.

You could also sit on a bench opposite a flower-bed to savor the fragrance of the tuberoses, lie in the grass, chat, laugh.

I particularly liked to isolate myself in a thicket to read and occasionally spy on the lovers.

In fact I thoroughly enjoyed following the evolution of certain idylls, from the first rendez-vous to the day of the fatal quarrel and of the disappearance of the two characters.

Sometimes a few weeks later, I would find one of them playing a new pastorale with a new partner.

There were also those liaisons that lasted ever since the beginning of the school year. To my eyes, they were detestable by the impression of monotony with which they risked blemishing the appearance of the garden.

What made this garden even more attractive to us were the bookish characters we all carried there. All the romantic or bucolic evocations from my literature classes or from my reading sought refuge there and became concrete, in order to quench the thirst created in us by the most beautiful verse we had studied.

*

Often, on evenings, to get to Sainte-Thérèse, instead of the main road, I took from Pont Démosthène, a short, sharp rise that climbed Morne-Pichevin and crossed a plateau from which one could see the town and the bay.

This way via Morne Pichevin was by far the shortest to get to Sainte-Thérèse.

There had sprung up, in that area, with the same liveliness, with the same proliferation, shacks of the same type as those in Sainte-Thérèse. But what I liked about this budding district was not only the convenience of reaching home more quickly by cutting through it, but most of all the spectacle of those people who, motivated by a need for well-being and independence, were building shacks helter-skelter, which their triumphant satisfaction made look as beautiful as any work done by pioneers.

It was a phenomenon that would have interested my mother, my grandmother. Unanimously, men had taken a resolution and, immediately, with the means that luck brought their way, began putting it into action.

No doubt those black people who, outside their regular working hours, gaily built those board shacks in the woods of this plateau, possessed even more inspiration, more strength and more drive to build real dwelling places and an entire city, conforming to the very dimensions and colors of the bold dream that inspired their sordid accomplishments.

Great was my grief at leaving the Sainte-Thérèse district.

My mother had received permission from her boss to allow me to spend a few weeks with her during the vacation and, at the instigation of one of her friends, had rented a room near to Route Didier. For as it turned out, at the height where Mr. Lasserous's house stood, there was, nestled in the undulation of the land, below the level of the road, a small agglomeration of some twenty or more shacks rented by the car drivers and maids of the district, living with their families or not housed by their employers for some reason or the other.

This black village was called Petit-Fond and belonged to whites who had little money and who had built it with that in mind, finding therein a sure, discreet and honest means of ensuring themselves some income.

In spite of their resemblance to those in Sainte-Thérèse and Morne-Pichevin, the shacks comprising that abominable island reminded me rather of Black Shack Alley.

Still I was at first delighted at the privilege my mother had had to be able to find a room there and to carry in an old, wobbly, arthritic truck the iron bed, the white wood table, the two chairs, the stool, the two shelves and the few rags and dishes that furnished our room in Sainte-Thérèse.

Long was my sorrow, too, over having lost my freedom. But with the reopening of school, my uneasiness at adapting to this new district disappeared. For didn't Route Didier, in the mouths of those who mentioned its name, possess all that was most wonderful, most desirable and respectable?

At any rate, the circumspectness, the conformity, the obsequiousness that characterised the attitude and the slightest conversations of the servants—the only people with whom I had any sort of contact—said enough about the submission they vowed to their masters and their respect for that place that they did their very best not to disturb in any way, ever mistrustful of their exuberance as black people, and compelling themselves to live as unobtrusively as possible.

Yet, one hardly ever saw the house-owners in Route Didier.

On mornings, at middays and on evenings, I would see in the back of luxury automobiles, a man with a pink complexion, comfortably installed. At times, it would be white women dressed like humming-birds. Or else it would be children looking like angels at Corpus Christi. Occasionally, I would hear them (the women in particular) give orders to their servants in a stuck-up, pretentious voice and in an accent that— I knew not how—associated platitude to pedantry.

The existence of those people was the occupation and essential *raison d'être* of the tenants in Petit-Fond.

I found myself with the latter amidst a category of black people that I did not know before.

No, Petit-Fond didn't resemble Black Shack Alley after all, and I couldn't be with my new neighbors the way I was with my old friends from Petit-Morne or from Sainte-Thérèse.

The people in Black Shack Alley and in Petit-Bourg toiled and moiled like slaves for the *békés;* they put up with them painfully, but did not bear any malice towards them. They did not prostrate themselves before them. Whereas those in Route Didier formed a devoted category, dutifully cultivating the manner of serving the *békés.*

Then, for me who up to that time had known only people working without respite, my amazement became greater and greater at the sight of that corporation whose task—determined by whom I had no idea— and sole concern consisted of doing for others what they could hardly do for themselves. And for what in return? Not even a salary commensurate with their effort. And despite it all, in that world, being a servant in a *béké's* house meant having a decent job.

I could not get accustomed to the passive indigence of the servants, unless I were to believe that people like my grandmother and my mother were duty-bound to take care of, to enhance, to prolong the life of another category of people who did not do and who did not think it their duty to do for them anything whatsoever in return.

I soon had as a pal a car driver from the district. We had become acquainted not in Petit-Fond where he lived, however, but on the road. We met often as I was on my way to school and he was passing in the car. He stopped and invited me to get in. He was no doubt aware that I was the son of Mr. Lasseroux's maid.

On every occasion, it would be a godsend because, four times a day, either in the heavy rain during the rainy season or in the sun of the dry season that softened the asphalt, I would have to trudge on foot the two kilometres that separated me from the town.

He was a young man, barely older than I. And irresistably gay! Always singing and humming. Since he was a bachelor, on those evenings when he left work pretty early, to my great joy, he used to come to see me. But at the same time I was very much afraid that he would be bored in my company. I was so enthused with literature—not stuck on literature, but in love with letters—that I was easily inclined to bring all the conversations round to works I had read or fictitious characters from my readings about whom I loved to talk.

But no, it was he who held sway with his songs and his crude jokes; he who set the tone of our conversations. He did not knock at my door to announce himself, but, once home, whistled a tune he had composed that had become our password and to which I echoed a reply. A few moments later he would arrive. He would push the door, finding me sitting at a table writing or reading beside my kerosine lamp.

"Hello, Jo," he would shout, "had a nice day?"

"Yes, and you?"

"Oh! as for me, those old *békés* tried to spoil my day, but you know,

I don't let evil thoughts enter my head."

"What happened then?"

"Oh! nothing. A *béké,* you know, always feels like whipping the black man serving him."

Atavism, I thought. Gestures must also be in the blood, must also be passed on.

He would sit on the bed to make himself more comfortable and, point-blank, come up with a funny story, anything at all: an ordinary everyday fact that he made enticingly amusing and entertaining.

His name was Carmen.

How embarrassing it was for me at first to call him by a girl's name, this pure-blooded hunk of a man! But little by little I ended up finding, on the contrary, that no other name fitted him better; and that this name even brought out that which was most masculine in him, that which was most rebellious, that which was most Bohemian at the same time, and that it would not at all have been well suited to a woman.

Carmen, it is true, by a series of long digressions in our conversations, had told me the story of his life.

Before him, all the male children his mother had given birth to had died. Some at birth, others somewhat longer afterwards. Four in all. And the girls already numbered five.

"My mother," he told me, "wasn't very lucky with boys. So, I was hardly born before my father rushed and gave me a girl's name, the first one perhaps that came out of his mouth: Carmen. My father was quite clever, for God knows I'm well entrenched in this life. For all that I've already endured! . . . "

Carmen was born on a plantation.

All he had told me about his childhood was so much like what I had been through in Petit-Morne that it seemed to me as if I'd played with him twelve years earlier.

But Carmen had not taken another turn the way I had. He had followed in its natural stages the destiny of one born in Black Shack Alley. He hadn't told me so in as many words but the traits he exhibited according to his mood suggested to me—judging from my own personal experiences—all the development of the twenty years he had spent on the plantation.

"Look at this," he said to me, pulling down his shirt collar. "You see that scar there, on my neck? Looking like the mark from a rope on the skin of a beast? Well! that's my first childhood memory."

"My papa, my maman, my five bigger sisters, everybody used to go to work. Right away, my two other sisters used to dump me on some rags on the floor in the shack, close the door, and go off to play with the other children on the plantation.

"So, one day, I was thirsty no doubt; I cried, screamed, creeping as far as the ray of light I could see below the door which had an opening to the bottom of it made by the dampness which had rotted away the wood; I pushed my head through the opening. But it was impossible to move forward and just as impossible to move back.

"I screamed and did all I could. The others were too far away to hear me, or paid scant attention to my screaming.

"I remained there a long time until that evening when my parents found me with my neck half sawn off by the door. You can imagine the commotion to get me out of there. I'm not aware of all that; it's my maman who told me about it. But I still have something to remind me of it; that doesn't lie."

Carmen often repeated that story, always in a different tone—sometimes with indignation, sometimes with sarcasm, at others with pride.

Another time, talking about an ox, Carmen told me:

"You know, when I was about seven, an ox walked on my back. At that time, I was a "shirt head" . . .

That meant that he would wear a shirt made of jute, covering his whole body, with the exception of his head, his arms and his feet, and his job was to walk in front of the teams to guide the oxen in the roads of the plantation.

One day, there had been such heavy showers that the feet of the workers, the hooves of the beasts and the wheels of the carts had dug up the 'traces' like a plough.

"At every step, splash! I sank down to my knees. The cart driver kept harrassing me with threats and curse words. I couldn't take it any longer . . . Can you imagine, walking like that, for hours on end, in a muddy stretch of land that gripped you around the ankles and prevented you from moving forward!

"Eh, wake up, faker," the cart driver shouted, "or I'll ram this goad up your ass. Look, I'm not going to get caught by the commander because you're blocking the oxen's path!

"My little legs couldn't hold out any longer, my head was splitting with fear, I toppled over and collapsed . . .

"It was the cart driver himself who came and hauled me out of the mud. He had jumped down from the cart as he saw the first ox place his foot on me. I don't know how I didn't end up with my spine broken!"

Carmen had been a mule driver, a fact that had earned him a long stay in the hospital, following a fall in which he had broken his shoulder-blade.

Then he had done his military service.

Oh! that was really the biggest event in his life.

"I had caught the dreaded disease; but I didn't play the fool; I told the doctor and it didn't last."

After his military service, as he liked Fort-de-France, he had remained there.

Then there were happy memories that he evoked at moments of serenity and when he was down in the dumps. For instance, those of nights aflame with fires and drums, those of innumerable, burning love affairs in the cane plantations. Or other more recent memories from Route Didier.

"Jo, imagine, old pal, that this morning . . . "

It often began in this way and was a story about a woman, a love story. For Carmen's existence was teeming with women.

"Women have always been a problem for me," he confided to me mischievously. "Think I was barely thirteen when 'big women' started their traps to have me satisfy whatever it was I aroused in them. That wasn't very lucky for me, for I have never been free to choose a woman. I've always been called, pursued, forced. I can assure you it's boring."

Thus, whenever he left me after a visit that seemed somewhat shortened, I immediately understood that he had a lover's rendez-vous. I had only to look as if I understood what was going on and he would whisper in my ear the name of the young maid he was going to see then and rush off with a hearty laugh, as if to poke fun at himself.

It could have been said that Carmen ran after women as a joke, so blatant did it appear that there was more fun than passion in his moves. So much so that he seemed to think that women were to make love to and laugh at afterwards.

Nevertheless, he was quite worried at times when a young girl he fancied began to get too fond of him, or when a woman he no longer bothered with took it into her head to go and abuse, right in the open street or in the middle of the Fort-de-France market, his latest conquest, the one he wanted to keep seeing for some time yet.

"But what can one do with them, these women? Screaming at each other, why? For something that doesn't belong to one or the other . . . "

Carmen ended up laughing at everything.

Some nights, Carmen came in whistling and, without speaking, pulled up a chair and began to beat out rhythms with his fingers on the edge of the table.

They were plantation songs that I also knew for the most part. But when he stopped whistling and switched to singing, his words were new to me. The black people on the plantations were so eager to sing and spread the songs that moved from district to district that they paid scant attention to the words, being content with the tune to which one of their songwriters adapted words, most often relating to some local bit of news.

Carmen continued, singing and whistling, softly beating out drum rhythms with such intense inspiration, such gaiety and sensual vigor, that I spent a long time listening to him, speechless, almost in a trance.

Suddenly, putting an end to his singing, Carmen got up like a gust of wind and said to me:

"Well! Jo, I'm going to bed."

"Already!"

"Yes, old pal, I hardly parked at all today. Then, it was hot."

Thereupon, he offered me his hand and said, with a yawn:

"See you tomorrow."

Often too, having stopped his music, Carmen would ask me straight off:

"Well! Jo, what's everyone talking about?"

It was then certain that he had some piece of news to give me. In general something about the *békés,* an amusing anecdote about himself or the reasons behind the dismissal of such and such a driver.

The fact remained that every visit from Carmen brought some new detail, thanks to which I got a closer and more detailed picture of Route Didier on a day to day basis.

I had already understood at least that it comprised the most affluent people, the most powerful whites in the country, descended from the Great-Whites of colonial times—at the same time the most harmful—on the one hand, and on the other, black servants, the only people with whom I was in contact without quite sharing their lives, and who were firmly convinced, *a priori,* of the superiority of these whites in power and in virtue.

Likewise, I knew the name of the owner of every villa, the bank or business place he went to by car every morning.

I saw that Route Didier was not only an area of aristocrats, but that from one end of that double row of stylish dwellings to the other there flowed the same blood, the blood of the *béké* race, that the offspring from one house could be found in the house across the street, married to that of the house next door; that a local white did not marry outside his local white clan. And that clearly confirmed the feeling I had that the inhabitants of the country were in fact divided into three categories: Blacks, Mulattoes, Whites (not to mention the subdivisions); that the first—by far the most numerous—were the cheap, common lot, like wild fruits, tasty, but too willingly doing without care; the second set could be considered as a grafted species; and the others, although ignorant, or uncouth for the most part, constituted the rare, precious species.

Of my last visit to Petit-Bourg, there remained one of those feelings of grief that overwhelmed me every time I began to think about M'man Tine's condition.

I had been startled to find her diminished by the withering clutches of misery. Her room, too, grew darker and more dilapidated. There were new rotten floor boards, new holes in the ceiling; the table, all distorted, its legs eaten away by the dampness. The picture was the same throughout the rest of Cour Fusil with, in the middle, its gutter stagnating with the water from the kitchens and body ablutions of all the inhabitants; similarly, the entire village, whose alley I found almost overtaken by grass and littered with piles of garbage. An empty plot of land where we used to play had been taken back by the factory to which it belonged and planted with sugar cane.

On the other side of the river, compact cane fields stood reaching over the water, ready to cross over and come and snuff out the village.

M'man Tine had fallen ill in the middle of the week. She complained of a pain in her left side that reached all the way to her back.

"A gas pain," the neighbors diagnosed.

At their advice, I made the patient garlic skin tisanes, which made her emit awful belches.

She also complained about her head. Ah! she could not stand the weight of her head, so heavy and painful it felt to her. So, Mam'zelle Délice wrapped it in *palma christi* leaves and soft candle.

Then there were her eyes.

"All of a sudden," she said, "it's as if a lamp has been blown out, at night, in a room, and here I am in utter darkness, with the ground giving out and moving from under me."

"Eyes, that's a bit ticklish," Mr. Assionis had said. "For that, you must have a li'l séance."

That Saturday night, since she had worked the first three days of the week, M'man Tine sent me to Petit-Morne to collect her pay for her.

In the ten years since we had left Black Shack Alley, I had never set foot in Petit-Morne and the memories I had of the place were even rather hazy. On taking the paths that led to it, I therefore felt a strange delight.

Despite the grief in my heart as a result of my grandmother's illness, I felt joy surge in me every now and then as I crossed, bare-footed, my head in the breeze, the countryside swept by wave after wave of sugar cane.

And I even recognised in the distance the trees, roads, savannahs and the mouths of the rivers I had so passionately frequented in former times, in the company of all my little naked, tattered, runny-nosed, scrofulous, hilarious or snivelling friends.

The sunset was similar in brilliance, in mellowness and in expression to all those I'd seen cast their halo around the hills.

Payments of wages had just begun. As they had not yet come to the weeders, M'man Tine's category, I stood a bit to the side, trying to remain unseen.

However, the crowd had noticed me and I could hear voices in whispers enquiring who I was. Fortunately, as the payment of wages continued, attention turned away from me.

Now, my curiosity and enthusiasm had disappeared, giving way to a feeling as gloomy, dreary and doleful as the scene, so familiar in the early days, that I was then witnessing.

It seemed as if I should recognise almost those workers by their names, by their voices; but I tried my best not to force the point too much. Perhaps I had doubts about what my reaction would be on once again seeing my childhood friends. If not, by what other act of cowardice? . . .

"Sonson-cross-eye!"

I recognised the man calling out the names.

" 'sent."

"Eighteen francs."

Still more names.

Some time went by.

"Marie-old-woman!"

" 'sent," I answered.

And I went up to the pay-window.

Everybody had turned towards me. A murmur spread through the crowd.

"You're collecting for her," the overseer said to me in patois (he was new, I didn't know him; Mr. Gabriel's replacement, no doubt).

"Yes, monsieur," I replied.

"Eleven francs fifty," he said.

And placing the point of his pencil on the tip of his tongue, he asked me:

"What's your name?"

"José! . . . I'm her son."

A great clamor of voices arose in the crowd around me.

"Just as I thought. See, it's José!"

And from among that pack of foul-smelling, dung-colored beings, earth-stained hands, the friendliest in creation, however, stretched out towards me, amidst the brightest smiles that happiness could bestow upon such glum faces.

I was being congratulated for having grown up. Some of them said to me:

"Heard you're in a fine school in Fort-de-France; that's very good."

Others challenged me to say what their names were to prove I still remembered them, and hugged me tightly when I managed to do so at the first shot.

I could only smile, squeeze their hands with all my might, allow myself to be pulled and tugged from left to right, intimidated by all those simultaneous bursts of affection.

But when, armed with the eleven francs fifty that had been given to me in payment for the three days work my grandmother had done, I found myself alone on the way home, I suddenly felt descend upon me the great weight of remorse—something both burdensome and vague like a feeling of the blues; indignation at my behavior; shame at a certain powerlessness of character on my part. It seemed to me that there had been something I could have said, that I hadn't even thought of . . .

At any rate, I had suffered.

I was now in the first year of my final class at school.

The *baccalauréat* appeared to us as a strait gate beyond which there existed the vastness that was offered.

I painfully observed on occasions that I was not a student like the others.

Geometry theorems, laws of physics, established opinions on literary works, nothing in all that managed to kindle any flame in me, in polarising my energy, in creating in me that intellectual zeal with which my school mates would endlessly discuss questions that seemed irrelevant to me.

Nor did I share the anxiety with which each one measured up his chances of success.

The subjects taught at the *lycée* did not inspire me in the least. I worked for working's sake. I endured them.

Until then, all I had been content to do was to move from class to class without any examination and to see my scholarship increase to the point of being a full scholarship at present.

I remained in a haze from which, impassively, I looked at those who shone with false brilliance, the dunces, the plodders. There were always, however, in every class one or two students whom I considered as having genuine value.

I belonged to no category. I was supposed to be good at English. Nevertheless, I didn't work at it particularly hard. I was rather average than weak in mathematics, because it took nothing out of me to learn my lessons and because I did them out of kindness for the teacher who, for his part, put so much of himself into his teaching.

Our History and Geography teacher talked too much, and in a tart, threadlike voice that reminded you of a constant drizzle. So, just as when it was raining, while he was doing his class, I would day-dream, my eyes staring into space.

In French, I was among those at the bottom of the class, but that didn't bother me.

Nothing ever seemed to me so well-conceived to turn you away from all study, from all reading itself, as those wretched little books called *Le Cid, Le Misanthrope, Athalie.*

One day the teacher said:

"We're going to study Corneille. Do you have your Corneille?"

Some did; others didn't.

"Le Cid, act I, scene 2."

Sometimes he himself read, sometimes he had one student read, with another giving the reply. More or less anyway. For, whether it was the teacher or the students who did the reading, it was so flatly, so indistinctly droned out, broken up, that we were all plunged into a dreadful daze.

At the end of the class, Mr. Jean-Henri, the teacher, dictated a text for homework on the 'Corneillean hero'. In the following class, *Horace* or *L'Avare*. Same old story.

I can't remember if it happened exactly like that, but such is the overall impression that that teaching left me. There were, however, students who obtained good grades and who passed for being strong in French. They consulted, it seemed, studies, manuals and model answers. For my part, once home, I would try to re-read *Le Cid*. After a while, I would find it much more interesting than I'd done in class. I was about to shout: "How beautiful!" but I didn't have the time for that bit of luxury; the next time we went on to *Horace*. No, I must have been too slow to catch on.

At times, I had ideas on the subject, but as I hadn't found them in any book, the way the older boys in the class did, I did not dare come out with them for fear of appearing stupid, and I tried in vain to doctor the notes taken in class to charm the teacher, if not to avoid being criticized. For the teacher loved quotations—proof that the student had done his research, had really worked. Well, too bad; I was just weak in French.

Only, I wasn't certain that many of those who were at the head of the class had any more of a flair for literature than I. You could tell from their discussions . . .

But, all in all, the level of the class was low in French.

"You have nothing in your heads," our teacher repeated every day.

Exasperated by our weakness, one day he gave as a subject for composition: "Your most moving childhood memory."

"Now you're talking!" I thought immediately. "This time, no

question of digging around in books."

Going back to Petit-Morne, I remembered the death of Médouze. Consumed by inspiration, I wrote my essay at one go. Then I meticulously set about correcting it, polishing it up, calling on all the recommendations on composition and style, sifting everything through the rules of spelling.

I was happy that I had devoted so much time to the assignment and that I had worked so hard on it.

One week later, results of the correction:

"Another disaster!" Mr. Jean-Henri announced. "How weak you are! Poor vocabulary, no syntax, no ideas. I've rarely seen students so indigent."

And he began to produce the better scripts—two or three. Then in bulk, the compositions of all the mediocre students. No sight of mine. Oh yes, at the last minute, just as I was in the depths of disappointment and despair.

"Hassam," he said in a deliberate manner.

I stood up. I would have blushed if it were possible to show up on my face.

"Hassam," Mr. Jean-Henri continued, unfolding my assignment, you're the most cynical chap I've ever met! When you have to do literary essays, you're never brave enough to consult the works recommended; but for an assignment as subjective as this one, it seemed easier to you to open a book and copy passages from it."

Lightning could not have dealt me a more violent blow.

A gush of heat burned my face, my ears were ringing, my vision became blurred. I thought that blood was going to rush from every opening in my head. My throat felt as if a rough rope was being pulled tightly around it.

"I didn't copy, monsieur," I stammered.

Holding my assignment open between his fingers, he spoke to the entire class.

"Listen to this . . . "

He read aloud, and in a sarcastic tone of voice, two sentences, three sentences.

"And then this," he continued . . . "And the little no-good is going to tell me he didn't copy? Didn't copy? Then it's plagiarised!"

"Monsieur, I can assure you I didn't . . . "

"Shut up!" he shouted, pounding the table.

He handed me back my assignment, his lips pursed in scorn, and added:

"At any rate, you no longer amuse me with this little game, for I don't like people making a fool of me. Here."

He was so indignant that the paper fell from his hand.

I went and picked it up and, back in my seat, I hid it in a book, without even having the courage to look at the comments written on it.

But that night, back in my room, I wanted to see what was scribbled in red ink. The passages the teacher accused me of having "copied from some books" were precisely those that were the most personal to me and which had come most directly, without any reminiscence.

I then felt pride urging me on to set to work in such a way as to produce consistently good assignments, until such time as the teacher was forced to recognise my honesty. But I smiled at his accusation. No, I preferred to agree to pass for a dunce in French. It was all the same to me.

That year the health of M'man Tine preoccupied me much more than the preparation of my *baccalauréat*. For some time, I had been haunted by the fear that my grandmother would die. It seemed to me that time wasn't passing quickly enough to bring me to the day when I'd start working so I could deliver my mother, and especially my grandmother, from dependency.

When I had left her the last time, M'man Tine had again gone back to the cane fields; but she no longer felt any strength within her; and if she continued to weed the tall grass, its roots firmly embedded in the black clay of the cane plantations, it was simply because misery did not choose death by violence, preferring to await, at the right time, the decisive completion of some apparently banal malaise.

I wrote to my grandmother every week, telling her over and over that I was soon going to leave school, no doubt to work in an office, and that when that happened, she and M'man Délia would both be re-united with me in my house. I sent her at the same time a pinch of tobacco gathered from the ends of cigarettes that Mr. Lasseroux left in his ashtrays and that my mother used to collect every day. And I was filled with a feeling of great relief at the end of the month when, having collected the one hundred and fifty francs from my scholarship, I went, with my mother's approval, to send her a postal order for twenty francs.

Sometimes too, when it was raining in November and the storm thundered away, M'man Délia would look up to the heavens and sigh aloud:

"Poor M'man Tine!"

I wouldn't say a word. My heart would become heavy and ready to break like the weather. If we were at the table, M'man Délia would stop eating, I would push my plate back and get up, clamping my jaws together so as not to break down.

Now, Carmen had become my best friend. Not only because we lived so close to each other and he shared so many secrets with me, but another reason was yet to come into play.

One evening, I was telling him, I think:

"Tomorrow, history essay; day after tomorrow, natural sciences essay . . . "

Carmen interrupted me:

"Jo, you don't find I'm an idiot?"

I burst out laughing.

"A real idiot, I tell you!" Carmen explained.

And he seemed to accuse himself thus, without any reason, innocently, but with utmost conviction.

"What do you mean, old pal?" I said at last.

"Listen," he continued, "look how long we know each other, how we frequent each without any fuss, how we talk and laugh and have fun together, and all this time, what has prevented me from asking you about a few li'l things? I'm sure you wouldn't have refused me . . . It's annoying, I can't sign my name. I never told you, I don't know why, but I don't even know my alphabet."

In fact, this request, despite its simplicity, struck me as a reproach. Why hadn't I been the one to offer my services to Carmen? Didn't I realise that he must have suffered from his illiteracy, all so obvious besides? Could I have any doubts about all the satisfaction he would have experienced in conquering it?

"But, Carmen," I cried, "what ever prevented me indeed from . . . "

Thus, Carmen became my pupil.

Things were still the way they were before—a whistle to warn me, the door he would push open. But from then on, he went straight to my writing table, opened his slim book, took his little blue or pink-covered exercise book.

I then showed him one by one, and each one over and over again, those small figures whose shapes and names were at first so impressive and difficult to remember. I tried my best to get him to hold a pencil between his fingers.

"It's funny," he told me, "that I can do anything I want with the steering wheel of a car in my hands, and I'm unable to make a little circle properly with a pencil as light as a straw. It's funny that, with the steering wheel in my hand, I can even steer the car along a bad piece of road without falling to my right or to my left, and I can't manage to guide my pencil between the two lines of the exercise book! . . . "

And there was on his face a sad smile that I had to quickly wipe off with a word or encouragement.

Which was greater—his joy at learning to read and to trace his letters, or mine at seeing my pupil improve with a rapidity that made me think more of the effectiveness of my teaching than of his intelligence?

It was he who had decreed that we would no longer speak patois, something I was reluctant to suggest to him. It was he who fixed to his liking the length of our sessions, even to the point of making me neglect my personal work to try to satisfy the zeal he showed for working.

Some evenings, he was not up to it. After a short written exercise, he would put away his text book, his exercise book, his other things in the place he had assigned them on my table. He would never take his stuff home.

"The women who come to see me like to dig around in my room too much," he explained.

And when he didn't leave right away, we would begin to talk, on the contrary, as if he'd just arrived.

However, Carmen had not, for all that he was now doing, toned down his ardent desire to run after women. You could also have said that since he began learning to read and write, he showed more boldness in many things. His tastes in love affairs had even changed. He was now taken up with a mulatto woman whose husband owned a large café near the square on the Savannah. An affair that had been going on for some weeks.

"Look," Carmen showed me, "all over my body is full of teeth marks she leaves when she kisses me so that during the day I can feel as I'm still with her, or so she says."

I was in stitches. Carmen must undoubtedly have found me too childish, rather silly.

"Don't laugh," he cried, "it's actually hurting me. Look, this bite on my shoulder, that's from two nights ago."

Or he would throw questions at me when I least expected them.

"Say, Jo, what's this thing called poetry?"

On the spur of the moment, I was once again caught off guard. I tried to do the best I could all the same. I took up a book, read a few lines of verse. I explained. Still, my demonstration left Carmen skeptical.

"Don't understand."

"What d'you mean you don't understand? Poetry, as I said, is . . ."

"But it can't be only that. This afternoon, she shouted: "Darling, darling, you are sheer poetry!"

I doubled up with laughter, my body wracked with a fit of coughing.

"Boy, you're stupid!" Carmen said, "stupid, I tell you!"

And when I finally calmed down, he continued:

"Well! as for me, at the time when she said that, it wasn't books or sonnets I was giving her."

"But poetry, Carmen," I continued, returning to my schoolmaster tone of voice, "is not only words, lines of verse, books. It can be any other thing that produces a similar effect."

"Then, she didn't say anthing wrong. I'm a poet."

He broke off with that woman because she was too much in love with him. About that time, it was another one from the same type of milieu, who was also responsible for Carmen once more testing my vocabulary. She called him: *"Mon violon d'Ingres."*

Like all the rich house-owners in Route Didier, Mr. Mayel, Carmen's boss, went to mass on Sundays in the district chapel, accompanied by his family in full strength.

For all that (and this Carmen had me swear not to repeat), on certain Fridays in the month, he had himself driven before dawn and through the remotest of roads, to see the old *sorciers* who, in their shacks on the hills, held at the disposition of whites and blacks alike the powers of black magic.

From time to time, he would have an evening get-together during which the poorer whites who lived in plain little houses in the shade of the beautiful villas would come, with their wives, like poor relatives, to help the mistress of the house, to serve as *maîtres d'hôtel* and discreetly enjoy the company of their rich co-religionists.

In addition, Mr. Mayel kept, in one of the semi-populous districts of the town, a young black girl who had had two little mulattoes by him. This woman was a sort of second boss for Carmen, a bastard boss he pretended to respect as much as Mme Mayel and who, in return, made some show of having much consideration and condescension for him.

Of course, being the mistress of a white man represented a very enviable situation for an ordinary lower-class woman in the West Indies, and even for some girls from the colored lower middle-class.

Beside the material advantages to be derived—jewels, little things for the woman herself or little bits of real estate—there was the impression, to one's own eyes and to those of all others, of being chosen, even of moving up the social ladder.

"And yet, Carmen, I don't see anything else but a manifestation of the same scorn contained in everything the creole white does when it comes to dealing with blacks. Don't you think that, in the final analysis, it's better for a black woman to be a servant in the *béké's* house and make love with a black man, rather than be held in reserve for the needs of a master who comes to relieve himself whenever, the night before, his lady has turned her back to him or because she's too old; and whom, even in the intimacy of love-making, you dare not call anything else but 'Monsieur'?"

When you think that those little bastard mulattoes, born of those unions, who don't even have the right to call 'papa' in public or to walk up to their *béké* fathers, grow up with the arrogance or not having a

black skin, and never miss an opportunity to hark back to the white side
of their origins . . .

Moreover, their mothers will help them to a large extent. Everyone
knows that when such liaisons produce children with the 'redeeming'
complexion, their mothers are only too proud that they—black like the
blackboard of the conscience of the *béké*—have contributed to what, in
the inferiority complex, is dear to the hearts of many West Indian
blacks: "Lightening the race."

For, to my great despair, I detected in Carmen's mind the attitudes
that betrayed all of those West Indian complexes, so contrary to all
dignity.

Carmen was silent for a long while.

"So, what to do?" he said "Sleep with all the *békés'* women,
until . . . "

And his hearty laughter filled the whole room.

Then he told me a story:

"I once knew in Macouba a *béké*—wasn't even very rich—which
possibly explains why he was shacking up under the same roof with a
black woman with whom he had five children, boys and girls. All of
which positively horrified his relatives.

"He died. While he was in the throes of death, he sent for the notary
and bequeathed all his worldly goods to his five children: a few plots of
land and a dozen head of cattle. The woman had always loved him very
much, and was very distraught to see him die. Now, seeing that he had
taken such good care of his children, she said to him:

" 'You're very generous. May you go to heaven. But if one day, by
some stroke of misfortune, the children were to lose what you're
leaving for them, what will they have from you?'

"And she implored him to recognise his five children, so that they
could keep the name of their father as the heritage least likely to perish.

"Well! true as I'm a fool sitting here, the old *béké* didn't accept. At
death's door though he was, he replied:

" 'My name never belonged to anyone but white people. It's not a
name for mulattoes.' "

*

It was nice, on mornings, walking all the way to school.

The air would be pure and the shadows still had the same charm
that captivated when I first arrived in Route Didier.

The gardens in particular remained constantly beautiful. In reality,
they did not seem to be of outstanding taste, but the hibiscus trees that
formed hedges around them, the large carpet-like lawns, the palm trees
in all different species, the blooming rose trees, the gleaming begonias,

the bougainvillaeas of insolent colors, wildly climbing up to the balconies, had an indescribable air of serenity and joy about them.

I knew the gardeners in almost all the houses that were on the route I took to school.

As I passed, I exchanged greetings with them from over the tops of the hedges and on Sunday afternoons I was sometimes delightfully surprised when one of them came by to see me.

Often, too shy to come by himself, one had brought a friend along, and they both arrived, friendly and reserved, almost respectful—to my great confusion.

"For a few days now," they would say by way of compliment and apology, "we've been promising to come and see you, but we didn't know if you'd like that. Anyway, we felt like it."

I would clear all the books and papers from my table so as to prepare the punch.

Their conversations slowly retraced their births on some hill or some plantation, their turbulent, easy-going childhoods, their experiences in the *petites-bandes* or the very little time they had spent in school, time that was cut short almost as soon as it started. They had all started from the same point, having followed the same path.

They too did not complain about anything. Their condition seemed justified in their eyes by the existence and presence of the *békés*—since there were *békés*, then their place had to be on top and on the shoulders of the blacks.

They admitted that the seventy-five or eighty francs they received every month, in addition to their meals, did not even meet the cost of a regular suit. But how they dreamed, for example, of learning to drive a car; becoming a driver, earning one hundred and fifty francs like Carmen; renting a room in Petit-Fond for fifty francs a month . . . of climbing the rungs of the servant world.

"And we can't humiliate ourselves again by going to work for the *békés* in old, ragged clothes. We must always be clean. We too have our pride."

Every now and then, on my way to the *lycée,* I would notice the absence of such and such a gardener from where I was accustomed to see him. That evening, Carmen would confirm that he had been fired; or that he had left of his own accord, alleging that he was going to see a relative of his who was sick and that he would return. Two days later, he would be replaced and his replacement, seeing me pass by always at the same times, would also exchange greetings of kindness with me.

So it was that one morning, catching a glimpse of the new gardener at the Villa des Balisiers, I jumped as if something in his look had struck me. However, the man was too far away for me to make out clearly the features of his face.

The following morning, he was again at the other end of the garden, a hose nozzle in his hand. I stopped. He turned towards me, looked at me, letting the stream of water spurting from the hose fall on the lawn.

Then he made a gesture, the same gesture as I; as if the same impression had bounced between him and me.

I wanted to get closer, but it was he who put down his hose and, in swift, agile strides, skipped over the beds and ran towards me.

"But it's Hassam!" he cried.

". . . Jojo!"

We stood still, facing each other.

I offered my hand, but he drew me vigorously to him and we embraced each other, patting each other on the shoulder.

Jojo's mouth, outlined by the thick line of a moustache, his broad shoulders and his body in his old khaki suit made me aware more than the figure I was hastily seeking, of the long years since we'd seen each other. I'd even have said he had grown more than I.

Though we were the same age, I looked like a mere adolescent beside him, so sun-burnt, so tough, so tall and strapping.

"Say, this is where you are, Hassam? Where are you working?"

"My mother works with Mr. Lasseroux."

But my reticence didn't go unnoticed and, glancing at the two books under my arm, he said:

"You're still at school?"

"Yes, at the *lycée.*"

I couldn't tell whether I had managed to inject into my reply the objective simplicity through which I wanted to erase any difference between my friend and me.

"Already got the *bachot?*" he asked me.

"I'm taking Part One this year."

"I'm glad," Jojo said.

In his eyes there remained a warm glow and he repeated:

"I'm glad for you, Hassam!"

That whole day I remained shaken by the shock of that encounter.

My joy at once again seeing my old boyhood pal was followed by my amazement at finding Georges Roc, son of Mr. Justin Roc, and Jojo who did not go to the village school without shoes, who lived in one of the loveliest houses in Petit-Bourg, whose parents had a car, a servant, . . . finding Jojo in Route Didier, working as a gardener, or rather as a houseboy, for, in Route Didier, gardener was the name given the man who did everything around the house.

It was as if Jojo had stopped living in order to appear before me that morning in a reincarnation that was one of the most unforeseeable.

All through that day, our encounter haunted my mind.

I wracked my brains over it.

I tried to understand, and I thought to myself that Georges Roc, son of the first foreman at the factory in Petit-Bourg, was also the son of Gracieuse, a black woman working as a weeder on a plantation, and that he had run away to his mother because in his father's house, in order to be brought up correctly, he was ill-treated, deprived of his freedom, forbidden to play with boys of his age and soundly beaten for the slightest error.

Then, from his mother's, in the country, no doubt near a plantation, he had taken the road fatal to all the little boys whose parents work in the canes.

There was no need for him to confide his secrets in me to understand how he had ended up where he was.

Give or take a few minor details.

*

"I was working in Pavillon, y'know," he told me, "that plantation near the Poirier factory. Well! during the harvest, I was a mule driver and, in the off-season, a ditch digger. There was a manager who, like most managers, doctored the figures on their books to make the blacks earn even less than the salary the *békés* sent for them. Now, thanks to my famous uncle Stephen, I still had something in my head which meant I wasn't quite a dumb sheep, and as I could see everything wasn't correct, every Saturday, as if it were the most casual and natural thing in the world, I would mutter under my breath: 'Thief!', just like that, without seeming to have done it on purpose.

"Then, one Saturday night, it was too much to bear.

"As no one wanted to listen to me, I shouted to all the workers who were gathered there: 'What the hell are you waiting for to set fire to the damn cane fields? Can't you see it's that that makes it miserable to be black!' "

"You, Jojo, you said that?"

"Sure, I said it, because I had suffering and rage like fire in my whole body. Immediately, the manager stopped paying and shouted to me: 'If you don't shut your damn mouth, I'll call the police right away.' But they couldn't scare me, y'know. As the saying goes: 'After good morning comes how are you?' And vexation for vexation: 'Just remain there, see if I don't plant a kick in you' backside,' the manager said to me.

"Y'know, a mulatto (and I have a bit of the blood in me, alas!) is always ready to shout 'dirty nigger' and to threaten to kick. But that night, every word fell on me like oil on fire. Then. there are times when one feels one is full to capacity, that one has to burst or explode.

"Then, the manager came out of his office. He came towards me. The whole crowd shouted in terror, but nobody dared to stop him. And crack! I felt the sharp kick of his shoe on my leg. No use telling you I didn't give him time to give me another one. Yes, before the overseer and the commander could step in, I had already cuffed him a good few times in his face. And, whoosh, I was gone.

"But they set the police after me. I was arrested.

"I did six months in prison, here, in Fort-de-France.

"After three months of detention, I was brought, along with other prisoners, to work in the gardens of the Secretary General of the Government.

"When I finished serving my time, I really wanted to go back to the country; for since last you saw me, it's as if my head has been through the flames of hell. Quite simply, I'm not afraid of anything; but I must be pointed out on every plantation. So, I ended up here. And now I've found you again.

"Life is real funny!"

I did not have anything to tell him. My life was insignificant.

*

I did not pass my examinations. I wasn't upset in the least, for that was the logical result of my school year. I had never understood why the things I had normally learned with the greatest of pleasure became so unpleasant to me the moment they became part of the syllabus of an examination.

My mother was very heart-broken over my failure.

Jojo and Carmen, who had put up money in advance to buy a bottle of champagne in anticipation of my success, did not want this champagne to remain on their hands—it was drunk to my future success.

Thereupon, I made out my time-table and started to work again, going over my books from the first page, and each one at the times I felt to be the most appropriate. I worked all day long and, on evenings, would take a walk on the road to admire the gardens and breathe the air they gave off—whenever I didn't have a visit from Carmen for his grammar and arithmetic exercises.

For his part, Jojo had taken a sort of subscription in reading material from my books. Since leaving school, he confessed to me, he had not read ten lines.

One night, as he looked at the few books bought, collected or received at random, and covered and arranged with rather touching care, perhaps, on shelves I had made from old boxes, he said to me:

"Jo, it'll be nice of you if you could see, when you have the time, whether among your books there isn't an old one you could lend me; one you'll hardly be needing, one that could interest me. I'll take good care of it."

I started by lending him the books I had devoured when I was in my first year. Jojo surprised me by the amount he could read in the little free time he had.

Carmen read much less, but reading produced in him a feeling of upheaval, a veritable charm in which he sometimes delighted for several weeks, in company with the characters of such and such a novel, or such and such a writer whose style, for instance, had plunged him into a state of deep rapture. On each occasion, he had to wait for his emotional state to be completely dispelled before asking me for another book. Thus, he remained God knows how long literally overwhelmed by the reading of *Batouala* by René Maran. He didn't like romantic novels. Nor did he have any weakness for adventure novels.

"When I'm in bed in hospital for months on end, you can bring me books like those. It'll help me to kill time."

In particular, he liked novels that made him regret he was not strong enough in 'writing' to do similar ones.

"I can assure you I wouldn't write for fun or to make you forget. I'd like to write books that would make people bite their thumbs till they bleed."

He liked Balzac, Gorki, Tolstoy, and condemned Jojo's affection for Pierre Loti.

But the day I had him read *Banjo,* by Claude McKay, he was beside himself with joy.

As if not to be outdone by me, Carmen and Jojo would take me to the cinema on Tuesday or Friday nights. In the largest cinema in Fort-de-France, the popular crowd that formed the clientele of those evening shows at reduced prices went to see the projection of the first combinations of sound and motion in the West Indies.

We would set off on foot after dinner.

Under an electric light, sparing and indigent, the interior of the cinema was always full, alive with boisterous shouting. The floor area, the stairs resounded and cracked under the feet of the members of the public who, before the start of the show, moved about in all directions, called out to one another, talked, shouted and erupted into bursts of laughter, as if each one had taken a bet to dominate everything by his voice alone.

The seats in the stalls were folding wooden chairs, arranged in rows on wooden blocks. This was where all the young ragged patrons, the untidily dressed, the brawlers, both men and women, with or without shoes, sat. It was there that we too sat. The most humorous, the most quarrelsome were always the same. A man would spot a woman by herself and would go over to touch her and whisper some rude words to her, to which she would reply with an eruption of curse words. A woman, on the contrary, would get up on a chair and begin to sing and dance, using her charms to urge the others on.

There was always someone who, no sooner inside, would bump into the first person on his way, square up and start a fight.

There were also the peaceful ones who, over in a little corner, would look on calmly and suspiciously.

The lights would go out one by one and everybody would scramble to the chairs to sit down.

At the first images on the screen, the cinema would become relatively silent. For all that, in the darkness, conversations and comments continued, attracting anonymous replies that clashed, exploding into violent discussions laced with jeers and threats.

In the long run, however, the atmosphere turned out to be inoffensive and even pleasant—simply foreign.

We discussed various things as we walked back from the cinema. Lively discussions that livened our pace and made us arrive so quickly that we lingered a while yet on the road to exhaust our topics, taking care to keep down the sound of our voices so as not to make the dogs start barking.

The "Black Shack Alley" style that characterized all that in this country was destined for the people or conceived by persons of dark complexions made me sad and indignant.

Shouldn't every enterprise in such a country also aim to promote the people?

Carmen, Jojo and I all enjoyed commenting on the films we had just seen and our discussions were never more impassioned than when the film had a black character.

For example, who was it who created for the cinema and the theater that type of black man, houseboy, driver, footman, truant, a pretext for words from simple minds, always rolling their white eyes in amazement, always with a silly irrepressible smile plastered on their faces, provoker of mockery? That black man with his grotesque behavior under the kick in his backside proudly administered by the white man, or when the latter had him hoodwinked with an ease that is explained by the theory of the 'black man being a big child?'

Who was it who invented for the blacks portrayed in the cinema and in the theater that language the blacks never could speak and in which, I am sure, no black man will manage to express himself? Who was it who, for the black man, agreed, once and for all, on those plaid suits that no black man ever made or wore of his own choice? And those disguises in shoes worn down at the heels, old clothes, bowler hats and umbrellas with holes in them, weren't they above all the sordid apanage of a section of the society that, in the civilised countries, misery and poverty made the sad beneficiary of the offscourings of the upper classes?

No, one could not manage every day to avoid a word or a deed bringing into question the dark nuances of the skin, which, in all milieus, determined sentiments and reflexes in the West Indies.

There was, near to the Savannah, a little bar where we often went to drink fruit juices. One day, we went in and the cashier, Mlle Adréa, a pretty brown-skinned woman with whom it was easy to exchange jokes, was continuing all by herself an argument she had just had, no doubt, with some customer. We arrived just in time to hear her say right in our faces: "That's why I don't hide the fact that I detest this race whose color I wear."

"Yet you wear the color with such charm," I told her.

"How do you expect me to like black people and to be proud I am one," she replied, still angry, "when every day I see them playing dirty tricks! Besides, except for my color, I'm not a black woman—I have the character of a white person . . . And I wonder what vice could have pushed my mother, who was already a beautiful mulâtresse, to dirty her bed with a black man!"

If I understood what had happened, a customer who, to top it all, happened to be black, had just provoked Mlle Adréa, for her mood showed nothing more than the irritability peculiar to the people in the warmer countries.

"Well! because of people like you, dear mademoiselle Adréa, I think that we black people are more to be pitied than hated, because, you see, I don't think there are in the world people who would deny their race because a person of the same color of skin as they behaved badly, in any way whatsoever. I don't think that any white person, for instance, ever shouted: 'I hate my race' when a white person committed some theft or murder—something that occurs quite often.

"That doesn't prevent white people who are not thieves or murderers from condemning the crime and the theft no matter who did them. So then, why, for some small misdemeanor by one of our people, are you so quick to disassociate yourself from all black people in the world and swear away our entire race?"

"You don't understand," said Adréa, outraged. "You don't understand me. It's so distressing to me to see someone who's already black doing something bad, even if it's only something trivial, that, in fact, on the spur of the moment, I'd throw my race into the fire. But you well know that, deep down inside, I'd not consent for anyone to criticize the race like this in my presence."

Indeed, I had often heard that type of reasoning. Didn't my mother tell me over and over again that it was already bad enough being black so that I was to avoid making the slightest mistake? Yes, I knew that everybody, white and black alike, agreed with the fact that the black man, invoking so little indulgence by his color, was tolerable only to the extent that he behaved like a saint.

In spite of everything, Adréa was a nice girl and admitted her mistakes as spontaneously as she had become angry.

So Carmen simply sentenced her to buying a round of lovely, fresh cane juice.

*

I passed the first part of my *baccalauréat* just as easily as I had failed it three months before.

I knew my work as I had studied it during the whole vacation with more application than during the regular academic year and had only to put into practice in the examination what I had learned.

My mother wept with joy.

Carmen and Jojo barged into my room, their arms bulging with bottles and food, and brought in little groups the maid, servant-boys, gardeners and drivers from the neighborhood to drink to my success.

Whereas I had always thought that I was going to be bubbling over with happiness, I could not get over how cooly I took it all. At most, a feeling of great relief. My joy was full and meaningful only when I went to deliver the good news to M'man Tine and kiss her as if it were she who had been successful. She had only one more year to wait before being delivered from the cane fields and from Cour Fusil. One more academic year!

And it was with this sole thought that I returned to the *lycée*, in the Philosophy class.

The year began in very mundane fashion, without promise.

I had no doubt I could be successful in my examination at the end of the year, but afterwards? I saw myself at the end of an impasse. How could I bring about in practical terms what I had hoped for and the promises I had made to M'man Tine? Possibly take one of those competitive examinations through which most of the *bacheliers* who had not received scholarships to study in France went into jobs in the civil service?

I did not feel attracted by any of those outlets. And the *lycée* was oppressive to me, making me weak.

I willingly studied my philosophy texts, even those I found irksome to read. But my favorite reading during that entire year in the Philosophy class consisted rather of works that were not part of the syllabus and pertaining to the lives of black people—those in the West Indies and in America; their history and the stories surrounding them. Those books had aroused in me more curiosity and deeper passion than all the stories of the lives of King This and King That, their wars and their deaths, that I learned and forgot continuously.

All the past of the black race, confronted with its present, was thus revealed to me as a challenge thrown out by history to this race, and such an observation made me throb with that vibrant pride that made people organize armed resistance.

Now, the only friends I had to discuss anything with were Jojo and Carmen. Christian, my old friend from my first year, was repeating his second part; and the others were too taken up with the preparation of their *bachot* to bother with books not on the syllabus and about which the teachers had never spoken.

I had, for some time now, lost all my taste for playing truant in the Jardin Desclieux or at Bord de Mer.

Whenever on a particular afternoon I did not feel like going to school, I simply remained in my room and read. Or else, over a sheet of paper, a pencil in my hand, I would daydream, listing the things I would have liked to study. Finally, as if to build castles in the air, what I would have liked to achieve; the material things I had to acquire: a little house with a nice little garden around it, a room with walls lined with books.

I also enjoyed, on certain Thursday afternoons for example, going to the square on the Savannah. Not so much as a stroller but as a spectator. For I had always experienced a feeling of malicious pleasure at the spectacle of people who could not live simply.

It was nearly always around the time when only a few old black nurse-maids, on benches, under tamarind trees, sat gossiping while, in the walks, children ran about and played. It was the time when the Savannah looked like a kindergarden.

If I did leave my bench, it was to go near the shore, for the sea was right there, nearby, and there would be a sail boat being pushed toward the town by the trade-winds that blew over the Caribbean Sea; or a cargo boat turning around, churning up the water in its wake and letting out into the air a stream of smoke and blasts of its whistle that conjured up in the setting sun mirages of Marseille, Bordeaux, Saint-Nazaire.

Around the Savannah, the cafés, with their offices. A typical scene in Fort-de-France. The day's work over, the body could unwind. Mind and heart, under the effects of a creole punch, were given over to relaxation, cheerfulness and spontaneous friendship. For I had wandered about, my hands in my pockets, in front of all the bars and drinking kiosks, and all I could hear was gusty laughter like the drawing of long bows on magnificent instruments, similar to the chests of black people; and the voices had that cordial tone that the smile, teeth, lips and eyes reflected.

Then I resumed my position on the bench.

By now, the Savannah was alive with a semi-elegant crowd in which the infants and their nurse-maids were lost.

And the walks, all too short, could scarcely hold the innumerable couples, those groups of friends who, to satisfy their need to go strolling, continuously moved up and down, looking as if they were interminably repeating the same dance step. You could almost say they were thoroughly enjoying executing multiple quadrilles, even those who, sporting an air of pride, were walking by themselves, trying their best to stand out from the crowd.

Others tried to be unobtrusive, taking the narrowest and shadiest of paths; and the grumpy, the misanthropes or the thinkers stood out of the way on the side of the Carénage bay, whereas the dreamers, their heads leaning over the water, were propped against the railing of the boulevard that skirted the port.

There was also that implacable gathering of the middle-aged gentlemen—newly retired, wearing cuffs and detachable collars, a respectable minority, representing a generation whose role was finished and who continued to harp continuously on their memories or their opinions on aspects of the contemporary world.

Along with punch drinking and cigarette smoking, the strollers in the savannah were also very fond of the charming habit of eating peanuts. Young girls, decked in *madras,* hawked them, distributing in all the walks.

And on certain evenings, for my most fervent excitement, there was this dark-eyed woman who, with two large gold rings in her ears, passed back and forth in the middle of the main walk, not looking at anybody, calm, as if she were alone in a huge park.

The role of the Savannah in the life of this West Indian town was gradually revealed to me, as I discovered the emulation, the vanity, the presumption for which it served as the stage, with its stars and its little figure-heads all eager and full of mimicry.

After one week of assiduous coming and going, this petty office clerk, whose mother took in washing, managed one night to get close to some "girl from a decent family," to say hello to her, to smile at her, to talk her and walk her back home. Perhaps he was not particularly fond of her, but that chance that she offered him to rise, at a ball—or even at a funeral—to the upper level of the colored lower middle-class, the feverish ambition of every young black man of humble origin in the West Indies! . . .

I was also very interested in the scene of the young *antillais*, fresh out of the Sorbonne or the Faculty of Medicine, strolling on the Savannah with his escort of admirers from whom he stood out by the knot of his tie or the cut of his jacket. Another one, from the same year, who had arrived by the same mail-boat, sat at a table in a café and evoked for those listening to him the Boulevard Saint-Michel, his café Dupont or the Jardin du Luxembourg.

Sons of modest civil servants or of small traders, no doubt, the two of them, having for five or six years been the recipient of a scholarship from the Colony, because their fathers served as yes-men for some deputies, they were now promoted to the upper class. Their parents would once more try to fix things so they could obtain the hand of a "girl from a decent family." Politics would come into the picture. To begin with, the mother—if it hadn't already been done—would give up her West Indian style of dress, which she nevertheless wore with dignity and even with much grace, but which, alas! made her look too much like the lower class people; she would make the sacrifice, for her son's future, of "wearing a hat." That concealed her origins somewhat, affirmed the new status in society and above all gave more assurance, whether she had to glance indifferently down at those below her, or smile up at those above her, or to enjoy, with her eyes half-closed, her own metamorphosis. As for the son, his main ambition was first of all a car. For a man who owned a car, no category of woman refused.

Priceless, that was the word to describe the Fort-de-France Savannah!

"Hello, Jo."

"Well, Carmen! What luck!"

"Monsieur is at Mme Chatran's in Rue Lamartine up to at least half past seven," my old friend told me. "So I came for a spin. I didn't expect to run into you . . . "

Carmen recognized people in the crowd.

"Over there," he pointed out, "the fellow in the straw hat with the l'il moustache—that's the chief accountant at Reynon's."

A little further on, he pinched me on my arm and whispered in my ear:

"There's the mistress of Ray-Carmin, the big-time trader; she's friendly with the woman who calls me 'sugar cane' . . . "

In spite of everything, Carmen was not very talkative that night.

While in the crowd, I didn't quite realize it. How could I detect anything whatsoever in that face that was constantly aglow with joviality? A face which, even when he was silent, maintained the warmth of all the laughter, of all the crude jokes, of all the humor that comprised the ineffable face of Carmen! So much so that I would have liked to see how that face expressed anger or violence.

But that night, sitting at the bar where Mlle Adréa had poured us two glasses of cold juice, I suddenly sensed a frightful feeling of dejection in Carmen's mood.

"Something's wrong?" I asked him.

"Oh! nothing," he replied.

Obviously, my question had surprised him.

"Nothing, of course?"

He remained visibly confused at having aroused my suspicions. He then replied:

"It's nothing, I tell you. But I'm going to tell you something."

He swallowed in one mouthful what was left in his glass, in a gesture that invited me to do likewise.

We went outside.

The crowd was still flowing by with the rhythm of the inward and outward rush of waves.

"You remember," he continued at last, "how I told you that sometimes for mere trivial matters Madame gets annoyed with me and does all sorts of stupid things to me? The other day, because she felt a slight bump in the car, she shouted: 'You can't see where you're going any more since your mind is not on your work; you're only thinking of dressing up like a prince to seduce the black women.' "

"And what did you say to that?"

"Nothing," Carmen said, "I felt like doing just one thing—parking the car at the side of the road, getting out and going somewhere else. So I said nothing. That passed. No, it never finished. Every time I was out with Madame alone, it was always some silly little thing like that to annoy me; to the point where I wondered whether sometimes she hadn't heard something about me. Which of the maids in the house could have told her that I visit Hortense, the housekeeper, in her room? For Madame may not exactly be a young woman, but she's not of the age where women become shrews.

"And hear what happened this morning. Normally, y'know, I drive Monsieur to Bord de Mer at eight o'clock, then I return for the money and the list Madame prepares later on, when she gets up, for me to buy things in the market. When I arrive, I remain in the yard, near the car, then as soon as she's ready, Madame calls me into the pantry and explains what shopping I have to do. And when she doesn't have anything to tell me, she simply sends me the pad and the money by Hortense.

"This morning she calls me. I go into the pantry. I find her in one of those large silk robes that *békés'* wives put on to remain in their bedroom, I think; and she tells me:

" 'You're here, Carmen? But I didn't have time to prepare the list. I'll give it to you directly.'

"She starts up the stairs and I remain standing there.

" 'But you can come up, Carmen,' she said, looking around.

"In fact, I thought I hadn't heard right. I can assure you I wasn't at all at ease.

"Yet another problem I thought.

"She enters her bedroom; I hesitate, you understand.

" 'Come in,' she says to me.

"It's as if I was a l'il boy all over again, fearing the scolding I was about to receive. I didn't know what on earth was going on."

Carmen fell silent, placed his hand on my shoulder and we stopped walking.

Then he took me away from the main flow of strollers, onto a side walk. I was so intrigued by all those precautions and the confidential tone his voice assumed, that what he was whispering to me changed before my eyes into the most thrilling of images.

The bedroom was bright, despite the curtains that filtered the sunlight behind the venetian blinds. Carmen was standing near the door that Madame had closed herself; and in the mirror-wardrobe, he saw himself—he, Carmen, the black driver, in his grey shantung suit, with his brick-red tie and his brown shoes sunk into the soft thickness of the carpet. There, in Mme Mayel's bedroom.

Madame was going to find fault with him and he tried his best—not through fright, but above all through politeness—to look calm and inoffensive.

Madame sat on the edge of the still unmade bed and said:

"You find my bedroom pretty, Carmen?"

"Yes, madame; very pretty."

"He had replied automatically, and it was afterwards that he noted to his surpise that the tone in which Madame now spoke to him betrayed no trace of annoyance.

Madame seemed delighted with the compliment. She looked at the black man and smiled. Then Carmen, out of politeness, cast his eyes at random on some trinket in the bedroom. Hadn't Monsieur told him one day: 'I don't want you looking me straight in my eyes—that's insolence!'? But he could feel Madame's eyes still riveted on him. He was all the more embarrassed as Madame prolonged the silence for no goodly reason.

"I hear," she said at last, "that you like women a lot."

Without raising his head, Carmen smiled and replied:

"My friends say so as a joke, Madame."

"A joke? Then it's not true, you don't like women?"

"I didn't say so, Madame."

"At any rate, you know they like you."

" 'Don't know, Madame."

Carmen kept his head down with a sly smile on his face. He was anxious to go, to jump behind the wheel of his car, to reach the market, to do his shopping, joking with the young women behind the stalls, and above all to meet, in the flesh, some of the young maids who had recently arrived in town and who would never refuse a rendez-vous. He was longing to leave that room where his boss thought it her right to question him about his private life, his life as a black man and as a servant, or apparently wanted to start up a conversation with him to which even her position as boss and as *béké* in particular did not entitle her.

He was burning with the urge to tell her: 'Madame, please give me the list and the money, will you?'

But there was this question of politeness. Politeness due to a boss, politeness imposed by the whiteness of her skin.

Then Mme Mayel said nothing further. But Carmen still felt her eyes on him, so acutely that he strained, in order to stand it, to follow the designs on the carpet on which he stood.

Her eyes went straight through him, burned him, touched him, like the hands of those women who so often enjoyed taking off his clothes and caressing him all over his body, as if to make him over to suit the ardor of their desire.

The whole scene also suddenly reminded him of Hortense. Yes, the day that Hortense had asked him to come to her room to fix the switch which was not working properly. The screws of the switch had in fact been loosened, and when Carmen had replaced them, he saw Hortense lying on the bed, her eyes closed, her legs invitingly offered.

So, all of sudden, the designs on the carpet grew fuzzy. Carmen felt all his blood boil within him. He looked up. Madame was no longer looking at him, she had sunk down on the bed, her eyes closed, her mouth half-opened in a sort of anguish that seemed to clutch at her bare throat as well as at her breast and her legs protruding through the silk of the blue dressing-gown . . .

Carmen stopped once more. Quite near to us, a couple passed by, silhouettes moving further on to blend into the tree trunks.

He continued:

"That night, she did not go visiting with her husband. She had herself excused. And when I was leaving, she made a sign to me to drop Monsieur then come back up and join her. It's bothering me a lot, for it's really not interesting—there's much better."

During the Carnival season, the villas in Route Didier were often gay with evening parties. Late into the night the open windows poured light, music, laughter and the clink of silver, the ring of porcelain and crystal, onto the gardens, all around the villa which then glittered like a huge jewel.

Whenever there were guests "at his house," Jojo, poor chap, was detailed since the day before to run multiple errands, along with the driver of the house; and on the evening of the party, in addition to the dishes to be washed, he had to spend hours turning the handles of the heavy freezers to make ice-cream. The two following days were devoted to various jobs cleaning up the house. It was no doubt for this reason that Jojo had not come to my place for several days.

From time to time I would see him on mornings and he would often tell me that that evening or the following one he had, on orders from his employers, to help the houseboy from some house where guests were expected.

And then, one night, he came—barefooted and in work clothes, because it was not Sunday.

He was not in a mood for laughing that night.

"I'd like a bit of advice," he said after a while.

"A bit of advice, Jojo!" I cried.

The mere sound of that word frightened me, for all its implications of responsibility, of infallibility. And I asked him, rather out of curiosity:

"Advice? on what?"

"Well! it's like this," he began. "I've made an arrangement with Pierre, the driver of the house. Every morning, I'll polish the car for him and, in return, he'll teach me to drive. Every time I go shopping with him, he'll give me the wheel to hold, and after a while, I could get my driver's license."

"Then you'll look for a job as a driver in Route Didier, Jojo?"

I don't know what nuance of reproach I had possibly let slip in my question, and Jojo protested sharply:

"But not for always. I'll start with that, but what I'd like is to work on my own—to have my own truck and transport merchandise to Bord de Mer . . . The main thing will be to obtain a truck on credit, payable in six months, for example. Like Maximin, who used to drive for Borry."

Jojo continued and I listened to him attentively, respectfully.

"From that," he said, "I could send for my mother, rent a room for her, then I could find me a good girl and get married. Possibly try to build a li'l house in Sainte-Thérèse . . . if I'm lucky."

He then stopped and asked me:

"What d'you think?"

He was sitting on the edge of my iron bed—which was too big for the room—his knees bent and the weight of his legs resting on his bare toes on the floor.

The truth was, I had absolutely no opinion on the matter.

But I admired the intensity and tenderness pulsating in the beautiful dream of my friend, so much so that, on reflection, any impression of banality disappeared and I understood Jojo and I told him sincerely:

"It's a fine plan. I'm sure you'll succeed."

Such was the advice Jojo wanted from me.

He spoke to me once more about the truck and his plan to transport merchandise as if he were pressing his dream on his heart and he left very late. He was in such high spirits that I placed my hand on his shoulder to share in his joy; he was in such a mood that I promised myself to wait a while before telling him that his dream was too simple, too silent and, above all, too solitary.

The following night, on my return from the *lycée*, I went to see my mother in Mr. Lasseroux's kitchen. Normally, we used to have dinner together, then I would wish M'man Délia goodnight and set off for my room in Petit-Fond. Now, that night, contrary to our usual pattern, the table had not been set as yet. The table had a thick, woolen covering and my mother, with an iron, was smoothening out clothes. She kissed me with a smile while continuing her ironing.

"Here, read this," she said, showing me a bit of folded blue paper near the stand for the iron.

M'man Délia's voice was not her natural one. I took the paper and opened it. 'Your mother sick, come right away.' It was from Mam'zelle Délice.

I looked at my mother. She had been crying.

"I could have left this afternoon," she told me, "if the message had come earlier. Tomorrow, I'll take the bus at five a.m. . . . . Ah! no, I can't take you. Already, in order to pay for my trip, I have to ask Monsieur for an advance. And I don't even know what I'll probably have to spend up there. I'll no doubt have to take her to the hospital and all that . . . . "

In a flash, I had lost my appetite. My mother went on ironing her dress and things for the trip, explaining what steps she had taken as far as I was concerned and with respect to her work in view of her absence.

The wife of a driver from Petit-Fond was to replace her. For my meals, I would do myself some eggs in my room. With those twenty cents, I would buy some bread. She was going to return two mornings later.

Alone, like a corpse, moaning on her old bed, shut up in her shack, that was how I pictured my grandmother in her sickness. So sick this time that Mam'zelle Délice, our old neighbor, had taken the supreme initiative of sending a telegram to my mother.

And I was not there, on this occasion, to go and fetch leaves in Haut-Morne or Féral: 'Around Mme Jean's garden, you should find some *guyapana*,' M'man Tine would have told me, 'the stem is red and the leaves a sort of yellowish green and tapered; it's good for chest colds.'

Sick, without my being there to make her a tisane and prepare that pap that was all she ate at that time.

And what was she suffering from this time?

"Don't think," she used to say, "my eyes will see you when you finish your exams. I won't be able to see the color of the first mouthful of bread you earn for yourself. My eyes are getting worse and worse. They're really bad. At times, it's as if I'm suddenly under a shower of ants so heavy that it blocks out the daylight."

True, sometimes her pipe would be on the table, right before her eyes, and she would be groping in all the recesses of the room, both arms stretched forward like antennas, calling upon St. Anthony to help her find it.

The thought that M'man Tine would go blind any day had me rather upset. What greater misfortune could then befall me?

All night long, the pounding of my heart and my clammy perspiration prevented me from sleeping. I felt like one thing alone—leaving immediately, at least at break of day, with my mother, to go and see M'man Tine and see for myself what state she was in.

"Mustn't worry yourself too much," Carmen said to me the next day, "old people, y'know, are like old cars—they keep on working out of sheer routine. And many times, they're stronger than brand new ones. Don't look so sad, man!

"Look, I'll tell you what happened to me today. Real madness . . . "

But if I did listen to Carmen's story, I don't think I fully appreciated it. Yet, Carmen knew how to add spice to the slightest little incident and make it into a juicy side-splitting story.

Jojo remained silent when I told him the news. Then he muttered simply:

"Poor Mam'zelle Amantine!"

At midday Carmen returned. I had not received any further news.

"Well!" he explained, "nothing serious. I can tell you now I was scared; for those sorts of messages: 'Maman sick, papa sick, come right away,' are often sent when everything's over. But from the time your mother herself didn't send to say anything, everything's fine."

But the following day my mother did not show up.

In spite of the reassurances of my two friends, I was tormented by the desire to leave. It was quite a pull from Fort-de-France to Petit-

Bourg on foot! And then I did expect, all the same, to see M'man Délia
arrive at any moment, to receive a telegram. Carmen himself would
probably come for me at the *lycée*.

And the day after that, still no sign of my mother.

Carmen gave me a franc to buy some bread.

That morning, the feeling that my grandmother was dead gripped
me.

However, my rather frantic imagination did not conjure up any
picture of an old mummified black woman, lying on her bed, whose
rags, so often washed and ironed in the sun, exuded for me a maternal,
engaging odor.

There was not the slightest picture of what the closed, inanimate
face of M'man Tine could be like.

I also thought about what the 'wake' was like, with the tenants of
Cour Fusil singing and praying. Assionis would be relating stories and
would play his drum with a soul full of compassion and with frenzied
inspiration.

I could see very distinctly the coffin, a gift from the *commune*—a
rough wooden box, blackened with smoke, that, in the little cemetery,
some hefty chaps would lower into the grave with ropes, making many
crude jokes to prevent the hearts of the on-lookers from shuddering at
the strange sound of the clumps of earth hitting the coffin.

All day long, my ears rang with the sound of that avalanche of hard
earth on the black coffin in the bottom of the grave.

My mother arrived early the next morning. She was wearing one of
her dresses I knew; but she had on her head a black *madras* with fine
white stripes. She didn't even have time to speak to me.

At the sight of that mourning, a shrill ringing started in my ears, and
at the same time my eyes became blurred. I threw myself on a chair, my
head held tightly in my arms against the table.

And that ringing bore painfully into my ears and the pounding of my
heart filled my chest from which, nevertheless, came a deep groan I
could not control.

It all lasted a few hours.

Jojo and Carmen came, stayed with me a long time, talked between
themselves, since it was impossible for me to reply to what they were
saying.

That was all.

When I was myself again, I still stubbornly persisted in picturing the
face of M'man Tine dead. That image would not come. I then tried to
replace it with that of Mr. Médouze stretched out like a black Christ on a

bare plank in the middle of his shack.

I was sure, all the same, that my mother had taken out the white sheet that M'man Tine kept so preciously in her clothes basket to be used on the day she died.

Certainly, her bed had been ceremoniously covered with this sheet and she had been placed in the middle of her black satin dress, the one she used to wear only twice or three times a year for ceremonies in the church. But not her face, nor the sink in her cheek where I would have kissed her.

Her hands.

It was her hands that appeared to me on the whiteness of the sheet.

Her black hands, swollen, hardened, cracked at every joint, and every crack incrusted with a sort of indelible mud. Cramped fingers, bent in all directions, their ends all worn and re-inforced with nails thicker, harder and more shapeless than the hooves of God knows what animal that had galloped on rocks, in scrap iron, in a dung heap, in mud.

. . . Those hands which M'man Tine used to wash carefully every night, more meticulously so on Sunday mornings, but which seemed rather to have gone through fire, beaten with a hammer on a stone, buried then uprooted with all the earth clinging to them; then soaked in dirty water, dried out in the sun over long hours and finally thrown there, with sacrilegious carelessness, on the whiteness of that sheet in the depths of that obscure shack.

. . . Those hands as familiar as the voice of M'man Tine, had fed me my dishfuls of crushed roots, had washed me clean with a tenderness that did not even lessen the roughness, had dressed me, had scrubbed my clothes on the stones of the river.

One of those hands had clutched my little hand one day to take me to school—I could still feel it.

They had never been pretty, obviously; they had seen so many blemishes, drawn and raised so many loads. And every day squeezed, scratched and clinging to the handle of the hoe, an easy prey to the fierce cuts inflicted by the cane leaves to create Route Didier.

*   *
*

Like every night since my heart was filled with the sadness of being a poor orphan, Carmen and Jojo came to see me.

They each sat in their usual places at the ends of the bed, their shoulders leaning on the head.

They spoke very little. Carmen knew only gay stories to tell. Not being sure he could amuse me in this fashion, he preferred, no doubt, not to say anything. Jojo, from time to time, asked me some trivial question about how I was now feeling, or about my studies; then he was silent for a long while.

I was the one who wished to rid them of their self-imposed gloom out of respect for my grief. I should, for example, tell them a story.

But which one?

The one which I knew best and which tempted me most at that time was quite similar to theirs.

It is to those who are blind and those who block their ears that I must shout it.